THE BEST OF THE NEW AND THE OLD

⋆ New and Old Stories by Masters of Science Fiction and Fantasy ⋆

⋆ New Stories by Emerging New Talents ⋆

⋆ PLUS Columns, Book Reviews and Interviews ⋆

⋆ Serializations of Great Novels & Stories ⋆

⋆ The Sargasso Legacy ⋆

I0608261

DON'T MISS OUT ON ANY ISSUE

SUBSCRIBE

www.GalaxysEdge.com/sub.htm

Or send a check for $37.74 for a one-year (six-issue) subscription
(save 10% off the cover price) with this form to :

Subscriptions: Galaxy's Edge

Arc Manor Publishers

P.O. Box 10339

Rockville, MD 20849

Currently, subscription to the paper edition is only available within the United States.

Your Name_____

Full Address_____

_____

_____

Ph. No._____ Email_____

GALAXY'S EDGE

EDITED BY MIKE RESNICK

ISSUE 12: JANUARY 2015

Mike Resnick, Editor
Shahid Mahmud, Publisher

Published by Arc Manor/Phoenix Pick
P.O. Box 10339
Rockville, MD 20849-0339

Galaxy's Edge is published every two months: January, March, May, July, September & November.

www.GalaxysEdge.com

Galaxy's Edge is an invitation-only magazine. We do not accept unsolicited manuscripts. Unsolicited manuscripts will be disposed of or mailed back to the sender (unopened) at our discretion.

Available by subscription (www.GalaxysEdge.com) or through your favorite online store (Amazon.com, BN.com, etc.).

ISBN: 978-1-61242-256-5

Advertising in the magazine is available. Quarter page (half column), $95 per issue. Half page (full column, vertical or two half columns, horizontal) $165 per issue. Full page (two full columns) $295 per issue. Back Cover (full color) $495 per issue. All interior advertising is in black and white.

Please write to advert@GalaxysEdge.com.

FOREIGN LANGUAGE RIGHTS: Please refer all inquiries pertaining to foreign language rights to Spectrum Literary Agency, 320 Central Park West, Suite 1-D, New York, NY 10025. Phone: 1-212-362-4323. Fax 1-212-362-4562

Contents

Sail to Success

a unique writers' workshop on board a luxury cruise ship

Intensive manuscript critique by
Toni Weisskopf (head of Baen Books)
and
Nancy Kress (bestselling, Hugo/Nebula-winning author)

PLUS

Writing and business (publishing) seminars by
Mike Resnick
Jack Skillingstead
Eric Flint
and
Eleanor Wood (head of Spectrum Literary Agency)

Class size restricted to only 22 students
December 7-11, 2015

All-inclusive pricing starting at $999 (as of January 2015; subject to change). Prices include cruise, food, entertainment
and all materials needed for the workshop.

www.SailSuccess.com

THE EDITOR'S WORD

by Mike Resnick

Welcome to the twelfth issue of *Galaxy's Edge*—and who'd have thought, twenty-four months ago, that we'd still be around and stronger than ever, that we'd have brought you not only the best stories by the new crop of writers but new stories by superstars like Larry Niven and Mercedes Lackey, that we'd be so popular abroad that there is now a Chinese edition of the magazine, and that we'd already have published *The Best Of Galaxy's Edge* in e-book and trade paperback forms.

Well, this issue should prove that we've no intention of slowing down. We have brand-new stories from Robert T. Jeschonek, Sandra M. Odell, Ron Friedman, and Zaslow Crane; new stories set in our Sargasso Containment universe by Tina Gower and Andrea Stewart; stories you may not have encountered by superstars Gardner Dozois, Maureen McHugh, and Jack McDevitt; the first part of a novella by Michael Flynn; Paul Cook's lauded book review column; Gregory Benford's science column; and Barry Malzberg's whatever-appeals-to-him column.

And, oh yes—we also have Robert A. Heinlein's classic story, "All You Zombies," the source material for the major motion picture *Predestination*. And while we were at it, Joy Ward got an interview with the writer/directors who created the film.

So sit back and enjoy—and remember our talented new writers at Hugo-nominating time.

Heinlein wrote some wonderful (and occasionally controversial) novels about military conflicts of the future, but he wasn't the first. That honor goes to H. G. Wells. whose *War of the Worlds* is generally considered to be the first serious novel about interstellar—well, interplanetary—war. Boiled down, it comes to this: the Martians come here, do a little serious devastation, scare the hell out of us, and then catch colds and die.

Never gonna happen. For one thing, given the weaponry that H. G. Wells and the movie give them, they'll never have to emerge from their ships before they've destroyed every last one of us and the battle is over—and as long as they stay in their ships, they're immune to the one indefensible weapon we have: our peculiarly human viruses.

And there's something else to consider. Let's not forget that Wells lived before the era of modern medicine. I think it's only logical to assume that any creatures, benevolent or hostile, that can traverse the void and reach planet Earth have doubtless developed their science—and especially their medical science—to the point where they can pinpoint and identify any dangerous germs in our atmosphere, and either develop some form of immunization to them, or create some way to annihilate them at the source, which is to say Earth, before invading us.

It's just common sense. You wouldn't invade the waters off the coast of Australia unless you had some protection against the great white shark. You wouldn't wander through a pride of hungry lions without protection. Hell, we don't send our soldiers into battle these days without protection against bullets, chemical agents, biological agents, everything we can think of.

So I think it's fair to say that our germs are not going to kill any extraterrestrial invaders once they get here.

Nope. We're going to kill them long *before* they get here. And by the very same means that we (or Earth, if you prefer) used to kill Wells' Martian invaders.

How?

Well, as likely as not, it'll be by accident.

You see, in recent years NASA has been examining ships, rovers, orbiters, everything that we send into space.

And guess what?

Neither the cold of space nor the heat of re-entry nor the direct gamma radiation from the sun kills every living thing on those objects.

Oh, there's nothing there that'll bother *us*—at least not so far. But that doesn't mean an alien race with an alien physiology isn't looking down a barrel loaded with newly-identified microbes from good old Planet Earth.

We've even got names for them.

For example, there's *Bacillus Odysseyi*, which has been found on the Mars Odyssey orbiter. Why is this noteworthy? Because the damned thing has been orbiting Mars for close to four years. It survived the 40-million-mile trip, it survived three years in orbit, it survived gamma radiation, and it's doing just fine, thank you.

Now, no one's ever been killed by *B. Odysseyi*, and probably no one ever will be. But that's not to say that it couldn't wipe out a squad of Wells' Martians or Edgar Rice Burroughs' green Tharks in an afternoon, depending on what particular germs they're vulnerable to.

Then there's *Bacillus Safensis*. This baby is not only found in the Jet Propulsion Lab's Spacecraft Assembly Facility (known as SAF, which gave it its name), but it is alive and well today on Spirit and Opportunity, the current Mars rovers.

So what do these—and a dozen other viruses that have survived the heat and cold and radiation of spaceflight—actually do?

Nothing much. They tend to go forth and multiply, like every other living thing, but they're not harmful to us. Hell, they've even been found in the water supply of the Mir space station. Astronauts drank it. They all survived.

But they're human astronauts, not Martian or Centaurian or Antarean astronauts. Or citizens.

Right. Citizens. Don't forget: we've sent out a few deep space probes, and we'll send out more. A couple have already left the solar system. They're not traveling fast, not by galactic standards, and it could take them a hundred thousand or even a million years to make planetfall somewhere out there—but they're going to arrive with a zillionth generation of perfectly healthy microbes and bacilli ready to find new homes.

Maybe the planet they touch down on won't have any life on it at all. (Which is okay by the fellow travelers; they can wait a billion years until some comes along.) Maybe it'll have life that's as unbothered by exposure to them as we are.

And maybe it will have life that finds them to be pure poison—life that, unlike the hypothetical invaders we discussed, is totally unprepared for a visit by microscopic creatures that can wipe them out, that will never know what hit them, that might indeed have been the friendliest folk in the galaxy.

All right. That's the non-fiction side of it. Those bacilli are out there, some of them aren't coming back, and sooner or later they're going to make contact with *something*.

Now let's look at the possibilities, science fictional today, but perhaps less so in the future.

We've got a million dedicated computer hackers, plus some truly powerful equipment in the hands of experts, searching the heavens every night for signals from other worlds—SETI, the Search for Extra-Terrestrial Intelligence. They're probably not going to discover any in my lifetime or yours, but sooner or later they're going to latch on to some signals, because we're finding out that just about every star in the galaxy has planets, and with tens of millions of G-type stars out there, the odds are that an awful lot of them have, or once had, or someday will have life. And some of it will be sentient. And some of that will be searching the skies for signs of life just the way we do.

So eventually we're going to make contact with them. If we like what they have to say, fine. If we don't … well, if we can trace their signals back to their source, we can send them a little present. Not the microbes that are living on the Mars rovers today, but rather some of the most powerful stuff we can whip up (after we lie to them about our physiology and hope they're telling us the truth about theirs).

And even if we don't know what their motives are, if meeting them at a neutral point in space is kind of like a blind date on a grand scale, it doesn't mean we won't go armed. Not with guns or lasers or any of that movie garbage; they'll be able to detect it from a light-year away. But with the most subtle weapons imaginable—Men, each carrying germs and viruses that we are immune to, each ready to transmit them by the simple act of breathing in and out.

Sounds pretty crude and heartless, I realize, and hopefully it will never come to that—but if your world is at risk, a visionary named Wells showed you that there is a far more efficient way of attacking the enemy than with a new generation of weapons, which history teaches us will be obsolete in a few years' time.

Much better to use a weapon neither time nor heat nor cold nor radiation has been able to kill.

There are going to be some alien immune systems that can't kill it either.

So how do we avoid killing off a friendly alien population?

We're working on it right now. NASA is aware that if enough of the bacilli I mentioned take root on Mars (or Venus, or Io, or any other world or moon in the solar system), we might one day discover life there, and if the bacilli have evolved or mutated enough, we'll never know that it came from Earth in the late 20th and early 21st centuries. So some of the NASA scientists have been given the task of learning how to terminate these microscopic agents that space can't kill.

They already know that if they hit them with a few million degrees of heat they can't survive—but neither can the equipment they live on, and it's counter-productive to melt a spaceship before it ever takes off just to make sure that it doesn't take any microscopic travelers with it.

But they're learning, and before long they'll find a method. And that's absolutely vital, because although Wells didn't know he was telling the truth, we already have the ability to destroy the bad aliens. Now we have to make sure we don't kill the good ones by accident.

Robert T. Jeschonek is a prolific author of short stories and articles, and has four novels to his credit, including the recent National Literature Award winner My Favorite Band Does Not Exist.

A LITTLE SONG, A LITTLE DANCE, A LITTLE APOCALYPSE DOWN YOUR PANTS

by Robert T. Jeschonek

I come back from the dead suddenly, the way I always do, with a great heaving gasp as air and light and consciousness rush into me all at once. "Easy now, Jody Lee." Binky the Bring-Back Bot says the same thing every time he resurrects me, the same damn thing. "Slow, even breaths, dear. In through the nose, out through the mouth."

Meanwhile, I'm twisting and flopping around naked in what I call the Humpty-Dumptynator—a rectangular glass box half-full of slimy blue goo and squirming anti-maggots. (They *give* life instead of *feeding* on it.) No matter how many times I've been through this—and believe me, there've been *thousands*—I still wake up with the same shock and nausea, spazzing out like this is my first freaking life restoration.

While at the same time, I know I've gotta get over it but fast, as Binky reminds me.

"Snap out of it, honey." The silver-skinned bastard jabs my left bicep with a hypo needle in the tip of his index finger, shooting me full of something that takes the edge off. "Remember, you've got another show tonight." He shoots me with a pale green light from his right eye, which is also soothing. "You have to die again in *three hours* if you want to get *paid*."

Once I get cleaned up, I go for a walk, trying to blow the stink off. My long black hair's tied in a ponytail, and I'm wearing a Selfie Suit, which looks like whatever I want depending on who's looking. A hot guy might see me in a little red dress, a not-so-hottie might see me in overalls … and I myself just see a casual black pantsuit.

I can't hold back a yawn as I walk through Tesseractus Prime 'cause it's just another pan-galactic mega-casino in just another multidimensional ho-tel-cathedral-singularity. It's the same old thing, the same old crowd, in the same old place.

And by that, I mean it's a looney tune wonderland to the zillionth power.

A unicorn centaur in a diaper gallops past, fleeing a flock of mocking blackbirds trying to bomb his horn with poop. A guy with an accordion-shaped body bounces by, burping filthy limericks every time his midsection crumples. A priest, a rabbi, and Hitler walk into the nearest bar, saying something about buying a dog a drink … and then they all turn into poodles.

Welcome to humanity circa 100,000 A.D., when science that might as well be magic makes all things possible. Everyone can be as wacky as they wanna be, in every imaginable way. The universe is one big joke … but nobody's laughing anymore.

And that's where *I* come in.

✿

"I have never been more miserable in my life." Standing onstage in the massive theater at the ho-tel-casino-cathedral, I gaze out at the crowd arrayed before me. It's a panoply of every silly, crazy, bizarre, surreal, and just plain *insane* character you can imagine … and everyone's laughing their heads off (some *literally*, if the heads aren't attached very well). "I mean it. I wish I were dead."

For a long moment, the roar of laughter and applause drowns me out. I stand there and let it flow around me, watching as the horde of ridiculous figures howls in hilarity.

A glowing purple clown in the front row blasts a bicycle horn and stomps his huge red shoes (which are also laughing). Beside him, a gorilla in a pin-striped suit hops up and down, making with the monkey shrieks and whipping banana peels and poo at the stage.

In other words, I'm *killing*. Again. Because I'm the best. I know what makes 'em laugh.

When the roaring dies down, I start talking again. "Seriously, I'm at the end of my rope." That gets a few titters from the crowd. "The more you people laugh, the more I long for oblivion." Cue a slew of scattered guffaws.

Then, a thing that looks like a giant pretzel with eyes instead of grains of salt zips up to the stage and flies around me a dozen times, laughing like a maniac. The audience follows suit with a roar that sounds ten times louder than before.

"Enough of this mortal coil!" The spotlight follows me as I stomp across the stage toward a long table covered by a red velvet shroud. "It is time to end my suffering!"

Everyone cheers and claps and howls with laughter as I pull the shroud from the table, revealing a selection of swords and knives. People shout out suggestions; some even teleport up beside me to point at the weapon of their choice. I shoo them all away and pick up the samurai sword.

"This is the end for me." I kneel on the stage and hold the sword out away from me, pointing the tip at my belly. "I go now to the big comedy show in the sky."

Hands shaking, I falter, and the crowd urges me on. I continue to hesitate, building suspense; it's all part of the act.

"I have the courage to do it at last!" I nod forcefully. "Death, I fear not thy sting!"

Then, before I can slide the sword through my stomach, there's a deafening boom from somewhere off stage. A cannonball blows through my midriff from side to side, cutting a swath where the sword was supposed to cut.

The top half of my body plops down to close the gap. For a moment, as the crowd gives me a standing ovation, I kneel there, my top and bottom halves disconnected but adjacent.

Then, the top half drops over backward, and the darkness of death swirls over me. I feel my mind sliding into the abyss like leftovers sliding from a plate into a trash receptacle.

And then I'm gone, into the great and fathomless unknown. Just like I am every time I do this—two shows a day, six days a week, 52 weeks a year.

✿

Three and a half hours later, I'm staring at a bowl of thin broth in one of the 100,001 ever-changing restaurants in Tesseractus Prime. The broth keeps telling me to eat it, *literally*—it's *conscious cuisine* with a mind of its own—but I can't force it down.

Binky the Bring-Back Bot put me back together just fine after the cannonball, but my stomach still remembers being blown apart just a little too well.

"Excuse me?" Just then, a horse's ass—an *actual* horse's ass, minus the horse—clops over to my table. "Have you seen a *setup* come this way? I seem to have lost mine."

Great, just what I need. Another lost punchline looking for the rest of his joke. "Can't help you, buddy." I stir my bowl of broth as if I'm actually going to eat it.

The broth gets all worked up and starts to yap. "Oh yes, oh *please* put me inside you, dear famous Jo Jawdropper! Eat me right *up*, you vixen!"

The tail on the horse's ass switches excitedly. I can see there's an eyeball staring back at me from its bunghole. "Ohmigod! I can't believe this! I'm talking to *Jo Jawdropper!*"

I never thought I could hate my stage name any more than I already do … but hearing it spoken in the squeaky whine of a horse's ass really does the trick. "Check, please!"

"No check yet!" screams the broth. "You've gotta *slurp me up* first!"

Just as I'm starting to freak out a little, someone clears his throat behind me. "Get lost, ass." His voice is as deep as the croak of a down-dirty drunk just before he turns himself sober so he can start drinking all over again. "*Amscray!*"

Turning, I'm surprised for two reasons: one, he's shorter than I imagined because of that voice, all of five-foot-five; and two, I recognize him, from his black leather jacket to his bald head to his bushy red mustache. I used to *work* with him, back in the day.

"Now git!" He stomps over and gives one of the horse's ass's butt cheeks a powerful slap. "Don't *make* me *kick* you!"

"*Kiss* my you-know-what," snaps the ass, and then he clops off through the restaurant.

"What an ass," says the guy. "Probably doesn't know *himself* from a *hole* in the ground."

"Well, well." I smile and hold out my hand. "If it isn't *The 'Stache.*"

The 'Stache (that's his stage name; he never told me his real name) gives my hand a hearty shake. "Long time no smell, JoJo m'dear."

"Thanks for the save," I tell him. "I guess that makes you my hero." Impulsively, I pull him into a big, grateful hug. It's been *such* a lousy day.

Meanwhile, the broth keeps yapping. "Slurp me up! Put me inside you! *Lick my bowl clean!*"

"Shaddup," snaps The 'Stache. "Or else!"

"Or else what?" says the broth.

"You know the one about the fly in the soup?" says The 'Stache. "Well, I'm gonna *show* you the one about the *soup* that *flies*. Across the *room*."

With that, the broth finally shuts up.

The 'Stache and I catch up while taking a late night stroll on Schrödinger's Catwalk—a promenade that might or might not occupy infinite locations and realities at any given moment.

Fountains of rainbow light cascade all around us, casting colorful glows on our faces. Within the light, I glimpse an ever-changing parade of images, flickering movies of people and events from all eras and alternate worlds.

For an instant, I think I catch a glimpse of The 'Stache and me in the old days, working the comedy circuit together … but then it's gone, or maybe it was never there at all.

"I was out of the biz for a while," says The 'Stache. "Didja know that?"

"You quit *show biz? For real?*"

He grins, flashing gold incisors through his over-abundant mustache. "For *ten years* real, Double-J."

"What was it like?"

"Not being on the road all the time, you mean? Not struggling to squeeze laughs out of a bunch of humorless fruitcakes every day of my pathetic life?" The 'Stache looks ahead of us and chuckles. "Why don't we ask *him*?"

"Ask me what?" It's an alternate version of The 'Stache with zebra stripes and elephant ears, loping toward us—one of the side effects of Schrödinger's Catwalk. You never know when you're gonna cross paths with another you from a parallel universe.

"Hey! Did I miss show biz when I gave it up for ten years?" says The 'Stache I came in with.

"You gave it up for *ten years*?" Other 'Stache punches original 'Stache in the shoulder on his way past. "What a maroon!"

Original 'Stache laughs and jerks a thumb at his doppelgänger as he walks off and vanishes. "That guy is such a *prick*, isn't he?"

"You're back in the game, aren't you?" I ask him. "That's why you're here, right? You're doing standup again."

"Maybe I'm just here to see *you*," says The 'Stache.

"So what made you do it? What made you want to get back onstage after ten years away?"

"Because I'm gonna be the greatest comic who ever lived," says The 'Stache. "And I'm gonna make it happen in a one-night-only performance, tomorrow night." He smiles and takes my hand. "You want in, JoJo? For old times' shake?"

"Sure." I say it with a smirk, waiting for the punchline. "How can I possibly say no?"

The 'Stache stops walking and faces me. "Dead serious here, partner. This ain't a *bit*."

"Izzat so?" Notice I haven't stopped smirking. "So how do you propose becoming the greatest ever in just one night?"

"I've done it before, haven't I?" The 'Stache winks and squeezes my hand.

"*Ten* years off the circuit is like a *hundred* years in *comedian time*." I pull my hand free and shake my head. "You're gonna have to sell your soul to Maxwell's Demon just to make a *comeback*, let alone become the *greatest*."

"Kiss my brain!" The 'Stache laughs and jabs a finger between his eyes.

"Huh?"

"Kiss it!" The 'Stache keeps jabbing. "Because it *knows*, darlin' JoJo. It has a *plan* that will set the worlds on *fire*."

Just then, someone taps me on the shoulder. Turning, I see an alternate me made of rippling green palm fronds. It hurts to look at her flashing gold bouffant hairdo, and she's chewing some kind of squealing gum or bite-sized creature, I can't see which.

"He's right, honey mustard," says Palm Frond Me. "Big Daddy here's got the goods."

"Hear that?" The 'Stache unveils his broadest grin yet. "If you can't trust your salad-based alternate self, who *can* you trust?"

I could say I don't want anything to do with Delusional Dudley Doofus here … but that would be a bald-assed lie. Truth is, he's got me curious; *anything* to break the boredom of my daily lives and deaths.

Not to mention, he and I used to be a *thing* once upon a once-upon. Maybe that's in the back of my mind a little, too.

Also *other* places, like ten feet away, where alt versions of me and The 'Stache just appeared *in flagrante delicto*. In the middle of the act, in other words, and I don't mean comedy.

So what does *my* 'Stache do? Gives 'em a standing-O, of course. "Yeah! Wooo! Bravo!" He whistles and claps for all he's worth.

It's been sooo long since I did what *they're* doing, I applaud, too. My alt-self, who's on top, laughs and shoots me a big thumbs-up.

Good thing I'm not the type who might get a funny idea from seeing something like that.

✿

So let's just say I get a funny idea after all, and the rest is history. And by history, I mean super-nasty sex.

So *sue* me. It's the first time in I don't know *how* long (literally) that I've done anything other than eat, sleep, kill myself, or rise from the dead. Breaking out of a rut is a good thing (or is that rutting till you break?).

Don't bother me about guilt and regret. This isn't our first time at the rodeo. Forget about illusions, too.

Not that *all* the mystery is gone. There's still a burning question hanging over us.

"Got any coffee?"

Not *that* one, though it's the first thing I ask him in the morning.

"So what's this plan of yours?" *That's* the one.

"You mean the plan where I ravish you?" says The 'Stache as he tickles my tummy. "Check and double-check."

Did I just *giggle*? I *never* giggle. "The *other* plan."

"You mean the one with the fifty porcupines, the nudist camp, and the case of bubble gum?"

Did I just giggle again? "The one about becoming the greatest comic who ever lived."

"Oh, *that* one." The 'Stache rolls over and kisses me. "It's a secret."

"A secret?"

"But who knows?" The 'Stache shrugs. "Maybe we can scare up an exclusive preview if you can pencil me in this morning."

"Hey, wait!" I laugh as he makes a grab for me. "What're you doing?"

"Sorry." He doesn't stop. "*I thought we meant pencil me in …*"

✿

"I know, right?" The 'Stache gives my shoulders a squeeze. "Kinda small, isn't it?"

"Yeah." I'm standing on the field of Hypercube Center, the biggest sports stadium in all of Tesseractus Prime. It's breathtakingly vast, stretching off for miles in all directions. "A real intimate venue."

"My thoughts exactly." The 'Stache gives me a peck on the cheek and undrapes his arm from my shoulders. He walks a few steps away and lets loose a loud whoop that echoes through the stadium. "I want everyone to feel like I'm close enough to reach out and touch."

"Then mission accomplished." Part of me keeps thinking he's pulling my leg, even after I saw his name on the marquee out in front of the place. How he got booked in a venue this big after so long away from the biz beats the hell out of me.

"I'll be a hot ticket, with so few seats to fill," says The 'Stache. "What're we lookin' at? Five thousand, max?"

"If that," I say, though of course we both know it's more like five *million*. "Guaranteed sell-out, I'd say."

"No need to beef up *this* bill." The 'Stache grins. "Though I *might* make room for *you*, if you need the work."

"Lemme think about it."

"I can always use an opening act." He shrugs. "Just sayin'."

"Very generous of you. Thanks loads."

"Fair warning, though. This'll be old school all the way." The 'Stache turns and gazes across the miles-long field. "Just a spotlight, a glass of water, and a microphone." He spreads his arms wide and looks up into the distant heights. "Plus a ginormous mother-lovin' communications array beaming to the fringes of the known freakin' universe in every possible signal and frequency."

Shading my eyes against the glare of the stadium lights, I can just make it out—a spindly silver grid hovering high above, punctuated with upturned disks and spiny antennae. How I completely missed it until now, I don't know; maybe it's got one of those Inexhaustible Apathy Filters that dims external stimuli to the brain based on natural human aversions to Getting Involved.

Whatever the reason, one thing's clear. "That thing's *huge*."

"It's all customized." The 'Stache proudly plants his hands on his hips. "I designed it myself and personally supervised the construction."

"You did?"

"I'm a cosmological engineer, Double-J," says The 'Stache. "I didn't spend those ten years away from show biz just workin' on my memoirs and keepin' it real, y'know."

"But how'd you pay for it? How'd you get permission to install it here?" I sweep an arm around to take in the field and seats. "How'd you get booked here *at all*, for that matter?"

"I made boatloads of money in cosmo-engineering." The 'Stache grins and nods. "Big projects mean big bucks. I worked on everything from Starhenge to the Great Space Roller Coaster, with plenty of hyperdrive bypasses in between." He waves for me to join him. "With the cash I made from my work and investments, I just *bought* the damn stadium and booked myself! Then I gave myself permission to install the array."

I walk over to stand next to him, looking up at the sprawling grid in the sky. "So what's it for? Streaming a pay-per-view special to the cosmos? Beaming a feed to distant primitive cultures so they'll come to worship you as a god?"

"It's something bigger and better than you can imagine." He puts his arm around me again.

Looking down, I slide him a frown. "Seems like a lot of trouble to go to. What's the punchline?"

"Wait and see," says The 'Stache.

"C'mon, tell me."

He shakes his head. "A punchline ain't worth much without the element of surprise, is it?"

I pop an elbow in his side. "What if full disclosure is a condition of my being on the bill?"

"Then I guess you'll miss out on being a headliner at the event of the millennium." Why the bleep is he still grinning? "No skin off *my* chin, Gunga Din."

Is this the part where I'm supposed to sigh and give in? Because damnit, that's exactly what I do. My curiosity couldn't *be* more piqued; my gut instinct is kicking the crap out of all my intuitions, taking their lunch money, and spending it on magic beans.

And yes, *Mom*, my *heart* might have something to do with it, too.

"All right," I tell him. "Good thing I happen to have the day off."

✧

That evening, Hypercube Center is filled to capacity and then some. Every seat in the stands is occupied, and every square inch of standing room on the field is packed. Even the sky is swimming with wall-to-wall spectators; everyone who can sprout wings or rotors or jets or antigravity nards is drifting overhead, angling for the best view in the house.

The only open space within that immensity is the stage itself. As The 'Stache promised, it's a bare bones affair, just a plain black square with a mike stand in the middle and a pitcher of ice water with two glasses on a skinny pedestal table nearby. Old school all the way.

Which begs the question: What's The 'Stache cookin' up? (And the corollary: What's he smokin'?) Without the ingredients of modern comedy—samurai swords, knives, guns, cannons, elaborate Rube Goldberg suicide machines—how the fun does he propose to get any laughs?

"Just go with it," he tells me when I ask him that very question. "Trust ol' Baba Looey here, he won't let you down."

I don't believe him for a second, but I feel better when he folds me in his arms for a pre-show hug. Even better when he stands on tiptoe to give me a long, loving kiss. Am I really that chickified that a little mush can drown out the voices of reason in my head?

Yes, apparently. The voices of reason are screaming for me to make like a banana and get the flock out of Dodge. But the next thing I know …

… I'm standing at the mike onstage, introducing The 'Stache.

Yay me, I get a standing-O all my own, just for being there. It takes a while for the applause to die down enough for me to be heard.

At which point, I put everything I have into singing The 'Stache's praises. I really pour it on, telling the crowd what a great comedian and unique talent he is—what an influence he's had on my career and those of so many others. I tell 'em how lucky they are that he's returned to the stage, what a privilege it is to be there to introduce him to the universe again. I tell 'em how great he is in bed, and how I'm probably mostly doing this because we're romantically involved, so don't blame me if he sucks, bites, and blows. (I skip that last part, but the mind readers out there might catch a whiff.)

Then I start applauding. "Ladies, gentlemen, invertebrates, intangibles, incomprehensibles, unmentionables, and all other lifeforms, artforms, and colorforms, I present to you the once and future comedy genius known far, wide, and in-between as *The* 'Stache!"

The crowd roars with deafening cheers and applause. I've done a great job warming them up; now it's up to him to close the deal.

The 'Stache bursts out from behind an Apathy Curtain that kept him invisible until now. Waving and grinning at the crowd like a beauty pageant contestant, he marches up and takes my place at the mike. Then he winks at me and gestures at a mark on the floor, a glowing red X ten feet behind the mike where he wants me to wait.

As I take my position and the crowd settles down, he starts talking.

"What is comedy?" That's how he starts. "It's what makes you laugh. And that changes through time as *humanity* changes."

The 'Stache spreads his arms wide to encompass the crowd around him—the millions of people who are listening in dumbstruck silence. He sounds more eloquent than usual, as if he's channeling his inner Einstein instead of his typical Wisenheimer. "Humans have evolved to a level where technology enables them to do so many things … things that would have been considered *magic* to their ancestors thousands—even *hundreds*—of years ago.

"And these human beings of today, so changed now from what they once were, have a very different definition of comedy. Since almost anything is possible to them, even commonplace … and every bizarre situation that might once have been the basis of a *joke* is now the basis of *reality* … they no longer laugh at what they once did."

At that moment, the crowd *shifts*. I can see and feel and hear it from the stage. The people in the stands and on the field and in the air have waited through what's amounted to a lecture so far, but they've passed the tipping point. It's just a matter of time until they turn ugly.

The question is, does The 'Stache know it's coming? And does he have something planned to head it off?

If he does, he gives no sign of it. "So what does it take to make humans laugh in this modern day and age?" He counts out the answers on the fingers of his right hand. "Cruelty. Shock. Atrocity.

"This is what their sense of humor has become. Laughing at someone mutilating or killing themselves." He shoots a glance in my direction.

Suddenly, a loud male heckler shouts from the audience. "What the Fermi are you *talkin'* about, 'they'?"

The 'Stache ignores the heckler and keeps talking. "But here's the irony … the *ultimate* irony, that *none* of them can see. In the course of their evolution to a *less* funny species, humans have stumbled upon the biggest *joke* of all time."

Again, the heckler calls out from the crowd. "What's with the 'them' and 'they'?"

A second heckler joins in. "*We're* human, and we're right *in front* of you."

The 'Stache ignores them. "It goes like this. It took billions of years for the universe to evolve … for the planet Earth to evolve in such a way that the conditions were optimal for sentient life to develop … and for that sentient life, *humanity*, to evolve to its current, highly advanced state. It has taken that long for human beings to reach a level of technological advancement that makes them masters of their own bodies and minds and the physical laws of the universe itself.

"Have they used this mastery to transcend their limitations and set out in search of greater knowledge? To probe the hidden mysteries of existence itself?"

Another heckler interrupts. "Why does he keep calling us 'they'?"

"What has humanity done?" continues The 'Stache. "They've used their *mastery* to turn themselves into a trillion variations on the same self-referential silliness … the same images of clowns and celebrities and fictional characters they've been recycling for the past ten millennia. They've got the power to become *gods*, and they're still pissing around in the same damn *kiddie pool*, laughing at the suffering of their fellow men and women.

"In this way, humanity itself has become the greatest *joke* in the history of the *universe!* The kind of joke that *my* audience will appreciate!"

By now, the crowd is restless to the point of open rebellion. I smell danger in the air like smoke from a fire.

There's a murmur through the crowd, a susurration of thousands of disaffected voices … but the shout of the first heckler still manages to punch through above them all. "For the last time, why do you keep calling us 'they'? We *are* humanity. We *are* your audience."

A dark smile curls its way across The 'Stache's face. "What the eff gave you *that* idea?"

The murmur of the crowd drops away as all ears lock onto his next words.

"I'm not *talking* to *you* people." The 'Stache points upward. "I'm talking to *them*."

"The airbornes?" asks the heckler. "The flying-room-only people?"

"Not even close." The 'Stache raises his arms overhead and spreads them wide. "I *should've* said I'm talking to *it*. The *universe*."

Just then, I remember the communications array he installed above the stadium, the one that's "beaming to the fringes of the known freakin' universe in every possible signal and frequency." I figured it would be streaming his show to people on distant worlds and vessels … but maybe I was thinking too small.

"*That's* who this whole show was *meant* for," says The 'Stache. "*You people* are just here to prove my *point*."

"You're full'a *shazbot*," shouts the heckler. "The *universe* isn't sentient!"

"Sure it is!" says The 'Stache. "And I just told it the funniest joke it's ever heard!"

Suddenly, a deafening blast of thunder crashes through the stadium, and everyone falls silent. The airborne audience scatters like cockroaches from a kitchen light, and everyone in the stands and on the ground looks up.

"Hear that?" The 'Stache hikes a thumb toward the sky. "I'd say *somebody's* getting the joke!"

There's another blast of thunder, and another—each progressively louder than the one before. The stars in the sky dance and swirl like gold dust in a prospector's pan, flashing in unnatural rhythms.

Down below, the ground rumbles and shakes. That sets the earthbound crowd in motion, as everyone stampedes toward the exits. Millions of screams rise together, exploding through the miles-long/miles-wide stadium in a tsunami of cascading terror.

Not that The 'Stache looks the slightest bit worried. His face is calm as he turns and gestures for me to join him.

I wonder if I ought to be fleeing for the exits instead, but I run to his side anyway. "What's *happening*? What *is* this?"

The ground shakes harder than ever, and the thunderous blasts keep coming. Every light in the stadium blows out at the same time, showering the crowd with sizzling shards of glass.

The 'Stache wraps his arms around me. "I'm *killing*, that's what!" He grins up at the reeling stars in the sky. "They freakin' *love* me!"

The booming thunder becomes a continuous roar. The stars spin faster and faster, and the ground splits apart. Thousands of fleeing audience members tumble into the widening crevices.

The 'Stache tightens his grip on me. "Don't worry, Double-J!" He has to shout for me to hear him over the cacophony. "You and I have nothing to worry about! We'll be fine!"

A powerful wind rushes past us, a hurricane wind—only it's not trying to blow us away. It's *sucking* everything upward, pulling people and pieces of stadium into the sky with inexorable, furious force.

"How can you *say* that?" My voice is a terrified shriek.

"Because!" says The 'Stache. "I haven't done an *encore* yet!"

Just as he says it, the wind hauls us off our feet. We both go tumbling toward the stars, still locked in our embrace as if that will save us somehow.

At some point after we leave the ground, I lose consciousness—which is probably a blessing, given the circumstances.

Then, I awaken in The 'Stache's arms. His eyes are locked on mine, and his smile is gentle.

"Hey there, sleepyhead." He kisses me softly on the cheek. "Rise and shine."

As awareness returns more fully, I realize our surroundings are calm. There seems to be no trace of the apocalyptic mayhem that engulfed Tesseractus Prime.

"Wait." I push away from him and look around. It's only then that I see where we are: in a transparent bubble, floating through uninterrupted white space.

"What is this?" My voice quivers when I say it.

The 'Stache runs his hand along the surface of the bubble, which flexes and stretches under his fingertips. "Nothing … yet."

I feel panic twisting inside me, straining to burst free. "What're you talking about? What just *happened*?"

"Pretty sure the *universe* just *laughed*," says The 'Stache.

"What do you *mean*, it *laughed*?"

"What do you think all the *noise* and *shaky-shaky* were about?" The 'Stache's eyes glitter as he grins.

Things still aren't making sense to me. The white space, the bubble … our *lives*, which somehow still exist. "But where *is* everything?"

"Out there somewhere." He waves dismissively at the milky void. "Compressed into a super-dense, super-heated ball of energy. The seed of a *new* universe, in other words."

"Wait, what?" Am I losing my mind here? Did he just tell me … "The universe *ended*?"

He waggles his hand and squints. "More like *reset*. It suddenly contracted …" He jams his hands together. "Now there's a *pause*, like a *breath*. And soon …" He makes a whooshing sound as he pulls his hands apart. "It'll *reboot*."

"Like a *big bang*, you mean?"

He touches the tip of his nose. "Exactamundo. There'll be a shiny new universe in place of the old one. Happens once every 14 billion years or so."

"And what about us?" When I press my hand against the bubble, it feels like a warm rubber balloon. "Why didn't *we* get mashed up with the rest of the old universe?"

"Funny you should ask." The 'Stache takes my hand. "It's been talking to me …"

"The universe."

"Yup. Apparently, it likes my work so much, it wants me to help set up the next version of itself. I mean the next *joke*."

My head is spinning. I'd think he's lost his mind if we weren't floating in a transparent bubble through some kind of white void after witnessing a cosmic apocalypse.

"So that's it then?" A hysterical giggle escapes my lips. "*Our* universe—the one we *knew*, our *home*—is just *gone?*"

"Gone forever." The 'Stache nods.

Again, a crazy giggle escapes me. "*Forever? Everything we know is gone forever?*"

"Yeah, and wouldn't ya know it?" The 'Stache laughs and shakes his head. "*Now* I'm hungry for *Chinese* all of a sudden!"

I think about it, chewing a fingernail. More giggles slip out.

"What is it?" asks The 'Stache. "What's so funny?"

I laugh a little harder now. "All those times I killed myself for comedy … and now here I am, a last survivor while everyone else is dead."

The 'Stache nods. "It's ironic, all right."

I keep laughing. "And you know what *really* cracks me up? I can't figure out whether the joke's on *them*, the people who are *gone* … or on *me*."

"Then everything's as it should be, Double-J. Remember the Groucho Marx Effect from physics: *A universe simple enough to be understood is too simple to produce a mind capable of understanding it.*

"Or as Groucho himself put it …" The 'Stache flicks an invisible cigar and waggles his eyebrows. "'I wouldn't want to belong to any club that would have me as a member!'"

Gardner Dozois is known primarily as an editor, winning an amazing 14 Best Editor Hugos during his time at Asimov's. *But Gardner's a writer too, and indeed won two Nebula Awards for short stories before winning any of his editing awards.*

COUNTERFACTUAL

by Gardner Dozois

"If we reach the Blue Ridge Mountains,
we can hold out for twenty years."
— General Robert E. Lee

Cliff's fountain pen rolled across the pull-out writing shelf again, and he sighed and reached out to grab it before it tumbled to the floor. The small ink bottle kept marching down the shelf too, juddering with each vibration of the car.

Writing on a train wasn't easy, especially on a line where the rail-bed had been insufficiently maintained for decades. Even forming legible words was a challenge, with the jarring of the undercarriage or a sudden jerk all too likely to turn a letter into an indecipherable *splat* or to produce a startled, rising line across the page, as if the ink were trying to escape the mundane limitations of the paper.

Scenery was a distraction too. Cliff had always loved landscapes, and he had to wage a constant battle against the urge to just sit there and look out the window, where, at the moment, pale armies of fir trees were sliding slowly by, while the sky guttered toward a winter dusk in washes of plum and ash and sullen red. But he'd be sharing this room tonight with three other reporters, which meant lights-out early and a night wasted listening to them fart and snore, so if he was going to get any writing done on the new Counterfactual he was working on for *McClure's*, it'd better be now, while his roommates were down in the bar with the rest of the boys.

Cliff opened his notebook, smoothed it, and bent over the page:

General Robert E. Lee put his hands on the small of his back and stretched, trying to shake some of the tension out of his aching spine. He had never been so tired, feeling every one of his fifty-eight years sitting on his shoulders like bars of lead.

For days, days that had stretched into an unending nightmare of pain and fatigue, he had struggled to stay awake, to stay erect in the saddle, as they executed a fighting retreat from the trenches and earthworks of Petersburg westward along the Appomattox River toward Lynchburg, Grant's Army of the James, which outnumbered his own forces four to one, snapping at their heels every step of the way. Thousands of his men had died along the way, and Lee almost envied the fallen—at least they could *stop*. But Lee couldn't stop. He knew that all eyes were on him, that it was up to him to put on a show of being indefatigable and imperturbable, tall in the saddle, regal, calm, and totally in command. His example and the pride it inspired, and the love and respect the men felt for him, was all that was keeping his ragged and starving army going. No matter how exhausted he was, no matter how bleak and defeated were his inner thoughts, no matter how hopeless he knew his position to be, no matter how much his chest ached (as it had been aching increasingly for days), he couldn't let it show.

They had stopped for the night in the woods near Appomattox Court House, too tired to even pitch tents. There had been almost nothing to eat, even for the staff officers. Now his staff huddled close to him in the darkness, as if they depended on him for light and warmth as much or more than the low-burning bivouac fire, ragged, worn-out men in tattered uniforms, sprawled on blankets spread on the grass or sitting on saddles thrown over tree-stumps, without even chairs or camp-stools anymore. Lee could see their eyes, gleaming wetly in the firelight, as well as feel them. Every eye was on him still.

The barking of rifles had started up again from General Gordon's rear-guard on the road behind them when the courier arrived. He was thin as a skeleton, like Death himself come to call. He saluted and handed Lee a sealed communiqué. "Sir, from General Grant."

Lee held the note warily, as if it was a snake. He knew what it was: another message from General Grant, politely suggesting that he surrender his army.

The question was, what was *he* going to say in return?

✧

The car jolted, shuddered, and jerked again while momentum equalized itself along the length of the train, and Cliff lifted his pen from the paper, waiting for the ride to steady again. What *was* he going to say in return? That was the problem.

He had an arresting central image, one that had come to him whole: Robert F. Lee surrendering the Army of Northern Virginia to General Ulysses S. Grant, the soldiers lined up somberly along a country road, heads down, some of the Confederates openly in tears, Lee handing his sword to Grant while a light rain fell, both men looking solemn and grim … How to justify it, though? Counterfactuals had become increasingly popular in recent years—perhaps because the public had been denied the opportunity to play soldier during the Great War—until they were now almost respectable as pulp stories went, and you could make decent money selling them. But in writing Counterfactuals, you had to provide some kind of tipping-point, some event that would have changed everything that came after—and it had to be at least superficially plausible, or the fans, armchair historians all, would tear you to pieces. Having the Confederates win the War was a common enough trope in the genre, and a number of stories had been written about how Lee had won at Gettysburg or had pushed on out of Virginia to attack and burn Washington when he had the chance, forcing capitulation on a terrified Union, but Cliff was after something more subtle—a tale where the Confederates still *lost* the War, but lost it in a different way, with different consequences as a result. It was hard to see what would have motivated Lee to surrender, though. True, he was nearly at the end of his rope, his men exhausted and starving, being closely harried by Union forces who were chasing him relentlessly West—but in the real world, none of that had brought him to the point of seriously contemplating surrender. In fact, it was at that very point when he'd said that he was determined "to fight to the last," and told his officers and men that "We must all determine to die at our posts." Didn't sound much like somebody who was ready to throw in the towel.

Then, just when things looked blackest, he had narrowly avoided a closing Union trap by breaking past Phil Sheridan at Appomattox Court House, and kept on going until he reached the Blue Ridge Mountains, there to break his army up into smaller units that melted into the wilderness, setting the stage for decades of bitterly fought guerilla war, a war of terror and ambush that was still smoldering to this day. It was hard to see what would have made Lee surrender, when he didn't contemplate it even in the hour of his most extreme need. Especially as he knew that he could expect few compromises in the matter of surrender and little or no mercy from the implacable President Johnson …

He was spinning his wheels. Time for a drink.

Outside, the sun had finally disappeared below the horizon, leaving only a spreading red bruise behind. The darkening sky was slate-gray now, and hard little flakes of snow were squeezing themselves out of it, like dandruff sprinkled across felt. He hoped that the weather didn't work itself into a real blizzard, one that might hold them up on the way back. Like everyone else, he wanted to get the ceremony over with and get back home before Christmas—even though all he really had to look forward to was a turkey sandwich at a Horn & Hardart's and an evening drinking in a journalist's hangout with many of the same people he was already sharing a train with in the first place.

Cliff stored his notebook in his carpetbag, and pushed out into the corridor, which was rocking violently from side-to-side, like a ship in a high sea, as the track-bed roughened. He made his way unsteadily along the corridor, bracing himself against the wall. Freezing needles of winter cold stabbed at him between the cars, and then stale air and the smell of human sweat swallowed him as he crossed into one of the coach cars, which was crowded with passengers, pinch-faced civilians in threadbare clothes, including whole families trying to sleep sitting up in the uncomfortable wooden seats. Babies were crying, women were crooning to them, couples were fighting, someone was playing a Mexican song on a beat-up old guitar, and four Texans in the stereotypical but seemingly obligatory Stetsons—Texans were being seen around more frequently these days, now that relations had been normalized with the Republic of Texas—were playing poker on one of the seats, with onlookers standing in the aisles and whooping with every turn of the cards.

There were three more coach cars to push your way through, and Cliff was glad to get beyond them into the alcoves between the cars, even though the cold air nipped at him each time. He never had liked noise and crowds, which was one reason why he'd always preferred small-towns to the big cities. With things the way they were, though, the big cities like Chicago and Minneapolis were where the work was, and so he had no choice but to live there, as long as the *Minneapolis Star* paid his bills.

Even out here, between the cars, you could smell the tobacco stink coming from the next compartment, and when he opened the door and stepped into the bar car, tobacco smoke hung in such a thick yellow cloud that you could barely see. Most of the newsmen on the train were in here, standing around the bar or sitting grouped on stools around the little tables. Like Cliff, most of them had shunned the dining car and brought bags of sandwiches from Chicago, to save their meager expense-account money for the bar.

Cliff was hailed with the usual derisive, mildly insulting greetings, and two of the boys squeezed apart to make room for him at the bar. He was well-enough liked by the other newsmen, although his hobby of writing Counterfactuals and Westerns, even the occasional Air War or Weird Fantasy, marked him out as a bit strange. Half of these guys probably had an unfinished draft of the Great American Novel stashed away in a drawer somewhere, but in public you were supposed to give lip-service to the idea that to a *real* newsman, the only kind of writing that mattered was journalism.

"Hey, Cliff," John said. "Finish another masterpiece?"

"Aw, he was probably just jerking-off," Staubach said.

Cliff smiled tolerantly and bought a round. He was already several drinks behind. The *wunderkind* from the *Chicago Tribune*—he was supposed to be nineteen, but to Cliff it didn't look like he could be more than thirteen—was trying to get an argument about The Gathering Clouds of War in Europe going with Bill, a big amiable Michigan Swede who rarely paid any attention to anything outside of the box-scores on the sports page, unless it was a racing form. "The United States will never get involved in a foreign war," the kid was saying, in his surprisingly deep voice. "Bryant kept us out of the Great War, and Hoover will keep us out of this one, too." He was short and pudgy, pasty-faced, with a sullen, cynical, seen-it-all air unusual in one so young. A few of the boys had held the fact that he was a New York Jew against him for awhile, but he was basically good-natured behind his gruff exterior, and smart as a whip, with just the kind of savage black humor that reporters liked, and so most of them had warmed to him.

He was trying to get a rise out of Bill, who had been incautious enough to express mild Interventionist sentiments a few times in the past, but Bill wasn't rising to the bait. "Guess England and Germany will just have to take care of de Gaulle without our help," Bill said amiably. "They're up to it, I guess."

"We've got enough problems of our own without worrying about de Gaulle," John threw in.

"Fuck de Gaulle and the horse he fucking rode in on," Staubach said. "Who's got the cards?"

"Language, gentlemen!" old Matthews said sternly. They all jeered at him, but they acquiesced, Staubach rephrasing his question to "Okay, who's got the *frigging* cards?" Although he was as erect and natty as ever, impeccably dressed, looking every inch the distinguished senior correspondent, Matthews had been drinking even harder lately than reporters usually drank, and was already a bit glassy-eyed. The kid was supposed to be his assistant, but everybody knew that he'd been writing his column for him, and doing a better job of it than Matthews ever had.

John had the cards, but they had to wait through another couple of rounds for one of the little tables to open up, as the more prosperous passengers, or those who were more finicky about their food, drifted off to the dining car up front. "Crowded in here," Cliff commented. "Where are all the politicians, though? You'd think they'd be nine-deep around the bar."

"Aw, they got a bar of their own, coupla cars up," Staubach said.

"Got the first three cars, all to themselves," Bill threw in, with a grin. "And a sergeant with a carbine on the platform outside, to make sure Lindbergh and the rest of them don't get bothered by the *hoi'poloi.*"

"Sure, little do they care that the poor bastard has to freeze his nuts off all the way to Montgomery," John said, which drew another admonishment of "Language!" from Matthews, although, as he was already more than half-fried, it was clear that his heart wasn't in it anymore. The bartender—who, on a train like this, traveling through the Occupied Territories, was likely to be a soldier in civilian clothes, with a carbine of his own tucked under the bar—grinned at them over Matthews's head.

At last a table opened up, and they settled in for their usual nickel-and-dime game of draw. Matthews kept fumbling with his cards, having trouble holding them in a proper fan, forgetting whose bet it was, and changing his mind about how many cards he wanted, and soon was the big loser—as big as it got in this penny ante game, anyway. Every time the kid lost a hand, he would curse with an inventive fluency that was almost Shakespearian, and that kept the rest of them chuckling. Since he never deigned to use the common "four-letter words," even Matthews couldn't really complain, although he grumbled about it. Bill played with his usual quiet competency and was soon ahead, although Cliff managed to hold his own and split a number of pots with him.

After about an hour and a half of this, the smoke and the noise, and the fact that Matthews was no longer able to keep from dropping his cards every time he picked them up, and was getting pissy about it, made Cliff deal himself out.

"Going back to the room," he said, "see if I can get a couple of pages done before the rest of you guys show up.

"Can't keep *Wild West Weekly* waiting," Bill said.

"Aw, he's just going to jerk-off again," Staubach mumbled, peering at his cards.

Cliff waved at them and walked away, moving a little more unsteadily than was entirely justified by the lurching of the car. Truth was, left to his own devices, Cliff wasn't that heavy a drinker—but if you were going to be accepted by the boys, you had to drink with them, and reporters prided themselves on their ability to put it away, another way in which the kid—who seemed to have a hollow trunk, as well as two hollow legs—fit right in in spite of his youth. Cliff could feel that he was at the edge of his ability to toss it back without becoming knee-walking drunk, though, which would lose him respect with the boys, so it was time to call it a night.

There was snow crusted on the footplates between the cars now, although it didn't seem to be snowing anymore outside. Cliff decided that he'd better clear his head if he was going to get any writing done, and walked back through the now-darkened coach cars and the sleeping cars to the observation platform on the back of the rear car.

It was bitterly cold outside, his breath puffing out in tattered plumes, but the snow had stopped, and the black clouds overhead had momentarily parted, revealing the fat pale moon. They were still moving through thick forest, the snow-shrouded ghosts of the trees gleaming like bones in the darkness, but now the ground on one side of the track fell steeply away, opening the world up to space and distance and the dimly perceived black bulks of nearby hills. There was a fast little mountain stream down there, winding along at the bottom of the slope, and in the moonlight he could see the cold white rills it made as it broke around streambed rocks.

The train slowed while going up the next long incline, and a dark figure broke from the trees, darted forward, and sprang onto the observation platform, grabbing the railing. As Cliff flinched back in shock, the figure threw a leg over the railing and pulled itself up. It paused, sitting on the top rail, one leg over, and looked at Cliff. It was a man, thin, clean-shaven, with a large nose and close-cropped hair bristling across a bullet-head, clutching a bindle in one hand. As Cliff gaped, the man smiled jauntily, said, "Evenin', sport!", and put one finger to his lips in a shushing gesture. Then he swung his other leg over the railing, hopped down to the platform, and sauntered by Cliff, giving him a broad wink as he passed.

Up close, even by moonlight, you could tell that his clothes were patched and much-mended, but they seemed reasonably clean, and although he exuded a brief whiff of sweat and unwashed armpits

and sour breath as he passed, it wasn't too strong or too rank. He couldn't have been on the bum for too long, Cliff thought, or at least he must have been finding work frequently enough to enable him to keep himself moderately clean. The tramp disappeared into the car without a backwards glance, presumably to lose himself among the coach-class passengers or find a water-closet or a storage cubical to hide in for the night. There were thousands of such ragged men on the road these days, drifting from place to place, looking for work or a handout, especially down here in the Occupied Territories; the economy was bad enough in the States, but down here, whole regions had never really recovered from the War in the first place, the subsequent decades of guerilla war and large-scale terrorism—with whole armies of unreconstructed rebels still on the loose and lurking in the hills, many of them by now composed of the children and grandchildren of the original soldiers—tending to discourage economic growth … especially with raiders knocking down new factories or businesses as fast as they sprang up, to discourage "collaboration" with the occupying forces.

Cliff knew that he really should report the tramp to the conductor, but it was difficult to work up enough indignation to bother, and in the end he decided not to even try. It was hard to blame him for wanting to be inside the train, where it was warm, rather than out there in the freezing night.

Up ahead, around a long curve, you could see the engine itself now, puffing out bursts of fire-shot black smoke like some great, stertoriously gasping iron beast. The smoke plume wrapped itself back around the observation platform, making him cough and filling his mouth with the ashen taste of cinders, and that, plus the fact that he was beginning to shiver, told him that it was time to go back inside himself. If his head wasn't clear by now, it wasn't going to be.

When Cliff got back to their compartment, though, it became obvious that it didn't matter whether his head was clear or not; he wasn't going to get any more writing done tonight. The conductor had already rearranged the compartment into its sleeping configuration, folding away the benches and lowering two bunks from each opposing wall, one stacked above the other. Somewhat surprisingly, his roommates were already back from the bar. Matthews, in fact, was already soddenly asleep on one of the lower bunks, gurgling and snoring, still fully clothed, although Bill was fussing with him, trying to get him undressed, with little success. Cliff gathered that the old man had passed out in the bar, or come near to it, and his compatriots had hauled him back to the roomette. Even out here, you could smell the booze coming off of him.

With the bunks folded down, there was hardly space enough for Bill and the kid to stand in the tiny compartment, and Cliff had to hover in the doorway, half out in the corridor, waiting for someone to make room for him. The kid at last got impatient with Bill's efforts to undress Matthews and bumped him aside, saying harshly "Oh, leave the poor old *pfumpt* alone." With a curious tenderness that belayed the gruffness of his tone, he took off the old man's shoes and stowed them under his bunk, and loosened his tie. "He'll just have to sleep in his clothes for once like the rest of us, instead of those stupid woolen pajamas."

As if to demonstrate, Bill climbed into the other bottom bunk—fully dressed except for his shoes; it was a good idea to keep your wallet in your pocket, too, since sneak-thieves were known to rifle through bags left on the floor in a compartment while the occupants slept—and put his hat over his eyes. Cliff slid inside, now that some floor space had opened-up, and closed the door on the corridor.

They had come down out of the hills by now, and stopped at a tiny station for no readily apparent reason. There was a small town out there, two or three streets of two-story storefronts laid out parallel to the tracks, some dilapidated old wooden houses with big overgrown yards set further back. The storefronts carried faded signs that said things like "Hudson's Hickory House" or "Brown Furniture Company," but none of them looked like they'd been open for awhile, and several had boarded-up windows. Nothing was moving out there except a dog pissing on a lamppole.

"What a dump!" the kid said, turning to look at Cliff. Up close like this, he had a habit of partially covering his mouth with his hand when he spoke; he was embarrassed about his teeth, which he never brushed, and were green. "No wonder all the colored folks moved up North."

"Getting lynched and shot and burned-out by Lee's Boys probably had something to do with it too," Bill said dryly, lifting his hat for a second. "Turn off the light. I want to get some sleep."

The kid vaulted up into the bunk above Matthews. Cliff took his shoes off, stuffed his carpetbag into his bunk to use as a pillow, shut off the light, and climbed into the other upper in the dark, nearly falling when the car lurched as the train started moving again.

Cliff lay awake in the darkness for awhile, feeling oddly apprehensive and jittery for no particular reason he could identify, listening to the snoring and moaning of his roommates, before the steady swaying movement of the car rocked him to sleep.

Even so, he'd wake up for a moment every time the motion of the train changed, slowing down or speeding up with a jerk and a lurch, opening his eyes to see, through the uncurtained top of the window, trees rushing by, the roofs of houses, bright lights on tall poles, more trees, and then his eyes would close, and he'd sleep again, the wailing of the train's whistle and the rhythmical clatter of its wheels weaving themselves through his dreams.

☼

By morning, they had outrun the winter. Here, it was still fall, no snow on the ground, browning multi-colored leaves still clinging to the hardwood trees. Further south still, on the Gulf Coast or at least in Florida, it was probably still summer, palm trees swaying in balmy breezes, but they weren't going that far. This was the last leg of their journey, with only a couple of hours left until they reached Montgomery.

The room steward brought them a pot of coffee. Sensitized by the kid's remarks of the previous evening, Cliff noticed that he was a Mediterranean immigrant of some sort—Italian, Greek; recent enough to still have a heavy accent—where before the War, he almost certainly would have been colored. It wasn't true that there were no colored people left in the Occupied Territories, of course—there were still families holding out here and there. But decades of large-scale terrorism had chased millions of them to the big cities of the North, where they had encountered other problems to replace the ones they'd left behind, and most of the medium-level jobs went to more recent (and reasonably white) immigrants like the room steward. Now the Open Door that had let people like the steward into the country was slamming closed as immigration policies were tightened, leaving millions of European refugees with nowhere to go. As someone whose father had immigrated from Prague only a generation before, Cliff sympathized with all of them, and with the exiled colored folk as well, unwelcome in either the South or North.

Bill slipped his shoes on and ducked out to fetch a bunch of doughnuts from the dining car. They ate while taking turns going to the WC at the end of the sleeper for sponge baths and to change into fresh clothes, although old Matthews was so glazed and hung-over that the kid had to guide him there and back, holding him by one arm. Bill teased him about this unmercifully, although he wasn't quite mean enough to ask the kid if he'd had to help Matthews bathe. He certainly had to help him dress, though, while Bill jeered, and Matthews, lost in his own world, stared at nothing anybody else could see. He clearly didn't have long to go before he reached the end of his rope, Cliff realized. Odds were that the kid would have his job before then anyway.

Outside, rundown white clapboard houses with incongruously large porches were slipping by, as well as burnt-out factories, cut banks of red clay, goats grazing in hilly yards, an occasional glimpse of a sluggish brown river. For the last half-hour, they crawled by a huge Army base, home of one of the occupying divisions, although little was visible beyond the high walls and barbed wire except the red roofs of the barracks, a water tower, a big industrial crane of some sort. There were guard-towers every few yards, with machine-gun emplacements at the top, giving the whole complex the look of a prison. Scrub woods, weed-overgrown lots, and heaps of rusting scrap metal for the next few minutes, and then the outlying freight yards for the Montgomery station began to roll past.

Montgomery was still a big city for this part of the world. It had been in Yankee hands since the end of the War, and although it had suffered several major raids in subsequent years from unreconstruct-ed Confederate forces, and had been shelled by terrorists more than once, it was still in pretty good shape. There were still a few bombed-out buildings visible in the center of town, but most of them were busily being repaired, and the sounds of construction—hammering, workmen shouting, buzz-saws whining—were a constant here. Outside the train for the first time in more than a day, Cliff wished he'd brought a heavier coat; it wasn't as cold here as it had been up the track, in the hill country, but it was still brisk, and the pregnant gray clouds that were sliding by overhead promised rain that he hoped would hold off until after the ceremony. The air smelled of dust and ozone.

He caught a glimpse of the Vice President going by, his handsome features looking strained and a bit grim; one of the youngest Vice Presidents in history, Lindbergh hadn't been given a lot to do after his charm, good-looks, and charisma had helped Herbert Hoover win the election, except to be trotted out on ceremonial occasions like this one that were important but not quite important enough to fetch the President out of the White House. He was accompanied by his son, a somber, silent little boy dressed like a miniature adult in suit and tie, and by the usual crowd of handlers and hangers-on, as well as by John Foster Dulles, Huey Long, Charles Curtis, and the rest of the senatorial party, and *their* people. All of the dignitaries were hustled into long black limousines and whisked away, the star reporters and big-name columnists—one of whom once would have been Matthews—scurrying after them, off to arrange interviews with local officials and whichever of the senators they could catch before they disappeared into backroom bars somewhere.

After the ceremony, there'd be the usual photo-op for clutch-and-grin shots of Lindbergh shaking hands with the outgoing Territorial Governor, Lindbergh and the pro-tem State Governor about to take office, Lindbergh and the Mayor, Lindbergh and the Mayor's big-breasted sister, and so on, and then, hopefully before it started pouring, they'd all rush back to the train station to file their stories via telegraph (there were no trunk lines through the Occupied Territories; it was difficult enough to keep the telegraph lines up). They'd all try to come up with some twist or angle on the same dry story, of course (Cliff hoped to get some pithy quotes from Huey Long, who'd been born in the Occupied Territories before moving North, carpetbag in hand, to seek his fortune, and who was a usefully Colorful Character, always good for a line or two of copy), and they they'd all pile back in the train and head back to Chicago, to be off to somewhere else a day or a week later. That was a reporter's life.

In the meantime, most of the newsmen crossed the tracks and headed for a café across the street from the station. It was just a dingy old storefront, with cracked and patched windows, the calendars on the walls the only decorations, but it was warm inside and smelled invitingly of cooking food. The pancakes and eggs weren't bad, either, although it was probably better not to know what animal the bacon had come from; even the bitter chicory brew that passed for coffee down here on the far side of the Embargo Line was tolerable. Most of the reporters ignored the grits, to the amusement of the local stringers who'd arranged to meet them here before the ceremony. Watching them, Cliff realized that although he had been born in Wisconsin and lived in Minneapolis, had only visited New York City once, and had never been to Boston in his life, he was a Yankee to the locals—they were all just Yankees to the locals, who didn't make any of the fine distinctions between them as to regional origins that they made amongst themselves, and who probably, truth be told, disliked them all equally. Cliff wondered if this boded well for the years ahead, when they'd all officially be fellow citizens once more, on paper, anyway.

Bill and Staubach and Hoskins from the *New York World* had started a political argument about just that, Bill thinking that officially readmitting Alabama to the Union (something that it had taken decades of economic sanctions and delicate negotiations to accomplish, in the face of Rebel reprisals against "collaborators" and a general population who were by no means wholeheartedly for the idea), as Virginia and the Carolinas and Arkansas had already been before it, as Mississippi and Louisiana and Georgia had *not*, was a good thing, putting more of the shattered jigsaw that had once been the Union back together—while Staubach and Hoskins thought that Reunification was a bad idea, that it would further

drag the economy of the U.S. down, that the nation was in fact better off *without* the disaffected former States, especially with federal troops quartered on them to make sure they stayed down.

Cliff lost interest in the too-familiar argument and started thinking about his Counterfactual again. How would the world of his story have differed from the real world? He toyed with the conceit that in that Counterfactual world there might *also* be a Cliff, struggling to write a Counterfactual story about *his* world, and yet another Cliff in the *next* world, and so on—a vision of a ring of Alternate Earths, in each of which history had taken a slightly different course. There was a story idea there. Maybe somebody manning a way station of some sort in some isolated location, maybe out in the rural Wisconsin hill-country where he'd grown up, a station which allowed travel between the Alternate Earths. It was too weird an idea for Thurber at *McClure's*, probably for most of the Counterfactual market, but it could maybe be done as scientifiction. He'd written a few scientifiction pieces at the beginning of his career for *Marvel Tales* and *Wonder Stories Quarterly*, although they didn't pay as well as Counterfactuals. For all his prim pseudo-Victorian stuffiness, Lovecraft at *Weird Tales* liked wildly imaginative stuff; maybe he'd go for it …

"Wake up, Shakespeare," Staubach said, punching his arm. "Time to get going."

The reporters gathered up their equipment—Cliff had earlier hauled his battered old Speed Graphic out of his bag; the *Star's* budget didn't stretch to sending a photographer as well—and shambled out through the streets of Montgomery. You could already hear a brass band playing in the distance.

There was a raised wooden stage set up in front of the State Capitol building, from whose white marble steps Jefferson Davis had announced the formation of the Confederacy (which was rubbing it in a bit too blatantly, Cliff thought, but nobody had asked him), with a podium and a microphone up front, and rows of cold-looking dignitaries sitting on camp-chairs lined up behind, including Lindbergh's little boy, who, sitting hunched up on himself, looked like he'd rather be inside drinking a cup of hot chocolate than sitting out here in the cold. No chairs for the color guard who surrounded the stage on two sides, weapons at port arms, or for the audience, who were packed-in in front of the stage in a disorderly mass. Not a bad turn-out for a chilly December day, Cliff thought as he and his compatriots wormed their way to the front, especially for a ceremony solemnizing a decision that by no means had the support of the entire citizenry. The real ratification ceremony would take place in Congress later, of course; this symbolic local ceremony was an excuse to literally show the flag, a big one center-stage that snapped in the wind. And to give the local yokels a chance to bathe in the reflected glory of Lindbergh and the other bigwigs.

The sky was still threatening, although a lacuna had opened up in the slate-gray clouds, splashing watery sunshine around. A brisk wind had come up, scattering trash and discarded sheets of newspaper like frightened birds. Bill cursed and seized his hat to keep it from flying away. The faces of the men in the brass band were stiff and red with cold, the cheeks of the trumpet player bulging grotesquely out, as though he'd bitten off something too big for him to swallow.

The band stopped playing. The Territorial Governor made a long, rambling, fawning introduction of Lindbergh, who then stepped forward to the podium and began speaking himself. His face was also red with cold, and he kept sniffing, as if his nose was running. He was holding his hat in one hand to keep it from blowing away, and the rising wind made his tie flap up into his face from time to time, requiring him to smooth it back down.

Cliff raised his camera and dutifully took a photo of him, and then stopped listening. Christ, he'd heard a lot of speeches in his life! Very few of them worth listening to. He'd crib quotations from the transcripts the Press Secretary would hand out later. Instead of listening, he fell into a reverie about his Counterfactual. He thought he'd seen a psychological justification for Lee surrendering rather than fighting on. Suppose, unlike what had happened in the real world, Lincoln *hadn't* been assassinated at the Second Inaugural ceremony by John Wilkes Booth, the well-known actor and radical Confederate sympathizer, who'd been lurking in the inaugural crowd with a pistol? Suppose that Lincoln had instead gone on to actually serve out his second term? In the real world, there was known to have been an exchange of notes between Lee and Grant in April 1865, discussing the possibility of surrender; Lee had refused to come to terms, and instead had vanished with his army into the Blue Ridge Mountains to wage a hide-and-seek campaign of large-scale guerilla war that had lasted far longer than even he could have possibly imagined that it would. Others had taken their cue from Lee, Joseph Johnson with his Army of Tennessee, the dreadful Nathan Bedford Forrest, the even more terrible John Mosby and William Clarke Quantrill, who had already been waging guerilla warfare in Missouri and "Bleeding Kansas." Jefferson Davis and the Confederate Cabinet had escaped into Texas, from where they'd continued to pursue the war for decades, until the Texans—always hard-pressed by Mexico on their southern border and out of patience with the arrogant high-handedness of the "Richmond Refugees"—had gradually lost interest in being a hold-out Confederate state and had reinvented themselves as a Republic instead.

But suppose Lincoln had still been President? It was well-documented that Lee and Lincoln had had great respect for each other as individuals, in an age where personal honor had been a real factor in human affairs. Suppose Lincoln had worked through Grant to mediate Lee's surrender, guaranteeing favorable terms for surrender and backing it with the force of his own personal word, terms that would enable Lee to surrender with some semblance of honor and dignity for himself and his hard-pressed men, terms that the vengeful Johnson never would have approved in *this* world? Would that have allowed Lee to justify the surrender of his army? And if Lee *had* surrendered, mightn't that have provided the cue for how others should act, just as Lee's defiant refusal to surrender had in the real world? If so, that one moment would have caused everything else to change …

It was in that moment that Cliff saw the tramp, the one from the train, standing a few yards away in the crowd, and from that instant on, he knew everything that was going to happen, detail for detail, like watching a play that you've previously seen rehearsed.

The tramp, staring up at Lindbergh intently, his sallow, unshaven face as blank as wax, the cords in his neck standing out with tension. He swallows once, twice, his prominent Adam's apple bobbing, and then his hand inches toward his coat.

Everything has gone into slow motion. Cliff wills himself to lunge forward, and feels his muscles begin to respond, but it's like swimming through syrup, and he knows that he'll be too late.

The tramp comes up with a gun, an old model Colt Navy .36. Practically a museum piece by now, but it's clean and seems in good working order. The weak sunlight splashes from the barrel as the tramp raises the gun, slowly, infinitely slowly, it seeming to ratchet up in discrete jerky intervals, like film being manually advanced frame by frame.

Cliff is swimming forward through the encrusted, resistant air, bulling through it as you'd breast your way through oncoming waves, and even as the breath for a warning shout is gathering itself in his lungs, he finds himself thinking, *It's not my fault! There's a dozen ways he could have gotten here!* Yes, but there was only one way he *did* get here, in this world, in this lifetime, and if he'd only reported him to the conductor last night, everything would be different …

Everything has stopped now, time freezing solid, and he sees it all in discrete snapshots.

A woman standing on the steps of the State Capitol building, holding up a baby so that it can have a better view. The baby is holding a rattle in one hand.

The trumpet player, cheeks no longer distended, lighting a cigarette and laughing at something the tuba player is saying.

Birds flying, caught on the wing, crossing the sky from left to right, something that would have been read as an omen in Ancient Rome.

John Foster Dulles saying something behind a raised hand, probably a scornful remark about Lindbergh's speech, to Charles Curtis.

Lindbergh's son scratching his nose, looking bored.

Lindbergh himself, pushing his tie out of the way again, a *moue* of annoyance crossing his face.

The tramp's face contorting into an intense, tooth-baring grimace of extreme, almost mortal, effort …

The gun fired.

At once, as if a sheet of glass had been shattered, time was back to normal, everything going *fast* again. Cliff staggered and almost fell, as other people in the close-packed crowd began to surge forward or back. The tramp's revolver barked twice more; the sharp reports hit the wall of tall buildings on the far side of the street and echoed back. Someone screamed, someone else shouted something incoherent. Then those nearest the tramp in the crowd swarmed over him, pulling his arm down. He disappeared under a knot of struggling men.

At the podium, Lindbergh staggered as if in concert with Cliff. His mouth half-open in shock, he grabbed the podium to keep himself upright, swayed, and then lost his grip and fell heavily to the stage. Some of the dignitaries had thrown themselves down at the sound of the first shot, Huey Long among them, but Charles Curtis had jumped up and grabbed Lindbergh's little boy as he threw himself forward with a scream, and was now wrestling with the child to keep him away from the body. Dulles had also stayed on his feet, and was now bending over the fallen Vice President, fumbling at him ineffectually with fluttering hands, his mouth working, although it was impossible to make out what he was saying over the rising roar of the crowd.

More screams, more shouts. Cliff could hear Bill, at his elbow, saying "Oh no! Oh no!" over and over again. Old Matthews looked as if someone had shot him as well, his face slack and ashen. The tramp was on his feet again, still struggling against a half-dozen men who were trying to wrestle him back down. His face was scratched and battered now, splattered with blood.

"The South will rise again!" the tramp shouted, before they could pull him down, "The South will rise again!" And Cliff realized with horror that indeed it *would*, that it would keep on rising again, and again, as it had ever since the ostensible end of the War, dragging the country down like a drowning man dragging his rescuer down with him … that the War would never be over, that his children and their children would still be fighting it when he had long since gone to dust, dealing with the dreadful consequences of it, even unto the fifth generation and beyond, world without end.

Was there another Cliff writing about this right now, he wondered numbly, in some other Counter-factual world where, unlike here, it was only a remote abstract possibility that had never happened, good for an hour's academic entertainment and nothing more?

Behind him, the kid had already regained his wits and was running for the train station to file the story, leaving Matthews and the rest of them gaping in the dust and the cold rising wind.

Zombies and Werewolves in space
What could possibly go wrong?

Sandra Odell's work has appeared in such venues as Jim Baen's Universe, Crossed Genres, Daily Science Fiction, Pseudopod, *and* Deep Cuts. *She is a Clarion West 2010 graduate, and attended Taos Toolbox in 2013.*

CURTAIN CALL

by Sandra M. Odell

The technician buffed my face, swapped my blue eyes for green, and lubed my joints. She polished my chest and used the reflection to touch up her make-up. "There you go, Ms. Starlight. Wha'd'ya think?"

I pranced and dipped in front of the mirror on the back of the dressing room door. "I think it's show time, baby cakes!"

I grabbed my wrap, and headed for the stage.

Onstage, Big Eddie Flashpoint did me right in that lady-loving baritone of his: "Luscious Ladies and groovin' Gentleamps, it's that time again, time for fast beats and slow heat. Put your hands together and make some righteous noise for The Joystick's Stainless Steel Siren, Miss Gina Starlight!"

Bright searchlights swept over the audience, catching neon silk suits, the chrome curve of bare shoulders. The boys came in on three, and I exploded onto the stage in silver and gold. I opened my arms and owned the house, every last erg. "Twilight Madame," "Gearing Up For Love," "Spark and Shine, Be Mine!" Sal Ballastern, bless his faulty pump, would have cried himself rusty to hear "Sweet Silver Sassy" for my second encore.

Benny Gracenote, the club owner, waited in my dressing room after the set. "Gina! Sweetheart! You were terrific!"

He came at me arms wide, all puckered up.

I wasn't having none of it. "Hold it right there, grabby gears." I gave him a palm to the chest. "We need to talk."

He bumped against the vanity table, rattling my polishes and oils. "Talk? What? Huh?"

"I want a new chassis."

Benny rolled his eyes. They clicked and popped in their sockets. "Gina, sweetheart, we've been over this be—"

"I want a new chassis."

"Times are tough all over. Money's tight, and—"

"Don't you give me none of that money's tight ma-larkey. I pull them in six nights a week, pack the house, double the drinks, right? Right?" I crossed my arms over my chest, better to show off the goods and hide them at the same time.

"Well …"

"You know I'm right."

Benny dropped his arms and looked away. "About that …"

He started in. Fewer customers, fewer receipts at the end of the night, tough times all around. I stamped my foot and demanded to know who did he think he was? Who did he think he could get that could sing half as good as I could? It's not like I was ever going to be—

"Replaced?" My hair snarled and rerouted. I pushed him into the vanity again. "What are you talking about? When? By who?"

"Gina, listen, sweetheart, it's not what you think." Benny reached for me and his handkerchief at the same time.

I brought my four-inch heel down on his instep. "Who?"

"Ow! Patsy—ow! ow!—Patsy Bellbottom."

"That factory knock-off?" I sat down, cleared my throat. Benny hurried to push in my chair. "What's she got that I ain't got?"

"Gina, Gina, it's not what you ain't, I mean, don't got, it's just that Patsy is, you know …"

"Lighter? A newer model? Has bigger heat sinks?" All the above.

Patsy had a spiff new composite chassis that needed less bracing under the stage, which meant lower insurance rates. Her heat sinks, well, word had it they was something to see.

"I was thinking of expanding and wanted, you know, fresh oil to liven up the place. And with your contract coming up, I just figured you might want a break, and the audience might want—"

I gave him my angry profile. "A body so tight it's got the plugs for the plays?"

"—something new."

I sniffed. I fingered a bouquet of copper carna-tions on the vanity, a gift from a sweetie in the audi-ence. Sal used to bring me flowers after every show until his wife found out he was rewiring me on the side. "After all I done for The Joystick, that you should treat me this way."

"Sweetheart, don't be like—"

"I signed on when this place was nothing but a plank bar and a fistful of stripped wires. I'm what keeps the customers coming back."

"Well, now—"

I grabbed my comb. "I done you a real favor, you know? All I'm asking for is a new chassis."

Benny put his hands on my shoulders. "It's busi-ness, Gina, nothing personal, you know that."

I made like I didn't know I was leaning against him. "Big deal."

"And, hey! I got great news. Me and some friends, we put our heads together, and I got a new oppor-tunity for you."

I sat a little straighter. A new opportunity? I loved The Joystick, but Benny knew some big names with bigger marquees. Maybe an upgrade, my name in lights. Maybe his way of making up for being such an insulated jerk. I combed the sparks into my hair. "Where?"

"The Cathode Ray!"

That was my last wire. I threw him out on his ear.

☼

I was so mad I couldn't see straight, and not sure who I'd shoot if I could. Has-beens and never-beens begged for scraps at The Cathode Ray.

Yeah, I had a cross-seated seam here and there, and my heat sinks were loose. My left knee froze some-times, and I'd snagged a couple wires under one arm. Didn't mean I hadn't done my good turns. Early on when I needed a back-up so's I could update my voice box and digitals, Benny asked if I could maybe do with a discount neural suite instead of going to a shop and I said sure. Sal had taught me some tricks with neural suites from his days in the upgrade in-dustry, so I didn't mind too much. I'd even taken a pass on my share of the box some nights just so's Benny could pay the band.

He wouldn't really drop me for Patsy Bellbottom, would he? I mean, I was the Stainless Steel Siren.

Saturday afternoon, Benny's girl sideboard pinged me on my way out the door to The Joystick. Said Benny was giving me the night off, that I could take it easy, maybe scope the Cathode Ray and chat up the band. Said he had someone else lined up, not to worry about it. Catch you later, toots.

I blew a gasket. That lout. That lousy, two-bit heel with a gap-toothed gear for an operating system! I stormed back up the stairs, made for a quick change of clothes, and headed back down to hail a cab.

Some new guy with a brass weave worked the door and let me by without a fuss. Maybe it was the hat and veil, or maybe he just pretended not to recognize me.

I found an out-of-the-way table. It took three tries before a waitress came my way. "Forty-weight and tonic, straight."

Five minutes later, she finally made it back with my drink. "Took you long enough," I said when she dropped my change on the table.

She shrugged, rolling back and forth on one of those new wheel upgrades. "Sorry about that. We got a new act tonight, so it's a full house."

I packed the house, too, but nothing like tonight's wall-to-wall. The quick headcount and crappy service ground my gears. "Do you know who I am?"

She didn't bat an eye—"Should I?"—and rolled away.

Life sure looked different from the audience pit, not near so's luscious and bright. No one noticed me. I wanted to shout, "Hey, you rubes! I'm over here!"

I sipped my drink and tried not to think about the postage stamp stage at the Cathode Ray.

When the lights finally dimmed, Big Eddie Flashpoint stepped through the curtain, all smooth silk and sleek chrome under the spotlight. He snuggled up to the microphone. "Ladies and Gentleamps, we have a special treat for you tonight. She is sweet, she is smooth, and she's here for what we hope is the first of many shows. Put your hands together for the luscious Motortown Songbird, Miss Patsy Bellbottom."

The room went dark and quiet. The boys came in on four with a low, honey-sweet bass and a cymbal sigh. A single spotlight, my spotlight, pierced the gloom center stage and there she stood, Miss Patsy Bellbottom, in a green sequined gown that hugged her curves like a factory floor lover. Copper hair, pol-ished skin, tight chassis, heat sinks out to here. No one said boo, not a one, then she lifted her head and began to sing.

The Motortown Songbird, that's what Big Eddie called her. She melted the room with Carter Bulbwright's "Turn Me On, Baby," then set the night moving with "Overcharged." "Little Copper Hen," "Gearshift Boogaloo," "Sparkler." She tied the tunes up in a bow and gave them to the audience. Her voice shot through the roof on its way to the stars. It dipped itself in the shadows and painted mercury kisses on every cheek. She had my voice from twenty years ago, modulated in ways I could only dream of anymore. She only stopped singing long enough to let the jackhammer applause die down, then went right back to it.

Me? I sat and watched. I couldn't do nothing else. Who needed the Stainless Steel Siren when the Motortown Songbird owned the room?

I caught sight of Benny stage right, all smiles and glad eyes. I wasn't being replaced, I was being sold for scrap.

Of course they'd set her up in my dressing room. I waited until all the factory boys went back up front for drinks, then I turned the knob and walked right in like I did after every set. I could have used the old service corridor that opened into the back of my closet, but the Stainless Steel Siren don't take the backdoor for nobody.

There were flowers everywhere—on the shelves, the vanity, tucked in the coatrack. They'd even tossed the pillows off the couch to make room for more bouquets.

Patsy didn't look up from applying her jeweler's rouge. "Listen, I'm about to go on again, so if you don't mind—"

"Hello, sweety."

She dropped her make-up brush and whirled around on the chair—my chair—eyes wide. "Oh! Miss Starlight."

I gave her my stage face, all smiles and bright eyes. Never let them see you leak, that's what Sal always said.

Patsy stood, smoothing her dress over her hips. "Sorry about that, I didn't, um—Come in, come in."

She cleared off a space on the couch, setting the flowers on the floor. "I mean, this is your dressing room and all so I really shouldn't tell you what to do."

"Thanks, but I'm not staying long." I straightened the wire-link doily on the edge of the couch. "I saw your show."

"You did?" Her eyes didn't have none of her smile.

Neither did mine. "You've got quite the chops on you. Nothing like mine, of course, but you could make it big someday."

"Of course." Her hands fluttered at her elbows, around her hair. "The Joystick's a big step up from the Cathode Ray, but Benny says the stars the limits." He said I was going to be a regular here.

That grimy, loose-chained, two-faced rat Benny. I locked my lips in a smile so's none of that slipped out. "Mmmm."

My lip lock must not have held, because she ducked her head and added, "Of course, we'd share stage time for awhile."

So's that's how it was going to be. I smiled again without so many teeth and made myself comfortable on the couch.

Patsy perched her pretty little self on the edge of the chair. "So." She let the word out slow like a low whistle. "You liked the show?"

I set my hat and veil beside me on the couch. "'Little Copper Hen' was nice. 'Overcharged' wasn't bad. Could have been a bit tighter."

Her smile faltered. "I have some of my best tunes coming up." She looked at my clock ticking its tock on the dresser.

"Yeah, but you got to wind them up tight right off so's they'll stick around."

That put a dent in her ego. She pursed her lips and swiveled her sleek little shoulders. "Benny swears I'll knock 'em dead."

"Sure you will. How'd you meet Benny, anyway?"

Patsy must have figured I wasn't that much of a problem. "He started coming to my shows at the Cathode Ray and we hit it off. One night he bought me a drink, and—"

A sharp knock, and the door opened. "Patsy! Sweetheart! Two—" Benny caught sight of me on the couch and all that schmarm went right out his tubes. "—minutes." He stepped inside, closing the door behind him. He straightened his tie. "Hey,

Gina. Wasn't expecting to see you here. Thought you'd be home, you know, resting."

I wanted to rest his face against the wall, the lousy cranker. "Resting or at the Cathode Ray?"

"The Cathode Ray's not that bad," Patsy said quick like. "You'll love it. They've got a great band."

Benny gave her a look, then turned back to me. "Now, Gina, don't be like that. I just thought you'd want a night off is all."

"That's all, huh? Funny—" I cut a look at his new pigeon. "—I thought I was going to have to share a stage."

This time they gave each other looks.

I stood and picked up my hat, giving Benny a good look at what he was letting go. When I came up, I could tell he'd liked what he'd seen. Patsy's pout told a different story. I said, "I'll see you tomorrow night, right?"

Benny cleared his throat like an engine with a bum ignition. "I thought Patsy might stay on for the rest of the week."

All the good will I'd ever had for Benny filtered right down the drain. He must've seen it in my face because he brought his hands up like so's to make amends. "Gina, sweetie, don't be like that, huh? It's business is all."

I brushed by him on my way to the door. "Yeah. Business."

☼

Benny never pinged to apologize. Not once, the lout. After a couple of days, I got a little tight in the head; I started to believe he was right. I mean, I was just a rundown singer, right? He handled the business.

One morning, I took a taxi downtown to drop in at the Cathode Ray for a looksie. The cabbie pulled up to the curb outside the club. "Here you go, lady. You want me to wait?"

"Sure." I set my hand on the handle, but couldn't open the door. Rust, broken bottles, and bits of wire littered the sidewalk. The marquee had chipped enamel and missing bulbs. The shops on either side had been boarded up, the walls covered in technicolor binary.

The cabbie looked at me in the rearview mirror. "You getting out, lady?"

"What do you care?" I said back, my face pressed against the window. "The meter's running."

An older model in a trench coat huddled by the front door, a sign propped against the stump of his third arm: WILL WORK FOR WASHERS. I could smell the desperation of the street, like smoked metal and burnt insulation. I knew that smell from way back.

That's how Benny wanted to play it? Fine. Back in the day, Sal made his bankroll in the upgrades industry, pretty pennies and patents to burn. I didn't know business, but I knew enough other things. Time to show Benny how we did things on the other side of the cabling.

I sat back against the seat. "Take me home."

The cabbie shrugged and pulled away from the curb.

✿

That night, I stopped off at the florist for a bouquet of gold-rimmed daisies, cheap like Patsy. I had the cabbie drop me off a block from The Joystick, and hoofed it through the back alleys to the service door.

The dumpster smelled like an oil pit, and a load of empty cans was set out beside it for the morning recycle. A look at my watch said Patsy should be on stage another five minutes, seven tops. I'd have to work fast.

I eased the door open and slipped into the dimly lit sink room. Busy kitchen drilling and clanging came from the door straight ahead, but the one I wanted was tucked behind the push brooms and mop buckets on the right. Quiet as I could, I moved everything to the side and jimmied the latch. The hinges creaked, and I locked, listening. The kitchen clatter didn't stop. I opened the door a bit more and slipped inside.

The corridor smelled like dust and dried metal polish. A bare bulb above my head showed the grease and skids of what had been The Joystick's start and now wasn't nothing but forgotten.

I hurried to the end of the corridor, and put my ear to the small door that opened into the dressing room closet. I listened hard. Nothing. I listened harder. Still nothing. Good.

I slipped into the closet, and eased the door shut behind me. Dresses, shoes, boas, doodads, none of them mine. I pushed to the front of the closet, listened again, then cracked the door. It didn't look like my dressing room no more. My clock, my shoe rack, my widgets, all gone. Didn't smell like mine, either, all cheap synthetics instead of my imported lubricants. Patsy lived there now. I checked my watch and headed out of the room.

The hall was showtime clear. I made it to Benny's office, knocked on the door, and slipped inside before anyone saw me. Benny looked up from his cast iron desk, and blinked in surprise. "Gina? What are you doin' here?"

His office was cozy with fancy chairs and cabinets. He was alone, just him and his ledgers. I clutched the strap of my bag, gave him my best smile, and shut the door behind me. "Heya, Benny. Long time no see."

Benny sighed and closed his book, marking his page with a scrap of aluminum. He came around his desk without so much as a smile. "Yeah, you're lookin' good. Have you been by the Cathode Ray? Dickie's been expectin' you."

I kept it cool. "I've been busy, you know, thinking and stuff." I held out the daisies. "I wanted to apologize."

The words stuck in my craw, but I said them with a smile.

Benny eyed the flowers like he expected a bee or something. "Listen, Gina, don't do this, okay? You don't got to apologize for anything."

"Sure I do. Last time I had my wires in a twist, and that ain't no way to say good-bye. This is good-bye, right?"

He didn't look so proud anymore, but he didn't look sad like, either. "Yeah, yeah it is, but no hard feelings, right? It's business is all, and I think you'll be a good fit for the Cathode Ray."

"I figured as much." I set the daisies on the desk, and palmed a glitcher out of my bag at the same time.

He looked at my shoulder bag. "What do you have there?"

"I need to get rid of some things to make ends meet. Maybe you'd be interested, you know, for Patsy." With my free hand, I reached for the clasp.

His lips curled in a quick smirk, then settled back into a frown. "That's fine, but maybe you should be going."

I brushed my hair behind my ear, setting the electrode between my fingers. "Is she doing okay?"

Benny locked a moment. "Fine."

"That's good." I took a half step toward the door. She's a good kid, you know? Stage work can take a lot out of a girl."

"She's fine. Listen, I really do need to—"

"Tell her to flash a bit of thigh every once in a while. That'll hold 'em for the next set."

"Fine, fine. Listen, you need to go. Talk to Barry at the bar, tell him I said to give you a free drink. Two drinks if you want, huh?"

He brushed by me on his way to the door, and I pushed the glitcher against the back of his head. Benny twitched and fell into my arms before he even got his hand on the knob.

I locked the door, jammed a chair under the handle so's it wouldn't move, then dragged him to the center of the room. Voices in the hall and a look at the clock said the first set was winding up. I didn't have much time.

The neural suite came out of the bag, and started up with the sharp smell of burnt circuits. It was an off-brand and way past its warranty, but I couldn't afford to be choosy now. I might not get another chance.

Still, I had a bad case of the what-ifs. What if the magnetic leads reversed and crunched my processor? What if someone broke down the door and pulled my plug before I finished?

I stared down at Benny with his big money suit and upgraded shoulders. He owed me big time for all I done for him. With a body like that, I could do what I wanted. Who needed music when I could be the one shining the spotlight? I'd show Benny the business all right.

I couldn't find the pop-switch to get at his processor. I searched under his hair, down his back, and finally found it behind his left eye. I opened Benny's head and poked around with a bobby pin to suss out his wiring. Leads, crossovers and splits, inputs and feeds. His processor flashed like crazy, but he couldn't so's much as bat an eyelash to stop me.

I struck gold at the bottom of a copper crease, or I hoped so anyway. I never got good with figuring blueprints. I set the bobby pin against a tiny silver plate and leaned over so's I'd be the last thing he ever saw. "Bye-bye, Benny-boy."

I pressed the bobby pin against the plate until I heard a click. Benny's body gave a ten-second jerk, then the light went out of his eyes as I purged him from his own system, easy-peasy. I could hear Sal laughing all the way to the bank.

Now came the tricky part. I wired myself to the neural suite and did the same to Benny.

Someone knocked on the door. "Mister Gracenote? We're out of solder, and there's none in stores." Knock-knock-knock. "Mister Gracenote?"

Of all the lousy—!

I made the last connections with a kiss and a bit, then stretched out on the other side of the box. I could feel my pump in the soles of my feet, I was that tight.

"He in there?" another voice said.

"Nah. Probably out front."

Footsteps, and then nothing.

My pump chugged right out of my chest. I hoped this worked. It had to work. It would work. I threw the switch.

The world tucked and curled down the tubes. Spinning, spinningingingingspinning. My toes got sucked through the white noise of my head into my time time pump exploding out my fingers along the roof of door sole of my shoes tumbling hairing my hear my hairhear where wear—

Knockcrickocking. A voice slar-away, far and a dayway: "Mushtor Greezhot? Buzz?"

Two hands lifted, mine?, which?, mine? Backforward which? Process slowing. Processing, process … ing … pro … cess … ing …

I ripped the wires out of my head, and the world went black.

☼

I came to with all my fingers and toes in the right place, and not.

Someone knocked on the door. "Benny?" Rattle-rattle went the knob. "Benny? You okay?"

Patsy Bellbottom. The Motortown Songbird.

"Is something burning?" Knock-knock. Rattle-rattle. "Open the door."

Burning? Insulation. Old circuits sharp like a knife carving me a new nose.

I turned my head to the door, and stared at a slab of metal dressed like me on the other side of the neural suite, wires streaming out of its head.

I lifted my hands, cleared my throat. "Hold on." Benny's throat, Benny's voice. My voice now. I could've burst out singing. "Hold on."

"Okay."

I got to my feet with no problem at all. In fact, I felt right at home. Lucky thing, too, because I had to do something with my old body. I picked it up and gave it a long look, crossed seams, bum knee, and all. So long, Gina Starlight. Hello, Benny Gracenote.

"Benny?" Patsy sounded kind of sulky on the other side of the door.

"I said hold on." I pushed the neural suite under the desk with my feet, then eased the old me into the oil cabinet without popping any cans. I set a pin through the handles to be safe. I'd dismantle myself later. Weird thought, made me kind of kinked. I shook it off and headed for the door.

Patsy gave me the side eye and her bottom lip. She wore a gold sequin shrug and not much else, hot from the stage. "About time. What's that smell?"

I stepped out of the office like nothing was wrong, pulling the door shut. "My book press went hinky."

"Is that why you weren't there after the set?"

A pack of admirers waited a few feet down the hall, ready with their flowers and smiles and compliments. Let them wait. I was in charge now, I was the one running the show. Maybe they didn't need the Stainless Steel Siren no more, but they needed Benny Gracenote because I had what they wanted. I had the Motortown Songbird.

"Yeah." I pulled her to me, and kissed her cheek, put an arm around her waist. I'd learn the books and maybe show her the ropes. I could get used to this. "No worries, baby cakes. It's business is all."

Maureen McHugh's first novel, China Mountain Zhang, *was a Tiptree winner and a Hugo and Nebula finalist. Maureen has won the Hugo for her story "The Lincoln Train." She is the author of four novels, a number of stories, and a collection, and is spending considerable time these days working for Hollywood.*

SPECIAL ECONOMICS

by Maureen McHugh

Jieling set up her boombox in a plague-trash market in the part where people sold parts for cars. She had been in the city of Shenzhen for a little over two hours but she figured she would worry about a job tomorrow. Everybody knew you could get a job in no time in Shenzhen. Jobs everywhere.

"What are you doing?" a guy asked her.

"I am divorced," she said. She had always thought of herself as a person who would one day be divorced so it didn't seem like a big stretch to claim it. Staying married to one person was boring. She figured she was too complicated for that. Interesting people had complicated lives. "I'm looking for a job. But I do hip-hop, too" she explained.

"Hip hop?" He was a middle-aged man with stubble on his chin who looked as if he wasn't looking for a job but should be.

"Not like Shanghai," she said. "Not like Hi-Bomb. They do gangsta stuff which I don't like. Old fashioned. Like M.I.A.," she said. "Except not political, of course." She gave a big smile. This was all way beyond the guy. Jieling started the boombox. M.I.A was Maya Arulpragasam, a Sri Lankan hip-hop artist who had started all on her own years ago. She had sung, she had danced, she had done her own videos. Of course M.I.A. lived in London, which made it easier to do hip-hop and become famous.

Jieling had no illusions about being a hip-hop singer, but it had been a good way to make some cash up north in Baoding where she came from. Set up in a plague-trash market and dance for yuan.

Jieling did her opening, her own hip-hop moves, a little like Maya and a little like some things she had seen on MTV, but not too sexy because Chinese people did not throw you money if you were too sexy. Only April and it was already hot and humid.

Ge down, ge down,
lang-a-lang-a-lang-a.
Ge down, ge down
lang-a-lang-a-lang-a.

She had borrowed the English. It sounded very fresh. Very criminal.

The guy said, "How old are you?"

"Twenty-two," she said, adding three years to her age, still dancing and singing.

Maybe she should have told him she was a widow? Or an orphan? But there were too many orphans and widows after so many people died in the bird flu plague. There was no margin in that. Better to be divorced. He didn't throw any money at her, just flicked open his cell phone to check listings from the market for plague trash. This plague trash market was so big it was easier to check online, even if you were standing right in the middle of it. She needed a new cell phone. Hers had finally fallen apart right before she headed south.

Shenzhen people were apparently too jaded for hip-hop. She made fifty-two yuan, which would pay for one night in a bad hotel where country people washed cabbage in the communal sink.

The market was full of second-hand stuff. When over a quarter of a billion people died in four years, there was a lot of second-hand stuff. But there was still a part of the market for new stuff and street food and that's where Jieling found the cell phone seller. He had a cart with stacks of flat plastic cell phone kits printed with circuits and scored. She flipped through: tiger-striped, peonies (old lady phones), metallics (old man phones), anime characters, moon phones, expensive lantern phones. "Where is your printer?" she asked.

"At home," he said. "I print them up at home, bring them here. No electricity here." Up north in Baoding she'd always bought them in a store where they let you pick your pattern online and then printed them there. More to pick from.

On the other hand, he had a whole box full of ones that hadn't sold that he would let go for cheap. In the stack she found a purple one with kittens that wasn't too bad. Very Japanese which was also

very fresh this year. And only one hundred yuan for phone and three hundred minutes.

He took the flat plastic sheet from her and dropped it in a pot of boiling water big enough to make dumplings. The hinges embedded in the sheet were made of plastic with molecular memory and when they got hot they bent and the plastic folded into a rough cell phone shape. He fished the phone out of the water with tongs, let it sit for a moment and then pushed all the seams together so they snapped. "Wait about an hour for it to dry before you use it," he said and handed her the warm phone.

"An *hour*," she said. "I need it now. I need a job."

He shrugged. "Probably okay in half an hour," he said.

She bought a newspaper and scallion pancake from a street food vendor, sat on a curb, and ate while her phone dried. The paper had some job listings, but it also had a lot of listings from recruiters. ONE MONTH BONUS PAY! BEST JOBS! and NUMBER ONE JOBS! START BONUS! People scowled at her for sitting on the curb. She looked like a farmer but what else was she supposed to do? She checked listings on her new cell phone. Online there were a lot more listings than in the paper. It was a good sign. She picked one at random and called.

✿

The woman at the recruiting office was a flat-faced southerner with buckteeth. Watermelon-picking teeth. But she had a manicure and a very nice red suit. The office was not so nice. It was small and the furniture was old. Jieling was groggy from a night spent at a hotel on the edge of the city. It had been cheap but very loud.

The woman was very sharp in the way she talked and had a strong accent that made it hard to understand her. Maybe Fujian, but Jieling wasn't sure. The recruiter had Jieling fill out an application.

"Why did you leave home?" the recruiter asked.

"To get a good job," Jieling said.

"What about your family? Are they alive?"

"My mother is alive. She is remarried," Jieling said. "I wrote it down."

The recruiter pursed her lips. "I can get you an interview on Friday," she said.

"Friday!" Jieling said. It was Tuesday. She had only three hundred yuan left out of the money she had brought. "But I need a job!"

The recruiter looked sideways at her. "You have made a big gamble to come to Shenzhen."

"I can go to another recruiter," Jieling said.

The recruiter tapped her lacquered nails. "They will tell you the same thing," she said.

Jieling reached down to pick up her bag.

"Wait," the recruiter said. "I do know of a job. But they only want girls of very good character."

Jieling put her bag down and looked at the floor. Her character was fine. She was not a loose girl, whatever this woman with her big front teeth thought.

"Your Mandarin is very good. You say you graduated with high marks from high school," the recruiter said.

"I liked school," Jieling said, which was only partly not true. Everybody here had terrible Mandarin. They all had thick southern accents. Lots of people spoke Cantonese in the street.

"Okay. I will send you to ShinChi for an interview. I cannot get you an interview before tomorrow. But you come here at 8:00 a.m. and I will take you over there."

ShinChi. New Life. It sounded very promising. "Thank you," Jieling said. "Thank you very much."

But outside in the heat, she counted her money and felt a creeping fear. She called her mother.

Her stepfather answered, "*Wei.*"

"Is ma there?" she asked.

"Jieling!" he said. "Where are you!"

"I'm in Shenzhen," she said, instantly impatient with him. "I have a job here."

"A job! When are you coming home?"

He was always nice to her. He meant well. But he drove her nuts. "Let me talk to ma," she said.

"She's not here," her stepfather said. "I have her phone at work. But she's not home, either. She went to Beijing last weekend and she's shopping for fabric now."

Her mother had a little tailoring business. She went to Beijing every few months and looked at clothes in all the good stores. She didn't buy in Beijing, she just remembered. Then she came home, bought fabric and sewed copies. Her stepfather had been born in Beijing and Jieling thought that was

part of the reason her mother had married him. He was more like her mother than her father had been. There was nothing in particular wrong with him. He just set her teeth on edge.

"I'll call back later," Jieling said.

"Wait, your number is blocked," her stepfather said. "Give me your number."

"I don't even know it yet," Jieling said and hung up.

The New Life company was a huge, modern looking building with a lot of windows. Inside it was full of reflective surfaces and very clean. Sounds echoed in the lobby. A man in a very smart gray suit met Jieling and the recruiter and the recruiter's red suit looked cheaper, her glossy fingernails too red, her buckteeth exceedingly large. The man in the smart gray suit was short and slim and very southern looking. Very city.

Jieling took some tests on her math and her written characters and got good scores.

To the recruiter, the human resources man said, "Thank you, we will send you your fee." To Jieling he said, "We can start you on Monday."

"Monday?" Jieling said. "But I need a job now!" He looked grave. "I … I came from Baoding, in Hebei," Jieling explained. "I'm staying in a hotel, but I don't have much money."

The human resources man nodded. "We can put you up in our guesthouse," he said. "We can deduct the money from your wages when you start. It's very nice. It has television and air conditioning, and you can eat in the restaurant."

It was very nice. There were two beds. Jieling put her backpack on the one nearest the door. There was carpeting, and the windows were covered in gold drapes with a pattern of cranes flying across them. The television got stations from Hong Kong. Jieling didn't understand the Cantonese, but there was a button on the remote for subtitles. The movies had lots of violence and more sex than mainland movies did—like the bootleg American movies for sale in the market. She wondered how much this room was. Two hundred yuan? Three hundred yuan?

Jieling watched movies the whole first day, one right after another.

On Monday she began orientation. She was given two pale green uniforms, smocks and pants like medical people wore and little caps and two pairs of white shoes. In the uniform she looked a little like a model worker—which is to say that the clothes were not sexy and made her look fat. There were two other girls in their green uniforms. They all watched a DVD about the company.

New Life did biotechnology. At other plants they made influenza vaccine (on the screen were banks and banks of chicken eggs) but at this plant they were developing breakthrough technologies in tissue culture. It showed many men in suits. Then it showed a big American store and explained how they were forging new exportation ties with the biggest American corporation for selling goods, Wal-Mart. It also showed a little bit of an American movie about Wal-Mart. Subtitles explained how Wal-Mart was working with companies around the world to improve living standards, decrease CO_2 emissions, and give people low prices. The voice narrating the DVD never really explained the breakthrough technologies.

One of the girls was from way up north, she had a strong Northern way of talking.

"How long are you going to work here?" the northern girl asked. She looked as if she might even have some Russian in her.

"How long?" Jieling said.

"I'm getting married," the northern girl confided. "As soon as I make enough money, I'm going home. If I haven't made enough money in a year," the northern girl explained, "I'm going home anyway."

Jieling hadn't really thought she would work here long. She didn't know exactly what she would do, but she figured that a big city like Shenzhen was a good place to find out. This girl's plans seemed very … country. No wonder Southern Chinese thought Northerners had to wipe the pig shit off their feet before they got on the train.

"Are you Russian?" Jieling asked.

"No," said the girl. "I'm Manchu."

"Ah," Jieling said. Manchu like Manchurian. Ethnic Minority. Jieling had gone to school with a boy who was classified as Manchu, which meant that he was allowed to have two children when he got married. But he had looked Han Chinese like everyone else. This girl had the hook nose and the dark skin of a Manchu. Manchu used to rule China until the Communist Revolution. (There was something in-between with Sun Yat-Sen but Jieling's history teachers had bored her to tears.) Imperial and countrified.

Then a man came in from Human Resources.

"There are many kinds of stealing," he began. "There is stealing of money or food. And there is stealing of ideas. Here at New Life, our ideas are like gold, and we guard against having them stolen. But you will learn many secrets, about what we are doing, about how we do things. This is necessary as you do your work. If you tell our secrets, that is theft. And we will find out." He paused here and looked at them in what was clearly intended to be a very frightening way.

Jieling looked down at the ground because it was like watching someone overact. It was embarrassing. Her new shoes were very white and clean.

Then he outlined the prison terms for industrial espionage. Ten, twenty years in prison. "China must take its place as an innovator on the world stage and so must respect the laws of intellectual property," he intoned. It was part of the modernization of China, where technology was a new future—Jieling put on her "I am a good girl" face. It was like politics class. Four modernizations. Six goals. Sometimes when she was a little girl, and she was riding behind her father on his bike to school, he would pass a billboard with a saying about traffic safety and begin to recite quotes from Mao. *The force at the core of the revolution is the people!* He would tuck his chin in when he did this and use a very serious voice, like a movie or like opera. *Western experience for Chinese uses.* Some of them she had learned from him. *All reactionaries are paper tigers!* she would chant with him, trying to make her voice deep. *Be resolute, fear no sacrifice and surmount every difficulty to win victory!* And then she would start giggling and he would glance over his shoulder and grin at her. He had been a Red Guard when he was young, but other than this, he never talked about it.

After the lecture, they were taken to be paired with workers who would train them. At least she didn't have to go with the Manchu girl, who was led off to shipping.

She was paired with a very small girl in one of the culture rooms. "I am Baiyue," the girl said. Baiyue was so tiny, only up to Jieling's shoulder, that her green scrubs swamped her. She had pigtails. The room where they worked was filled with rows and rows of what looked like wide drawers. Down the center of the room was a long table with petri dishes and trays and lab equipment. Jieling didn't know what some of it was and that was a little nerve-wracking. All up and down the room, pairs of girls in green worked at either the drawers or the table.

"We're going to start cultures," Baiyue said. "Take a tray and fill it with those." She pointed to a stack of petri dishes. The bottom of each dish was filled with gelatin. Jieling took a tray and did what Baiyue did. Baiyue was serious but not at all sharp or superior. She explained that what they were doing was seeding the petri dishes with cells.

"Cells?" Jieling asked.

"Nerve cells from the electric ray. It's a fish."

They took swabs and Baiyue showed her how to put the cells on in a zigzag motion so that most of the gel was covered. They did six trays full of petri dishes. They didn't smell fishy. Then they used pipettes to put in feeding solution. It was all pleasantly scientific without being very difficult.

At one point everybody left for lunch but Baiyue said they couldn't go until they got the cultures finished or the batch would be ruined. Women shuffled by them and Jieling's stomach growled. But when the lab was empty Baiyue smiled and said, "Where are you from?"

Baiyue was from Fujian. "If you ruin a batch," she explained, "you have to pay out of your paycheck. I'm almost out of debt and when I get clear—" she glanced around and dropped her voice a little—"I can quit."

"Why are you in debt?" Jieling asked. Maybe this was harder than she thought, maybe Baiyue had screwed up in the past.

"Everyone is in debt," Baiyue said. "It's just the way they run things. Let's get the trays in the warmers."

The drawers along the walls opened out and inside the temperature was kept blood-warm. They loaded the trays into the drawers, one back and one front, going down the row until they had the morning's trays all in.

"Okay," Baiyue said, "that's good. We'll check trays this afternoon. I've got a set for transfer to the tissue room but we'll have time after we eat."

Jieling had never eaten in the employee cafeteria, only in the guesthouse restaurant, and only the first night because it was expensive. Since then she had been living on ramen noodles and she was starved for a good meal. She smelled garlic and pork. First thing on the food line was a pan of steamed pork buns, fluffy white. But Baiyue headed off to a place at the back where there was a huge pot of congee—rice porridge—kept hot. "It's the cheapest thing in the cafeteria," Baiyue explained, "and you can eat all you want." She dished up a big bowl of it—a lot of congee for a girl her size—and added some salt vegetables and boiled peanuts. "It's pretty good, although usually by lunch it's been sitting a little while. It gets a little gluey."

Jieling hesitated. Baiyue had said she was in debt. Maybe she had to eat this stuff. But Jieling wasn't going to have old rice porridge for lunch. "I'm going to get some rice and vegetables," she said.

Baiyue nodded. "Sometimes I get that. It isn't too bad. But stay away from anything with shrimp in it. Soooo expensive."

Jieling got rice and vegetables and a big pork bun. There were two fish dishes and a pork dish with monkeybrain mushrooms but she decided she could maybe have the pork for dinner. There was no cost written on anything. She gave her *danwei* card to the woman at the end of the line who swiped it and handed it back.

"How much?" Jieling asked.

The woman shrugged. "It comes out of your food allowance."

Jieling started to argue but across the cafeteria, Baiyue was waving her arm in the sea of green scrubs to get Jieling's attention. Baiyue called from a table. "Jieling! Over here!"

Baiyue's eyes got very big when Jieling sat down. "A pork bun."

"Are they really expensive?" Jieling asked.

Baiyue nodded. "Like gold. And so good."

Jieling looked around at other tables. Other people were eating the pork and steamed buns and everything else.

"Why are you in debt?" Jieling asked.

Baiyue shrugged. "Everyone is in debt," she said. "Just most people have given up. Everything costs here. Your food, your dormitory, your uniforms. They always make sure that you never earn anything."

"They can't do that!" Jieling said.

Baiyue said, "My granddad says it's like the old days, when you weren't allowed to quit your job. He says I should shut up and be happy. That they take good care of me. Iron rice bowl."

"But, but but," Jieling dredged the word up from some long forgotten class, "that's *feudal*!"

Baiyue nodded. "Well, that's my granddad. He used to make my brother and me kowtow to him and my grandmother at Spring Festival." She frowned and wrinkled her nose. Country customs. Nobody in the city made their children kowtow at New Years. "But you're lucky," Baiyue said to Jieling. "You'll have your uniform debt and dormitory fees, but you haven't started on food debt or anything."

Jieling felt sick. "I stayed in the guesthouse for four days," she said. "They said they would charge it against my wages."

"Oh," Baiyue covered her mouth with her hand. After a moment, she said, "Don't worry, we'll figure something out." Jieling felt more frightened by that than anything else.

Instead of going back to the lab they went upstairs and across a connecting bridge to the dormitories. Naps? Did they get naps?

"Do you know what room you're in?" Baiyue asked.

Jieling didn't. Baiyue took her to ask the floor auntie who looked up Jieling's name and gave her a key and some sheets and a blanket. Back down the hall and around the corner. The room was spare but really nice. Two bunk beds and two chests of drawers, a concrete floor. It had a window. All of the beds were taken except one of the top ones. By the window under the desk were three black boxes hooked to the wall. They were a little bigger than a shoebox. Baiyue flipped open the front of each one. They had names written on them. "Here's a space where we can put your battery." She pointed to an electrical extension.

"What are they?" Jieling said.

"They're the battery boxes. It's what we make. I'll get you one that failed inspection. A lot of them work fine," Baiyue said. "Inside there are electric ray

cells to make electricity and symbiotic bacteria. The bacteria breaks down garbage to feed the ray cells. Garbage turned into electricity. Anti-global warming. No greenhouse gas. You have to feed scraps from the cafeteria a couple of times a week or it will die, but it does best if you feed it a little bit every day."

"It's alive?!" Jieling said.

Baiyue shrugged. "Yeah. Sort of. Supposedly if it does really well, you get credits for the electricity it generates. They charge us for our electricity use, so this helps hold down debt."

The three boxes just sat there looking less alive than a boombox.

"Can you see the cells?" Jieling asked.

Baiyue shook her head. "No, the feed mechanism doesn't let you. They're just like the ones we grow, though, only they've been worked on in the tissue room. They added bacteria."

"Can it make you sick?"

"No, the bacteria can't live in people." Baiyue said. "Can't live anywhere except in the box."

"And it makes electricity."

Baiyue nodded.

"And people can buy it?"

She nodded again. "We've just started selling them. They say they're going to sell them in China but really, they're too expensive. Americans like them, you know, because of the no global warming. Of course, Americans buy anything."

The boxes were on the wall between the beds, under the window, pretty near where the pillows were on the bottom bunks. She hadn't minded the cells in the lab, but this whole thing was too creepy.

☼

Jieling's first paycheck was startling. She owed 1,974 R.M.B. Almost four months' salary if she never ate or bought anything and if she didn't have a dorm room. She went back to her room and climbed into her bunk and looked at the figures. Money deducted for uniforms and shoes, food, her time in the guesthouse.

Her roommates came chattering in a group. Jieling's roommates all worked in packaging. They were nice enough, but they had been friends before Jieling moved in.

"Hey," called Taohua. Then seeing what Jieling had. "Oh, first paycheck."

Jieling nodded. It was like getting a jail sentence.

"Let's see. Oh, not so bad. I owe three times that," Taohua said. She passed the statement on to the other girls. All the girls owed huge amounts. More than a year.

"Don't you care?" Jieling said.

"You mean like little Miss Lei Feng?" Taohua asked. Everyone laughed and Jieling laughed, too, although her face heated up. Miss Lei Feng was what they called Baiyue. Little Miss Goody-goody. Lei Feng, the famous do-gooder soldier who darned his friend's socks on the Long March. He was nobody when he was alive, but when he died, his diary listed all the anonymous good deeds he had done and then he became a Hero. Lei Feng posters hung in elementary schools. He wanted to be "a revolutionary screw that never rusts." It was the kind of thing everybody's grandparents had believed in.

"Does Baiyue have a boyfriend?" Taohua asked, suddenly serious.

"No, no!" Jieling said. It was against the rules to have a boyfriend and Baiyue was always getting in trouble for breaking rules. Things like not having her trays stacked by 5:00 p.m., although nobody else got in trouble for that.

"If she had a boyfriend," Taohua said, "I could see why she would want to quit. You can't get married if you're in debt. It would be too hard."

"Aren't you worried about your debt?" Jieling asked.

Taohua laughed. "I don't have a boyfriend. And besides, I just got a promotion, so soon I'll pay off my debt."

"You'll have to stop buying clothes," one of the other girls said. The company store did have a nice catalogue you could order clothes from, but they were expensive. There was debt limit, based on your salary. If you were promoted, your debt limit would go up.

"Or I'll go to special projects," Taohua said. Everyone knew what special projects was, even though it was supposed to be a big company secret. They were computers made of bacteria. They looked a lot like the boxes in the dormitory rooms. "I've been studying computers," Taohua explained. "Bacterial computers are special. They do many things. They can detect chemicals. They are *massively* parallel."

"What does that mean?" Jieling asked.

"It is hard to explain," Taohua said evasively.

Taohua opened her battery and poured in scraps. It was interesting that Taohua claimed not to care about her debt but kept feeding her battery. Jieling had a battery now, too. It was a reject—the back had broken so that the metal things that sent the electricity back out were exposed and if you touched it wrong, it could give you a shock. No problem, since Jieling had plugged it into the wall and didn't plan to touch it again.

"Besides," Taohua said, "I like it here a lot better than at home."

Better than home. In some ways yes, in some ways no. What would it be like to just give up and belong to the company? Nice things, nice food. Never rich. But never poor, either. Medical care. Maybe it wasn't the worst thing. Maybe Baiyue was a little … obsessive.

"I don't care about my debt," Taohua said serenely. "With one more promotion, I'll move to cadres housing."

Jieling reported the conversation to Baiyue. They were getting incubated cells ready to move to the tissue room. In the tissue room they'd be transferred to the protein and collagen grid that would guide their growth—line up the cells to approximate an electricity generating system. The tissue room had a weird, yeasty smell.

"She's fooling herself," Baiyue said. "Line girls never get to be cadres. She might get onto special projects, but that's even worse than regular line work because you're never allowed to leave the compound." Baiyue picked up a dish, stuck a little volt reader into the gel and rapped the dish smartly against the lab table.

The needle on the volt gauge swung to indicate the cells had discharged electricity. That was the way they tested to see the cells were generating electricity. A shock made them discharge and the easiest way was to knock them against the table.

Baiyue could sound very bitter about New Life. Jieling didn't like the debt, it scared her a little. But really, Baiyue saw only one side of everything. "I thought you got a pay raise to go to special projects," Jieling said.

Baiyue rolled her eyes. "And more reasons to go in debt, I'll bet."

"How much is your debt?" Jieling asked.

"Still seven hundred," Baiyue said. "Because they told me I had to have new uniforms." She sighed.

"I am so sick of congee," Jieling said. "They're never going to let us get out of debt." Baiyue's way was doomed. She was trying to play by the company's rules and still win. That wasn't Jieling's way. "We have to make money somewhere else," Jieling said.

"Right," Baiyue said. "We work six days a week." And Baiyue often stayed after shift to try to make sure she didn't lose wages on failed cultures. "Out of spec," she said and put it aside. She had taught Jieling to keep the out of specs for a day. Sometimes they improved and could be shipped on. It wasn't the way the supervisor, Ms. Wang, explained the job to Jieling, but it cut down on the number of rejects, and that, in turn, cut down on paycheck deductions.

"That leaves us Sundays," Jieling said.

"I can't leave the compound this Sunday."

"And if you do, what are they going to do, fire you?" Jieling said.

"I don't think we're supposed to earn money outside of the compound," Baiyue said.

"You are too much of a good girl," Jieling said. "Remember, *it doesn't matter if the cat is black or white, as long as it catches mice.*"

"Is that Mao?" Baiyue asked, frowning.

"No," Jieling said, "Deng Xiaoping, the one after Mao."

"Well, he's dead, too," Baiyue said. She rapped a dish against the counter and the needle on the voltmeter jumped.

✿

Jieling had been working just over four weeks when they were all called to the cafeteria for a meeting. Mr. Cao from Human Resources was there. He was wearing a dark suit and standing at the white screen. Other cadres sat in chairs along the back of the stage, looking very stern.

"We are here to discuss a very serious matter," he said. "Many of you know this girl."

There was a laptop hooked up and a very nervous-looking boy running it. Jieling looked carefully at the laptop but it didn't appear to be a special projects computer. In fact, it was made in Korea. He did something and an ID picture of a girl flashed on the screen.

Jieling didn't know her. But around her she heard noises of shock, someone sucking air through their teeth, someone else breathed softly, "*Ai-yah.*"

"This girl ran away, leaving her debt with New Life. She ate our food, wore our clothes, slept in our beds. And then, like a thief, she ran away." The Human Resources man nodded his head. The boy at the computer changed the image on the big projector screen.

Now it was a picture of the same girl with her head bowed, and two policemen holding her arms.

"She was picked up in Guangdong," the Human Resources man said. "She is in jail there."

The cafeteria was very quiet.

The Human Resources man said, "Her life is ruined, which is what should happen to all thieves."

Then he dismissed them. That afternoon, the picture of the girl with the two policemen appeared on the bulletin boards of every floor of the dormitory.

✿

On Sunday, Baiyue announced, "I'm not going."

She was not supposed to leave the compound, but one of her roommates had female problems—bad cramps—and planned to spend the day in bed drinking tea and reading magazines. Baiyue was going to use her ID to leave.

"You have to," Jieling said. "You want to grow old here? Die a serf to New Life?"

"It's crazy. We can't make money dancing in the plague-trash market."

"I've done it before," Jieling said. "You're scared."

"It's just not a good idea," Baiyue said.

"Because of the girl they caught in Guangdong. We're not skipping out on our debt. We're paying it off."

"We're not supposed to work for someone else when we work here," Baiyue said.

"Oh, come on," Jieling said. "You are always making things sound worse than they are. I think you like staying here being little Miss Lei Feng."

"Don't call me that," Baiyue snapped.

"Well, don't act like it. New Life is not being fair. We don't have to be fair. What are they going to do to you if they catch you?"

"Fine me," Baiyue said. "Add to my debt!"

"So what? They're going to find a way to add to your debt no matter what. You are a serf. They are the landlord."

"But if—"

"No 'but if.'" Jieling said. "You like being a martyr. I don't."

"What do you care?" Baiyue asked. "You like it here. If you stay you can eat pork buns every night."

"And you can eat congee for the rest of your life. I'm going to try to do something." Jieling slammed out of the dorm room. She had never said harsh things to Baiyue before. Yes, she had thought about staying here. But was that so bad? Better than being like Baiyue who would stay here and have a miserable life. Jieling was not going to have a miserable life, no matter where she stayed or what she did. That was why she had come to Shenzhen in the first place.

She heard the door open behind her and Baiyue ran down the hall. "Okay," she said breathlessly. "I'll try it. Just this once."

The streets of Shanghai were incredibly loud after weeks in the compound. In a shop window, she and Baiyue stopped and watched a news segment on how the fashion in Shanghai was for sarongs. Jieling would have to tell her mother. Of course her mother had a TV and probably already knew. Jieling thought about calling, but not now. Not now. She didn't want to explain about New Life. The next news segment was about the success of the People's Army in Tajikistan. Jieling pulled Baiyue to come on.

They took one bus, and then had to transfer. On Sundays, unless you were lucky, it took forever to transfer because fewer buses ran. They waited almost an hour for the second bus. That bus was almost empty when they got on. They sat down a few seats back from the driver. Baiyue rolled her eyes. "Did you see the guy in the back?" she asked. "Party functionary."

Jieling glanced over her shoulder and saw him. She couldn't miss him, in his careful polo shirt. He had that stiff party-member look.

Baiyue sighed. "My uncle is just like that. So *boring*."

Jieling thought that, to be honest, Baiyue would have made a good revolutionary, back in the day. Baiyue liked that kind of revolutionary purity. But she nodded.

The plague-trash market was full on a Sunday. There was a toy seller making tiny little clay figures on sticks. He waved a stick at the girls as they passed. "Cute things!" he called. "I'll make whatever you want!" The stick had a little Donald Duck on it.

"I can't do this," Baiyue said. "There's too many people."

"It's not so bad," Jieling said. She found a place for the boombox. Jieling had brought them to where all the food vendors were. "Stay here and watch this," she said. She hunted through the food stalls and bought a bottle of local beer, counting out from her little horde of money she had left from when she came. She took the beer back to Baiyue. "Drink this," she said. "It will help you be brave."

"I hate beer," Baiyue said.

"Beer or debt," Jieling said.

While Baiyue drank the beer, Jieling started the boombox and did her routine. People smiled at her but no one put any money in her cash box. Shenzhen people were so cheap. Baiyue sat on the curb, nursing her beer, not looking at Jieling or at anyone until finally Jieling couldn't stand it any longer.

"C'mon, *meimei*," she said.

Baiyue seemed a bit surprised to be called little sister but she put the beer down and got up. They had practiced a routine to an M.I.A. song, singing and dancing. It would be a hit, Jieling was sure.

"I can't," Baiyue whispered.

"Yes you can," Jieling said. "You do good."

A couple of people stopped to watch them arguing, so Jieling started the music.

"I feel sick," Baiyue whimpered.

But the beat started and there was nothing to do but dance and sing. Baiyue was so nervous, she forgot at first, but then she got the hang of it. She kept her head down and her face was bright red.

Jieling started making up a rap. She'd never done it before and she hadn't gotten very far before she was laughing and then Baiyue was laughing, too.

Wode meimei hen haixiude

Mei ta shi xuli

tai hen xiuqi—

My little sister is so shy

But she's pretty

Far too delicate—

They almost stopped because they were giggling but they kept dancing and Jieling went back to the lyrics from the song they had practiced.

When they had finished, people clapped and they'd made thirty-two yuan.

They didn't make as much for any single song after that, but in a few hours they had collected 187 yuan. It was early evening and night entertainers were showing up—a couple of people who sang opera, acrobats, and a clown with a wig of hair so red it looked on fire, stepping stork-legged on stilts waving a rubber Kalashnikov in his hand. He was all dressed in white. Uncle Death, from cartoons during the plague. Some of the day vendors had shut down, and new people were showing up who put out a board and some chairs and served sorghum liquor; clear, white and 150 proof. The crowd was starting to change, too. It was rowdier. Packs of young men dressed in weird combinations of clothes from plague markets—vintage Mao suit jackets and suit pants and peasant shoes. And others, veterans from Tajikistan conflict, one with an empty trouser leg.

Jieling picked up the boombox and Baiyue took the cash box. Outside of the market it wasn't yet dark.

"You are amazing," Baiyue kept saying. "You are such a special girl!"

"You did great," Jieling said. "When I was by myself, I didn't make anything! Everyone likes you because you are little and cute!"

"Look at this! I'll be out of debt before autumn!"

Maybe it was just the feeling that she was responsible for Baiyue, but Jieling said, "You keep it all."

"I can't! I can't! We split it!" Baiyue said.

"Sure," Jieling said. "Then after you get away, you can help me. Just think, if we do this for three more Sundays, you'll pay off your debt."

"Oh, Jieling," Baiyue said. "You really are like my big sister!"

Jieling was sorry she had ever called Baiyue "little sister." It was such a country thing to do. She had always suspected that Baiyue wasn't a city girl. Jieling hated the countryside. Grain spread to dry in the road and mother's-elder-sister and father's-younger-brother bringing all the cousins over on the day off. Jieling didn't even know all those country ways to say aunt and uncle. It wasn't Baiyue's fault. And Baiyue had been good to her. She was rotten to be thinking this way.

"Excuse me," said a man. He wasn't like the packs of young men with their long hair and plague clothes. Jieling couldn't place him but he seemed familiar. "I saw you in the market. You were very fun. Very lively."

Baiyue took hold of Jieling's arm. For a moment Jieling wondered if maybe he was from New Life, but she told herself that was crazy. "Thank you," she said. She thought she remembered him putting ten yuan in the box. No, she thought, he was on the bus. The party functionary. The party was checking up on them. Now that was funny. She wondered if he would lecture them on Western ways.

"Are you in the music business?" Baiyue asked. She glanced at Jieling who couldn't help laughing, snorting through her nose.

The man took them very seriously though. "No," he said. "I can't help you there. But I like your act. You seem like girls of good character."

"Thank you," Baiyue said. She didn't look at Jieling again, which was good because Jieling knew she wouldn't be able to keep a straight face.

"I am Wei Rongyi. Maybe I can buy you some dinner?" the man asked. He held up his hands. "Nothing romantic. You are so young, it is like you could be daughters."

"You have a daughter?" Jieling asked.

He shook his head. "Not anymore," he said.

Jieling understood. His daughter had died of the bird flu. She felt embarrassed for having laughed at him. Her soft heart saw instantly that he was treating them like the daughter he had lost.

He took them to a dumpling place on the edge of the market and ordered half a kilo of crescent-shaped pork dumplings and a kilo of square beef dumplings. He was a cadre, a middle manager. His wife had lived in Changsha for a couple of years now, where her family was from. He was from the older generation, people who did not get divorced. All around them, the restaurant was filling up mostly with men stopping after work for dumplings and drinks. They were a little island surrounded by truck drivers and men who worked in the factories in the outer city—tough grimy places.

"What do you do? Are you secretaries?" Wei Rongyi asked.

Baiyue laughed. "As if!" she said.

"We are factory girls," Jieling said. She dunked a dumpling in vinegar. They were so good! Not congee!

"Factory girls!" he said. "I am so surprised!"

Baiyue nodded. "We work for New Life," she explained. "This is our day off, so we wanted to earn a little extra money."

He rubbed his head, looking off into the distance. "New Life," he said, trying to place the name. "New Life …"

"Out past the zoo," Baiyue said.

Jieling thought they shouldn't say so much.

"Ah, in the city. A good place? What do they make?" he asked. He had a way of blinking very quickly that was disconcerting.

"Batteries," Jieling said. She didn't say bio-batteries.

"I thought they made computers," he said.

"Oh yes," Baiyue said. "Special projects."

Jieling glared at Baiyue. If this guy gave them trouble at New Life, they'd have a huge problem getting out of the compound.

Baiyue blushed.

Wei laughed. "You are special project girls, then. Well, see, I knew you were not just average factory girls."

He didn't press the issue. Jieling kept waiting for him to make some sort of move on them. Offer to buy them beer. But he didn't, and when they had finished their dumplings, he gave them the leftovers to take back to their dormitories and then stood at the bus stop until they were safely on their bus.

"Are you sure you will be all right?" he asked them when the bus came.

"You can see my window from the bus stop," Jieling promised. "We will be fine."

"Shenzhen can be a dangerous city. You be careful!"

Out the window, they could see him in the glow of the streetlight, waving as the bus pulled away.

"He was so nice," Baiyue sighed. "Poor man."

"Didn't you think he was a little strange?" Jieling asked.

"Everybody is strange anymore," Baiyue said. "After the plague. Not like when we were growing up."

It was true. Her mother was strange. Lots of people were crazy from so many people dying. Jieling held up the leftover dumplings. "Well, anyway. I am not feeding this to my battery," she said. They both tried to smile.

"Our whole generation is crazy," Baiyue said.

"We know everybody dies," Jieling said. Outside the bus window, the streets were full of young people, out trying to live while they could.

They made all their bus connections as smooth as silk. So quick, they were home in forty-five minutes. Sunday night was movie night, and all of Jieling's roommates were at the movie so she and Baiyue could sort the money in Jieling's room. She used her key card and the door clicked open.

Mr. Wei was kneeling by the battery boxes in their room. He started and hissed, "Close the door!"

Jieling was so surprised she did.

"Mr. Wei!" Baiyue said.

He was dressed like an army man on a secret mission, all in black. He showed them a little black gun. Jieling blinked in surprise. "Mr. Wei!" she said. It was hard to take him seriously. Even all in black, he was still weird Mr. Wei, blinking rapidly behind his glasses.

"Lock the door," he said. "And be quiet."

"The door locks by itself," Jieling explained. "And my roommates will be back soon."

"Put a chair in front of the door," he said and shoved the desk chair toward them. Baiyue pushed it under the door handle. The window was open and Jieling could see where he had climbed on the desk and left a footprint on Taohua's fashion magazine. Taohua was going to be pissed. And what was Jieling going to say? If anyone found out there was a man in her room, she was going to be in very big trouble.

"How did you get in?" she asked. "What about the cameras?" There were security cameras.

He showed them a little spray can. "Special paint. It just makes things look foggy and dim. Security guards are so lazy anymore no one ever checks things out." He paused a moment, clearly disgusted with the lax morality of the day. "Miss Jieling," he said. "Take that screwdriver and finish unscrewing that computer from the wall."

Computer? She realized he meant the battery boxes.

Baiyue's eyes got very big. "Mr. Wei! You're a thief!"

Jieling shook her head. "A corporate spy."

"I am a patriot," he said. "But you young people wouldn't understand that. Sit on the bed." He waved the gun at Baiyue.

The gun was so little it looked like a toy and it was difficult to be afraid, but still Jieling thought it was good that Baiyue sat.

Jieling knelt. It was her box that Mr. Wei had been disconnecting. It was all the way to the right, so he had started with it. She had come to feel a little bit attached to it, thinking of it sitting there, occasionally zapping electricity back into the grid, reducing her electricity costs and her debt. She sighed and unscrewed it. Mr. Wei watched.

She jimmied it off the wall, careful not to touch the contacts. The cells built up a charge, and when they were ready, a switch tapped a membrane and they discharged. It was all automatic and there was no knowing when it was going to happen. Mr. Wei was going to be very upset when he realized that this wasn't a computer.

"Put it on the desk," he said.

She did.

"Now sit with your friend."

Jieling sat down next to Baiyue. Keeping a wary eye on them, he sidled over to the bio-battery. He opened the hatch where they dumped garbage in them, and tried to look in as well as look at them. "Where are the controls?" he asked. He picked it up, his palm flat against the broken back end where the contacts were exposed.

"Tap it against the desk," Jieling said. "Sometimes the door sticks." There wasn't actually a door. But it had just come into her head. She hoped that the cells hadn't discharged in awhile.

Mr. Wei frowned and tapped the box smartly against the desktop.

Torpedinidae, the electric ray, can generate a current of two hundred volts for approximately a minute. The power output is close to one kilowatt over the course of the discharge and while this won't kill the average person, it is a powerful shock. Mr. Wei stiffened and fell, clutching the box and spasming wildly. One … two … three … four … Mr. Wei was still spasming. Jieling and Baiyue looked at each other. Gingerly, Jieling stepped around Mr. Wei. He had dropped the little gun. Jieling picked it up. Mr. Wei was still spasming. Jieling wondered if he was going to die. Or if he was already dead and the electricity was just making him jump. She didn't want him to die. She looked at the little gun and it made her feel even sicker so she threw it out the window.

Finally Mr. Wei dropped the box.

Baiyue said, "Is he dead?"

Jieling was afraid to touch him. She couldn't tell if he was breathing. Then he groaned and both girls jumped.

"He's not dead," Jieling said.

"What should we do?" Baiyue asked.

"Tie him up," Jieling said. Although she wasn't sure what they'd do with him then.

Jieling used the cord to her boombox to tie his wrists. When she grabbed his hands he gasped and struggled feebly. Then she took her pillowcase and cut along the blind end, a space just wide enough that his head would fit through.

"Sit him up," she said to Baiyue.

"You sit him up," Baiyue said. Baiyue didn't want to touch him.

Jieling pulled Mr. Wei into a sitting position. "Put the pillowcase over his head," she said. The pillowcase was like a shirt with no armholes, so when Baiyue pulled it over his head and shoulders, it pinned his arms against his sides and worked something like a straightjacket.

Jieling took his wallet and his identification papers out of his pocket. "Why would someone carry their wallet to a break in?" she asked. "He has six ID papers. One says he is Mr. Wei."

"Wow," Baiyue said. "Let me see. Also Mr. Ma. Mr. Zhang. Two Mr. Lius and a Mr. Cui."

Mr. Wei blinked, his eyes watering.

"Do you think he has a weak heart?" Baiyue asked.

"I don't know," Jieling said. "Wouldn't he be dead if he did?"

Baiyue considered this.

"Baiyue! Look at all this yuan!" Jieling emptied the wallet, counting. Almost eight thousand yuan!

"Let me go," Mr. Wei said weakly.

Jieling was glad he was talking. She was glad he seemed like he might be all right. She didn't know what they would do if he died. They would never be able to explain a dead person. They would end up in deep debt. And probably go to jail for something. "Should we call the floor auntie and tell him that he broke in?" Jieling asked.

"We could," Baiyue said.

"Do not!" Mr. Wei said, sounding stronger. "You don't understand! I'm from Beijing!"

"So is my stepfather," Jieling said. "Me, I'm from Baoding. It's about an hour south of Beijing."

Mr. Wei said, "I'm from the government! That money is government money!"

"I don't believe you," Jieling said. "Why did you come in through the window?"

"Secret agents always come in through the window?" Baiyue said and started to giggle.

"Because this place is counter-revolutionary!" Mr. Wei said.

Baiyue covered her mouth with her hand. Jieling felt embarrassed, too. No one said things like 'counter-revolutionary' anymore.

"This place! It is making things that could make China strong!" he said.

"Isn't that good?" Baiyue asked.

"But they don't care about China! Only about money. Instead of using it for China, they sell it to America!" he said. Spittle was gathering at the corner of his mouth. He was starting to look deranged. "Look at this place! Officials are all concerned about *guanxi*!" Connections. Kickbacks. Guanxi ran China, everybody knew that.

"So, maybe you have an anti-corruption investigation?" Jieling said. There were lots of anti-corruption investigations. Jieling's stepfather said that they usually meant someone powerful was mad at their brother-in-law or something, so they accused them of corruption.

Mr. Wei groaned. "There is no one to investigate them."

Baiyue and Jieling looked at each other.

Mr. Wei explained, "In my office, the Guangdong office, there used to be twenty people. Special operatives. Now there is only me and Ms. Yang."

Jieling said, "Did they all die of bird flu?"

Mr. Wei shook his head. "No, they all went to work on contract for Saudi Arabia. You can make a lot of money in the Middle East. A lot more than in China."

"Why don't you and Ms. Yang go work on Saudi Arabia?" Baiyue asked.

Jieling thought Mr. Wei would give some revolutionary speech. But he just hung his head. "She is the secretary. I am the bookkeeper." And then in a smaller voice, "She is going to Kuwait to work for Mr. Liu."

They probably did not need bookkeepers in the Middle East. Poor Mr. Wei. No wonder he was such a terrible secret agent.

"The spirit of the revolution is gone," he said, and there were real, honest-to-goodness tears in his eyes. "Did you know that Tiananmen Square was built by volunteers? People would come after their regular job and lay the paving of the square. Today people look to Hong Kong."

"Nobody cares about a bunch of old men in Beijing," Baiyue said.

"Exactly! We used to have a strong military! But now the military is too worried about their own factories and farms! They want us to pull out of Tajikistan because it is ruining their profits!"

This sounded like a good idea to Jieling, but she had to admit, she hated the news so she wasn't sure why they were fighting in Tajikistan anyway. Something about Muslim terrorists. All she knew about Muslims was that they made great street food.

"Don't you want to be patriots?" Mr. Wei said.

"You broke into my room and tried to steal my— you know that's not a computer, don't you?" Jieling said. "It's a bio-battery. They're selling them to the Americans. Wal-Mart."

Mr. Wei groaned.

"We don't work in special projects," Baiyue said.

"You said you did," he protested.

"We did not," Jieling said. "You just thought that. How did you know this was my room?"

"The company lists all its workers in a directory," he said wearily. "And it's movie night, everyone is either out or goes to the movies. I've had the building under surveillance for weeks. I followed you to the market today. Last week it was a girl named Pingli, who blabbed about everything, but she wasn't in special projects.

"I put you on the bus, I've timed the route three times. I should have had an hour and fifteen minutes to drive over here and get the box and get out."

"We made all our connections," Baiyue explained.

Mr. Wei was so dispirited he didn't even respond.

Jieling said. "I thought the government was supposed to help workers. If we get caught, we'll be fined and we'll be deeper in debt." She was just talking. Talking, talking, talking too much. This was too strange. Like when someone was dying. Something extraordinary was happening, like your father dying in the next room, and yet the ordinary things went on, too. You made tea, your mother opened the shop the next day and sewed clothes while she cried. People came in and pretended not to notice. This was like that. Mr. Wei had a gun and they were explaining about New Life. "Debt?" Mr. Wei said.

"To the company," she said. "We are all in debt. The company hires us and says they are going to pay us, but then they charge us for our food and our clothes and our dorm and it always costs more than we earn. That's why we were doing rap today. To make money to be able to quit." Mr. Wei's glasses had tape holding the arm on. Why hadn't she noticed that in the restaurant? Maybe because when you are afraid you notice things. When your father is dying of the plague, you notice the way the covers on your mother's chairs need to be washed. You wonder if you will have to do it or if you will die before you have to do chores.

"The Pingli girl," he said, "she said the same thing. That's illegal."

"Sure," Baiyue said. "Like anybody cares."

"Could you expose corruption?" Jieling asked.

Mr. Wei shrugged, at least as much as he could in the pillowcase. "Maybe. But they would just pay bribes to locals and it would all go away."

All three of them sighed.

"Except," Mr. Wei said, sitting up a little straighter. "The Americans. They are always getting upset about that sort of thing. Last year there was a corporation, the Shanghai Six. The Americans did a documentary on them and then western companies would not do business. If they got information from us about what New Life is doing …"

"Who else is going to buy bio-batteries?" Baiyue said. "The company would be in big trouble!"

"Beijing can threaten a big exposé, tell *The New York Times* newspaper!" Mr. Wei said, getting excited. "My Beijing supervisor will love that! He loves media!"

"Then you can have a big show trial," Jieling said.

Mr. Wei was nodding.

"But what is in it for us?" Baiyue said.

"When there's a trial, they'll have to cancel your debt!" Mr. Wei said. "Even pay you a big fine!"

"If I call the floor auntie and say I caught a corporate spy, they'll give me a big bonus," Baiyue said.

"Don't you care about the other workers?" Mr. Wei asked.

Jieling and Baiyue looked at each other and shrugged. Did they? "What are they going to do to you anyway?" Jieling said. "You can still do big exposé. But that way we don't have to wait."

"Look," he said, "you let me go, and I'll let you keep my money."

Someone rattled the door handle.

"Please," Mr. Wei whispered. "You can be heroes for your fellow workers, even though they'll never know it."

Jieling stuck the money in her pocket. Then she took the papers, too.

"You can't take those," he said.

"Yes I can," she said. "If after six months, there is no big corruption scandal? We can let everyone know how a government secret agent was outsmarted by two factory girls."

"Six months!" he said. "That's not long enough!"

"It better be," Jieling said.

Outside the door, Taohua called, "Jieling? Are you in there? Something is wrong with the door!"

"Just a minute," Jieling called. "I had trouble with it when I came home." To Mr. Wei she whispered sternly, "Don't you try anything. If you do, we'll scream our heads off and everybody will come running." She and Baiyue shimmied the pillowcase off of Mr. Wei's head. He started to stand up and jerked the boombox which clattered across the floor. "Wait!" she hissed and untied him.

Taohua called through the door, "What's that?"

"Hold on!" Jieling called.

Baiyue helped Mr. Wei stand up. Mr. Wei climbed onto the desk and then grabbed a line hanging outside. He stopped a moment as if trying to think of something to say.

"'A revolution is not a dinner party, or writing an essay, or painting a picture, or doing embroidery'," Jieling said. It had been her father's favorite quote from Chairman Mao. "'… it cannot be so refined, so leisurely and gentle, so temperate, kind, courteous, restrained and magnanimous. A revolution is an insurrection, an act of by which one class overthrows another.'"

Mr. Wei looked as if he might cry and not because he was moved by patriotism. He stepped back and disappeared. Jieling and Baiyue looked out the window. He did go down the wall just like a secret agent from a movie, but it was only two stories. There was still the big footprint in the middle of Taohua's magazine and the room looked as if it had been hit by a storm.

"They're going to think you had a boyfriend," Baiyue whispered to Jieling.

"Yeah," Jieling said, pulling the chair out from under the door handle. "And they're going to think he's rich."

It was Sunday, and Jieling and Baiyue were sitting on the beach. Jieling's cell phone rang, a little chime of M.I.A. hip-hop. Even though it was Sunday, it was one of the girls from New Life. Sunday should be a day off, but she took the call anyway.

"Jieling? This is Xia Meili? From packaging. Taohua told me about your business? Maybe you could help me?"

Jieling said, "Sure. What is your debt, Meili?"

"3,800 R.M.B.," Meili said. "I know it's a lot."

Jieling said, "Not so bad. We have a lot of people who already have loans, though, and it will probably be a few weeks before I can make you a loan."

With Mr. Wei's capital, Jieling and Baiyue had opened a bank account. They had bought themselves out, and then started a little loan business where they bought people out of New Life. Then people had to pay them back with a little extra. They had each had jobs—Jieling worked for a company that made toys. She sat each day at a table where she put a piece of specially shaped plastic over the body of a little doll, an action figure. The plastic fit right over the figure and had cut-outs. Jieling sprayed the whole thing with red paint and when the piece of plastic was lifted, the action figure had a red shirt. It was boring, but at the end of the week, she got paid instead of owing the company money.

She and Baiyue used all their extra money on loans to get girls out of New Life. More and more loans, and more and more payments. Now New Life had sent them a threatening letter saying that what they were doing was illegal. But Mr. Wei said not to worry. Two officials had come and talked to them and had showed them legal documents and had them explain everything about what had happened. Soon, the officials promised, they would take New Life to court.

Jieling wasn't so sure about the officials. After all, Mr. Wei was an official. But a foreign newspaperman had called them. He was from a newspaper called *The Wall Street Journal* and he said that he was writing a story about labor shortages in China after the bird flu. He said that in some places in the west there were reports of slavery. His Chinese was very good. His story was going to come out in the United States tomorrow. Then she figured officials would have to do something or lose face.

Jieling told Meili to call her back in two weeks—although hopefully in two weeks no one would need help to get away from New Life—and wrote a note to herself in her little notebook.

Baiyue was sitting looking at the water. "This is the first time I've been to the beach," she said.

"The ocean is so big, isn't it."

Baiyue nodded, scuffing at the white sand. "People always say that, but you don't know until you see it."

Jieling said, "Yeah." Funny, she had lived here for months. Baiyue had lived here more than a year. And they had never come to the beach. The beach was beautiful.

"I feel sorry for Mr. Wei," Baiyue said.

"You do?" Jieling said. "Do you think he really had a daughter who died?"

"Maybe," Baiyue said. "A lot of people died."

"My father died," Jieling said.

Baiyue looked at her, a quick little sideways look, then back out at the ocean. "My mother died," she said.

Jieling was surprised. She had never known that Baiyue's mother was dead. They had talked about so much but never about that. She put her arm around Baiyue's waist and they sat for a while.

"I feel bad in a way," Baiyue said.

"How come?" Jieling said.

"Because we had to steal capital to fight New Life. That makes us capitalists."

Jieling shrugged.

"I wish it was like when they fought the revolution," Baiyue said. "Things were a lot more simple."

"Yeah," Jieling said, "and they were poor and a lot of them died."

"I know," Baiyue sighed.

Jieling knew what she meant. It would be nice to … to be sure what was right and what was wrong. Although not if it made you like Mr. Wei.

Poor Mr. Wei. Had his daughter really died?

"Hey," Jieling said, "I've got to make a call. Wait right here." She walked a little down the beach. It was windy and she turned her back to guard protect the cell phone, like someone lighting a match. "Hello," she said, "hello, mama, it's me. Jieling."

Copyright © 2008 by Maureen McHugh

Ron Friedman's stories have appeared in Daily Science Fiction, the Age of Certainty *anthology, and received Honorable Mentions in the Writers of the Future Contest in 2011, 2013 and 2014.*

GAME NOT OVER

by Ron Friedman

Molten lava flowed through Death Valley, bypassing islands of glowing flint and brimstone. The air stank of sulfur and decaying corpses. Dark acid clouds were scattered throughout the amber sky. Occasionally, vengeful lightning discharged fury against the agonized soil.

In short, it was a wonderful day, thought Esh.

The small fire imp stopped in front of the magma pit.

"Go away," boomed a voice.

"But, Mistress!" said Esh, taking a step back.

"You dare to defy my words?"

Esh looked at the she-daemon who rose out of the boiling hollow. She was a good-looking mistress. Her dark hair fell in waves over her shoulders. Her pitch-black eyes shone like the abyss, reflecting intelligence and wisdom. With her feminine horns and folded bat-like wings, no mortal woman even came close to Sheda's beauty.

"Satan demands your presence, Mistress." Esh bowed. "Humans have infested his den."

"Again?" Sheda sighed.

Esh shrugged, staring at the she-daemon.

"This human infestation problem is growing beyond …"

Suddenly, she groaned. Black marks appeared on her forehead.

"What's wrong, Mistress? Aren't you feeling well?"

She grabbed Esh's hand and squeezed it tight. "My belly … I feel … ill." Esh saw her face turning green. "It's so painful …"

Esh felt helpless. "Shall I call for aid? Perhaps Satan can help."

"Curses!" She shook her head. "I think I'm being summoned."

"Summoned? That's horrendous. Who dare …"

"It's those damn sorcerers from Earth," whispered Sheda, still holding her abdomen. "Why can't they solve their own problems? Why do they need to involve us daemons in their puny affairs? I don't care who this wizard is. I swear I'm going to eradicate him! Damnation shall fall upon his soul."

In that instant, Sheda vanished into thin air.

Sharp pain hit Esh in his stomach. The whole of Gehenom began to spin. Smoke and steam engulfed his small body. Something pulled him into oblivion.

Slowly, Esh regained his vision. His first thought was to fly out of there. The fire imp fluttered his tiny wings. Something smashed into him. He flinched in pain and charged again, only to be subjected once more with grief by that cursed, invisible barrier.

"We're trapped," said a charming soprano voice.

"Mistress, what happened to us?"

Sheda said nothing.

Esh looked downward. Both he and Sheda floated helplessly above a glowing pentagram which was painted on the floor. The dim illumination intensified the direness of their situation. This wasn't Gehenom. In fact, this place didn't look like anything he had ever seen in any of the upper plains. They were in a cold, dark, flameless dungeon.

Around them he noticed a few broken tables, traces of blood, body parts, smashed armor, shields and other shattered weapons of war.

Furthermore, there was her. The one which was complete. The only non-mutilated body. Her beautiful yet motionless statue looked alive; frozen inside a large amber cube, a seven-foot-long rectangular prism.

"I wonder what happened here," said Esh.

Before Sheda had a chance to respond, Esh heard chains rolling, followed by rusty axles squeaking. He turned to see a figure in red robes entering the dungeon.

The figure halted at the center of the hall. Then it bowed. A deep voice greeted them, "May you burn in Hell for all eternity."

Sheda looked at the figure, her face red, her eyes blazing anger mixed with flames. "Damn you!" she exclaimed, spitting venom. "Burning in Hell is exactly what I had in mind before your intervention." She shook her head fiercely, pointing her finger at

the figure. "You summoned us to this cold filthy place. Speak your words and send me back to Gehenom!"

The figured bowed once more. "Forgive me, Mistress. I hold nothing but the greatest respect to you. I would have never called you to this mortal plain of existence if it wasn't for a matter of grave importance."

Sheda burst into rolling laughter. "You can remove your hood, Nakam. It is transparent to my kind."

The figure bowed again and took off his head covering.

Esh flinched at the sight. Nakam's face was rotten and decayed. His nose and both ears were absent. Bones could be seen through the eroded flesh. Little hair remained on the semi-exposed skull. What intimidated Esh most were two glittering diamonds in the sockets which were supposed to host eyes. Nakam ground his teeth in an incomprehensible gesture. If it wasn't for the missing lips, Esh would have sworn Nakam was smiling.

"I don't think he is human," whispered Esh.

"Esh, dear," Sheda chuckled, "this one is Nakam, the Lich Emperor of Sham-Rahok."

Nakam took another step toward the pentagram. "I see there is no fooling a great daemon such as you, mistress Sheda."

"What is it that you want of me?" she barked impatiently.

Nakam rubbed his skull, nodding toward Sheda. "My lady and your daemonic shape-changing ability could be helpful for this task."

"You're pathetic if you think I would help." She looked around at the carnage, at the maiden elf, then at the pentagram.

Fire sparks trickled down Esh's forehead. The flare burning within his chest pounded. He flinched at the thought of what Nakam might do to them if Sheda declined the offer. When nothing happened, he swallowed flames.

"Now," Sheda put her hands on her hips, "by the names of all the daemons and devils in Hell, send us back to the abyss."

Nakam just stood there in silence.

"I gave you an order, Lich."

"Mistress Sheda,"—Nakam coughed and shook his head—"if you'll allow me to speak, I shall explain myself." He rolled his diamond eyes upward. "Surely, you don't think I went through all the trouble of summoning you here just so I would send you back."

Esh tried to read Sheda's expression. She seemed ready to explode.

"What I want you to look into," said Nakam, "is who this elf is and who these invaders are."

All Hell broke loose. Thunder, lightning, fire shook the pentagram. Unimaginable shrieks and inconceivable screams filled the space around Esh. He shut his eyes and held his hands against his tiny ears. It didn't help. The noise was immensely strong and the flashes strikingly bright. His small body was pushed and sucked, shattered and smashed, shoved and scratched, squished and smote, yet the force field remained intact.

"Send us back to Hell, you miserable piece of zombie excrement! I shall slay you. I shall scorch the earth, dealing death and destruction of apocalyptic proportions. I shall suck your life force and banish your soul. Even the Hell of all Hells is too good a place for a miserable worm-infested scum like you." Sheda attacked the invisible barrier with all her might. But to no avail.

Seeing that the force field held against her attacks, Sheda's rage subsided. Esh opened his agonized eyes. The Lich Emperor stood outside the pentagram in a stoic calmness.

"As I said before,"—Nakam bowed—"I called upon you to resolve a serious matter that shouldn't be taken lightly. Our universe is at stake. All of us are in danger, mortals, undead and daemons alike."

Sheda stared at Nakam, and so did Esh. Then she spoke softly. "Release the force field and I shall listen more."

Nakam shook his head, "Only after you swear your allegiance and promise to investigate the origin of this elven maid."

Sheda paused for a long moment before she nodded. "Three days," she groaned. "Release me and I shall be in your service for three days. Then the deal is off."

"I promise you," she whispered to Esh, "a day shall come when Nakam shall pay for his insolence."

"No doubt, Mistress."

Nakam came closer, stopping in front of Sheda. He scanned her as if his diamond eyes could see whether she was telling the truth. "Deal." He snapped his fingers and the glow radiating from the pentagram vanished.

The daemon slowly stepped outside the barrier. Her facial expression changed from anger to surprise and then to happiness. "Free! At last."

Then it was anger once more. She spread her wings wide and hovered above Nakam, exposing her fangs. Lightning bolts discharged within her claws. "Now you shall witness the powers of Hell descending upon you. I shall smite you into oblivion."

"Mistress," screamed Esh in panic, "remember the last time you lost your temper?"

Sheda hesitated.

"Let us first hear what Nakam has to say," said the fire imp. "If you don't like it, you can always smite him into oblivion then."

The Lich reached into his robe, pulling out an old-looking scroll.

"In recent months," explained Nakam, "my domain has been invaded time and again by these adventurers."

Esh nodded, examining the elven beauty who lay inside the cube. The maid had braided long blonde hair. She wore a green wool jacket, and a dagger was attached to her belt. He looked closely at the motionless body; his jaw froze in surprise. Her eyes were open wide, and her pupils moved back and forth.

"I spoke with other lords across the continent," added Nakam. "Vampires, mummies, orc kings and even human warlords. All share the same tragedy."

"Which is?"

"Adventurers!" Nakam muttered, lowering his voice to a bass. "We lived happily in our own realms, minding our own business. These invaders," said Nakam, spitting on the floor as he spoke the words, "came out of nowhere with one purpose in mind: killing and pillaging. No one is safe from these evildoers. Not even I."

"Fascinating," hissed Sheda. "Satan had similar complaints. Tell me more."

"They appear in the Temple of the Combined Elementals. From there, they set on a voyage of rampage against the inhabitants of this land."

"Your Imperial Highness," Esh coughed, "have you noticed her eyes?" He pointed his finger at the elf. "They're moving."

The Lich fixed his diamond eyes on the tiny fire imp. "Of course they are."

A few tiny sparks flashed. Esh said nothing.

"That's the only way to hold those adventurers confined," said the Lich. "I have tried several times to imprison them. After a brief moment, they all vanish. However, when showing them captivating illusions, they'll remain confined, at least for a short while."

"How?" Esh asked.

"Dream—one of my best illusions. Nevertheless, we only have a few hours before she shall find even the greatest of dreams boring; then, she too shall disappear."

"These invaders of yours," asked Sheda, "what kind of creatures are they?"

"Demi-humans," replied the Lich. "Most are humans, some are elves, not to mention the occasional dwarves."

"I meant what profession they hold, hmmm, besides being thieves and murderers?"

"Ah," replied Nakam. "Paladins, warriors, rangers, wizards, clerics—you know, the usual trades."

Sheda stared at the frozen elven lady. "She is an abomination. It's as if she is a sort of …"

"Of what?" Esh and Nakam asked simultaneously.

"Unnatural."

The she-daemon bent over the cube, gazing at the body inside. "I could shape-change myself into someone like her."

"Splendid." Nakam's diamond eyes brightened. "I knew I made the right choice when I summoned you."

"Don't ever do it again," snapped Sheda.

"Finally," Nakam said, his shiny sparks glittering, "the riddle of the invaders shall be unveiled." He paused for a moment. "Start to polymorph; we don't have much time …"

✧

"How do I look?"

Esh looked at the elven body which was his daemon mistress. He looked at her pointy ears, her bright complexion, the braided blonde hair and the simple clothing. "Beautiful. A fair Lady." Realizing he might have offended her, he immediately corrected himself. "For an elf."

"Perfect!" Nakam clenched his teeth within his lipless skull. "With your new look, you might be able to penetrate the Combined Elementals Temple."

"Come, Esh," said Sheda. "Let's waste no time. We have a mission to complete."

The small fire imp landed on Sheda's shoulder. Traces of smoke appeared on her wool jacket as it began to burn.

A blow hit Esh. He smashed on the floor.

"Idiot!" Nakam snapped. "An elven lady can't wander around town with a fire imp as her companion, especially while wearing a flammable outfit."

Esh looked upon himself. There was something to Nakam's logic. "But I must accompany my mistress," he cried.

"Not as a fire imp!" Nakam said.

"So how would I go?"

"I can transform you into a small animal." There was a hint of contempt in Nakam's voice. "Something suitable for elven females, possibly an owl or a frog."

"But what if the mistress wishes to speak to me? I must be able to talk."

"Hmmm," mumbled Nakam as he scratched an exposed piece of his skull. "Perhaps you're right."

✧

Disguised as a parrot, Esh stood on Sheda's right shoulder while she walked the streets in her new elven body. As they advanced toward the temple, merchants, beggars and a large number of nobles greeted them with the same dumb smiles.

"Mind your own business, mortals." Sheda smirked.

"It feels strange walking upon human streets." Esh struggled to speak in his new birdlike shape.

"Ha-ha," agreed Sheda. "Last time I tried that, people ran away screaming, except for a few stupid ones who actually tried to attack me."

"Aye," agreed Esh. "Daemons are always hated and feared. I wonder why." Using his beak, he scratched an itch below his feathery wing.

"You're pathetically naive."

"Why?" Esh asked. "All we want to do is to be left alone in Gehenom. If humans want to be upset about something, why don't they pick on the wizards who summoned the daemons in the first place?"

His voice sounded so awkward with the high-pitched twittering—damn his parrot's beak.

The houses on both sides of the road were two stories high. In most, the second floor was bigger than the ground level; supporting beams prevented the upper deck from collapsing into the open sewage. The open sewers scent was not as good as the sulfuric acid and brimstone Esh was used to, yet he couldn't complain.

It wasn't long before they reached the Combined Elementals Temple. It was a remarkable building made of marble, perhaps twenty stories high. Nobody knew how many levels extended below ground. The gate was open and Esh saw no guards.

Sheda walked toward the entrance. She climbed the stairs and—bang! An invisible barrier blocked their path. Sheda tried once more. She tried to throw stones. Nothing could enter the temple.

"Perhaps we should ask someone," suggested Esh. "Maybe this beggar knows the secret."

Sheda nodded, and climbed down the staircase to meet the tramp. He was an old man in ragged clothing.

The beggar extended his hand. "Can you spare a couple of coppers for a poor old man who lost his daughter?"

"Silence, old fool," snapped Sheda. "Tell me how to enter the Temple."

"How can I tell you anything, if you want me to be silent?"

Sheda grabbed the beggar and lifted him with one hand. "Tell me what I want to know, or I shall smash your spine and banish your miserable soul to Hell."

"I seek no confrontation," begged the beggar. "I shall answer thy questions, free."

"How do I get in?"

The beggar looked at her with his eyes wide open. "All you have to do is to climb the stairs and enter the black gate."

"Are you as blind as you are a fool?" Sheda said, her voice like ice. "My way was blocked."

"Anyone who stepped out of the temple may enter."

"What if one never stepped out of the temple?"

The beggar kept silence for a short while. "That's impossible. I saw you come out of the gate a day before yesterday. You were kind enough to provide me a gold piece, don't you remember?" The beggar paused for a moment. "I was the fellow who told you where the pub was; the one with your friends."

Sheda shook the beggar once more. "Are you saying only those who came out may enter?"

"Aye."

"Can you enter?" she asked, putting her index finger on his chest. Esh recognized the tone. It meant danger.

"Of course not. I'm a local."

Sheda dropped the beggar angrily. "Didn't I tell you to remain silent?"

"Can you spare a couple of coppers for a poor …"

Esh shut his eyes close as a sudden flash blinded his sight. A deafening explosion almost knocked him off Sheda's shoulder. When he opened his eyes, all that was left of the beggar was a crumbling heap of ash.

"That shall teach him respect," said Sheda.

Esh looked around, expecting the city guards to jump them. Nothing happened. The many nobles and few merchants just continued with their daily business wearing their silly smiles, as if frying people with lightning bolts was a normal occurrence.

Sheda shook her head. "This whole mission smells like a waste of my valuable time. Damnation bestowed upon Nakam."

"What about the 'friends' mentioned by this, hmm, thing?" Esh stared at the heap of ash. "Perhaps we could find some clues if …"

"Let us seek that pub."

✿

Esh scanned the patrons in the pub. Most seemed ordinary folks like knights, priests, rich merchants, a street beggar and a couple of palace guards.

Sheda seated herself at one of the empty tables. "I've had enough of this mystery. I miss Hell."

"I wish I could help, Mistress," replied Esh, still standing on her shoulder.

She turned to the bartender. "Fetch me some sulfuric acid. Make it boiling!"

"I'm sorry, lady," the bartender replied, staring at the elven maid. "We don't carry that drink. Would you be satisfied with some warm tea instead?"

"Baah!" Sheda said. "Bring me the strongest stuff this miserable establishment has to offer."

"Aye, my lady," the bartender bowed.

The door slammed open. The inn was flooded with light so strong that for a moment, Esh had to shut his parrot eyes.

Most of the tavern's occupants simply ignored the new arrivals. Esh and Sheda examined them closely.

There were three.

The first one covered himself, head to toe, with golden full plate armor. He held a huge rectangular shield. On his back, he carried at least three backpacks, an enormous two-handed sword, a large lance, a longbow and no fewer than ten quivers packed with arrows. He wore a polished golden crown, spotted with gems so bright that looking at them pained Esh's eyes.

The second person also wore heavy full plate armor. This one was fat, and unlike the first, his armor was as black as coal. The large shield he carried was decorated with an image of snow-covered mountains. In his right hand he held a bulky staff. Atop his many backpacks Esh could identify a huge flail, and in his belt the fellow carried a sling. This individual wore a sizable necklace; many beads and prayer books peeked from his pockets.

The third character wore a blue robe and a purple pointy hat that could only be seen on wizards. His equipment was fundamentally different from his comrades' gear—he had but a single backpack, and his only weapon was a tiny dagger stuck in his belt. Strangely, two shining gems orbited his head. They reminded Esh of moons orbiting a world up in the upper plains of existence. A black cat trailed behind the skinny human.

"Perhaps these are the 'friends' the beggar spoke of," whispered Esh.

"Hi, Susan." The human with the golden armor waved his hand at Sheda. "I was trying to call you last night. Why didn't you answer? Did you forget about the barbecue?"

Esh froze. "Susan" definitely wasn't a typical elven name. And what did barbecue stand for? Esh had never heard of such a word. He hoped barbecue had something to do with fire.

"Hmmm," mumbled Sheda. "I was preoccupied at the Lich palace. He captured me."

"And I thought you were playing hard to get," he chuckled. "I'll text you tonight."

"I'll be delighted." Sheda glanced at Esh and shrugged.

Esh wanted to scratch his head hearing these funny words. Unfortunately, his parrot wings didn't allow that luxury, and he dared not use his feet.

The other two humans came closer. The blue-robed wizard stared at Sheda closely. "Were you at the Lich palace the whole night?"

"Aye."

"Captured?"

Sheda nodded.

"Sweet Jesus," the wizard said, while his black cat rubbed at his legs. "Why didn't you just log out and start fresh at the temple?"

Esh wondered what by the name of Asmodeus that wizard was talking about.

"You tell me," Sheda said.

"You didn't want to lose your experience points?"

Sheda nodded.

"You didn't have to be up all night, you know," the wizard continued. "You could have called support. I was killed twice at the palace. I e-mailed the company, and they restored all my items. By the way, we're thinking of going back there. Wanna join? We could use a good thief."

"A thief?" Icicles formed in Sheda's eyes. "You dare to call me a thief? I shall obliterate you for your insolence."

"Mistress!" Esh whispered in panic. "Remember the mission."

The one with the golden plate smiled. "You talk funny, Susan. A true role player! Anyway, about that Lich, are you in? We could use your help. Nakam is a first rate AI."

"AI?" Sheda raised an eyebrow.

The wizard punched himself on his forehead. "What's the matter with you, Susan? I thought you were a geek. AI—Artificial Intelligence." His hands extended wide, as if he was talking about the most trivial thing in this plain.

"Ah, yes, that kind of AI. Sorry, I forgot," Sheda replied. Her voice sounded awkward and unconvincing.

"So?" The golden-plate warrior stared at Sheda. "Are you in?"

Sheda ignored him as she addressed the wizard. "Some daemons are also incredibly smart. Are you implying they too have artificial, um, intelligent?"

The wizard nodded.

Esh was confused. These humans were talking about the creatures of this world as some sort of artificial … something. This was madness.

"Are you claiming that all the locals," said Sheda, "all those who didn't come out of the temple, are nothing but …" She fell silent. Then she whispered in Esh's ear. "These humans must have drunk too much elixir of lunacy. Continuing this parley is a waste of my precious time. We should go home."

"Susan,"—the wizard sounded surprised—"didn't you read the game manual? All the local creatures are an interactive part of the software."

"Of course I read them." Sheda played along with their psychosis. "I'm, as you said, a good, hmm … role player. This body is the avatar of an entity from the real world." She pointed at her elven body, mocking the wizard. "The one where humans can invoke, barbecues and software, while the inhabitants of this place are nothing but a brainless artificial creation. Right?"

The wizard chuckled.

Sheda stood up and walked toward the exit. "I'm afraid I must bid you farewell, gentlemen. I have more important business."

The human with the golden plate shouted after her, "What kind of business? The Lich? What did he promise you?"

Sheda turned her head. "Nakam promised me my freedom."

The man looked at her, "Eh?"

"The freedom to go to Hell."

✿

The dazzle in Nakam's diamond eyes dimmed. "I've suspected that for the longest time. And don't fool yourself. It's much worse than what I initially expected."

"Have you lost your mind?" said Esh, hovering above Sheda in his original fire imp shape. "These humans are insane beyond redemption. Are you saying there is a shred of truth in their ill mind?"

Nakam just stood there, shaking his head. "I have other sources that confirmed this story. Our plains of existence are indeed nothing but a sophisticated creation. And we are mere creatures designed to entertain the players who enter our world."

Sheda, back in her she-daemon form, glared in red. She shoved Esh aside with one hand, and with the other, she grabbed Nakam's fragile neck and lifted him in the air. "Explain yourself!"

"In your absence," Nakam said without flinching, "I linked to this maiden's mind. I read her memories. I saw the world she came from."

"Carry on!"

Nakam just gestured at the elven maid frozen inside the transparent cube.

"It can't be true." Sheda dropped the Lich to the ground, her eyes as dead as the abyss. "I've fulfilled my part of our agreement. If you choose to believe in the maiden lunacy, it's your choice. I demand that you hold your part of the bargain, and send me back to Gehenom."

"Our world,"—Nakam clanged his teeth—"with all its plains, is nothing but a game. A game which could be turned off at any moment. We," he pointed at himself, then at Sheda, "can be turned off at any time."

"Mistress?" Esh said, wondering where Sheda was heading. "Nakam sounds very convincing."

"Is he?" said Sheda, pointing her claw at Nakam. "The Emperor Lich can be as delusional as the invading humans. I know what I am. I know where I belong. I'm acquainted with the nature of this world. I claim my right to return home. Enough with this lunacy."

"The deal spoke of three days." Nakam said calmly. "You are still in my service for two more." He pointed his rotten finger at the dreaming elven maid. "We need to find a way to send you to the place where these beings come from. We must bring an end to their reckless rampaging through our world. Only then could I afford to free you of your oath."

Esh remained speechless. Sheda seemed a little unsure of herself.

"Can you send me to the invaders' realm?" Sheda calmed herself down. "I'll get to the bottom of this insanity."

"I'm afraid that's impossible," Nakam replied flatly. "Nobody is that powerful; not in the entire world. Besides," he said, pointing at the elf, "at any moment she'll be bored with my inceptions, and then she'll rematerialize to her primary reality."

Esh noticed the anger mounting in Sheda's face. He must do something before she erupted. "Is there anything we can do? Perhaps take control of Susan's body in her world?" He snuck a worried glimpse at his mistress.

Nakam's gaze nearly froze Esh in midair. "You mean Dybbuk? Hmm, highly unlikely, yet …" The Lich clenched his teeth and then nodded. "Esh, you're a mastermind! We must hurry." He spun toward the exit. "I'll be back shortly. Perhaps I'll be able to transfer your consciousness after all."

☼

It has been told that, for a short while, all magic was drained in the empire of Sham-Rahok. Mystical creatures, minions and slaves, sorcerers, wizards and witches, all lent their strength. It took a whole day and a whole night collecting and channeling the magic mana. Nonetheless, when the sun came forth on the second day, the deed had been done. It was told, in that day, Nakam's laughter was heard for the first time within the land of Sham-Rahok.

☼

Esh, Nakam and Sheda stood around the sleeping maid. A hefty sphere of glowing blue mana floated above in the air. This was a concentration of magical energy beyond Esh's wildest dreams.

"Remember," said Nakam, "it requires all three of us to subdue Susan in her own dream. Only together we could …"

A blast threw Esh, smashing his tiny fire body against the wall. Three columns of green smoke appeared near the entrance.

Esh's fire heart almost extinguished when he recognized the images inside the dissolving green smolders. These were the three adventurers they met in the pub.

A series of fireballs exploded. A hurricane of lightning bolts and acid arrows turned the hall into a turmoil of molten chaos.

"If Susan's body dies," cried the Lich, "all shall be lost."

"Esh, release the magic sphere!" Sheda screamed.

"Quickly," cried Nakam. Desperation could be heard in his voice. "I can't hold them much longer."

"I can't," shouted Esh. He watched in horror as the blue wizard moved to block his way.

The adventurer waved one of his wands. Fire engulfed Esh's little body.

Stupid human, thought Esh. You don't fight fire with fire. In a swift maneuver, Esh flew through the flames and punched the sphere. Everything exploded.

☼

Esh found himself in an open, never-ending field of sunflowers. A small water stream ran nearby.

Where am I? How did I get here? Could this be Susan's dream?

Instead of an answer, he heard a call from afar. "Stay away from me, witch."

He sprang through the air. Soon, he hovered above two women, grappling and thumping at each other. The one he didn't recognize punched his beloved Sheda. The she-daemon fell to the ground motionless.

Dream or no dream, he must help his mistress.

"Help," shouted the other, as then she turned and ran away.

"She is Susan," whispered Sheda. "We're in her dream. Get her before she wakes up. Hurry …"

Esh charged at the escaping young woman.

Susan's image began to vanish. She was already partly transparent when Esh finally caught her. In spite of her fading body, Susan successfully blocked Esh with a desperate thump.

He heard Sheda coming from behind. Were they too late? Someone grabbed him, and the sunflowers vanished.

☼

The pain was unbearable and so was the stench. His limbs were stiff. He couldn't see a thing. It felt like being in a different plain, and in a new shape, again. Something covered his eyes. He felt his throat yearning for water, an alien sensation for a fire being who always feared water. And what was that awkward sting in his lower abdomen? Esh released the pressure. Wet liquid flowed down his legs, soaked into some uncomfortable cloth wrapped around them. The sting was gone. What a relief.

He felt weak and shaky. "Mistress, are you here? Did our consciousness manage to possess Susan's body in her reality?"

Someone laughed out loud. The voice formed within his head. "What do you know? It seems that Nakam and the three human invaders were right after all."

"Mistress?"

"This body is a disaster," echoed Sheda's voice. "This careless woman hasn't eaten, drunk or slept for two days. And the smell … Disgusting."

"I'm on vacation," came a third feminine voice which must have been Susan's. "You're not my mom. I don't have to listen to you."

Esh wondered what was going on. He wished someone would turn on the lights.

A horrific scream deafened Esh. He'd never heard someone that terrified. "Stop that." Susan begged. "Please."

Esh recognized the terror in her voice.

Sheda's laughter filled his head. "Foolish girl. I'm a daemon from the game you've been playing. An AI daemon. Now I control your body."

"But … That's impossible …"

Someone slapped Esh's face, at least his new body's face. The pain was sharp, yet bearable.

"Silence!" exclaimed Sheda. "Obey or be destroyed."

Esh realized he was in Susan's body. And that this body was now shared by three consciousnesses—his, Sheda's and Susan's. There was little doubt who was in control.

Sheda used Susan's hands to take off a strange-looking helmet this body was wearing. And Esh regained his sight. He blinked as his eyes adjusted to the light.

The helmet was covered by mysterious runes. Esh was amazed to see it was connected by a string to a bizarre black box. Another device was tied by a black rope to the box; one with many-colored buttons.

"Virtual Reality," Susan's mouth said aloud as their shared eyes stared at the runes. "I wonder what that means."

Esh look around as Sheda moved Susan's head. They were in a room. He saw a bed, many books, a pot with some plants and another glass covered black device; a few buttons decorated its bottom.

"Toshiba," said Sheda.

"For God's sake, what's happening to me?" Susan's shaky and weak voice was heard inside his head.

His hand slapped his cheek, again. "Silence, slave, or inferno shall rain down upon your worthless soul."

Esh was horrified; Sheda's impulsiveness might kill their shared body in this reality. He feared to speculate what the consequences might be. "Susan, calm down." Esh projected his words to the other consciousness. "You must not cross the mistress' words, please."

Susan's voice inside his head fell silent.

"Obedient," said Sheda victoriously. "Now tell me where I can find the software entity that created the game. My home game. I'm going to pay that entity a visit, and make sure my game shall be around forever." She picked up a set of keys from the desk, and walked toward the door. "I have a whole new world to conquer." She burst into vicious laughter.

Original (First) Publication
Copyright © 2014 by Ron Friedman

A Classic Revived
Includes the prequel story,
"The Ballad of Lost C'Mell"

The late Robert A. Heinlein was the Guest of Honor at three different Worldcons. He won four Hugos, all for Best Novel, while alive, and won still more Retro-Hugos after his death. A giant in the field, he was the first writer chosen by SFWA to be a Grand Master.

❋ Publisher's Note ❋

"All You Zombies—" was written in July 1958. This is important to keep in mind reading the story since the story deals with time travel. 1958 is the "present."

"ALL YOU ZOMBIES—"

by Robert A. Heinlein

2217 Time Zone V (EST) 7 Nov 1970 NYC—"Pop's Place": I was polishing a brandy snifter when the Unmarried Mother came in. I noted the time—10.17 p.m. zone five or eastern time November 7th, 1970. Temporal agents always notice time & date; we must.

The Unmarried Mother was a man twenty-five years old, no taller than I am, immature features and a touchy temper. I didn't like his looks—I never had—but he was a lad I was here to recruit, he was my boy. I gave him my best barkeep's smile.

Maybe I'm too critical. He wasn't swish; his nickname came from what he always said when some nosy type asked him his line: "I'm an unmarried mother." If he felt less than murderous he would add: "—at four cents a word. I write confession stories."

If he felt nasty, he would wait for somebody to make something of it. He had a lethal style of infighting, like a female cop—one reason I wanted him. Not the only one.

He had a load on and his face showed that he despised people more than usual. Silently I poured a double shot of Old Underwear and left the bottle. He drank, poured another.

I wiped the bar top. "How's the 'Unmarried Mother' racket?"

His fingers tightened on the glass and he seemed about to throw it at me; I felt for the sap under the bar. In temporal manipulation you try to figure everything, but there are so many factors that you never take needless risks.

I saw him relax that tiny amount they teach you to watch for in the Bureau's training school. "Sorry," I said. "Just asking, 'How's business?' Make it 'How's the weather?'"

He looked sour. "Business is okay. I write 'em, they print 'em, I eat."

I poured myself one, leaned toward him. "Matter of fact," I said, "you write a nice stick—I've sampled a few. You have an amazingly sure touch with the woman's angle."

It was a slip I had to risk; he never admitted what pen names he used. But he was boiled enough to pick up only the last. "'Woman's angle!'" he repeated with a snort. "Yeah, I know the woman's angle. I should."

"So?" I said doubtfully. "Sisters?"

"No. You wouldn't believe me if I told you."

"Now, now," I answered mildly, "bartenders and psychiatrists learn that nothing is stranger than the truth. Why, son, if you heard the stories I do—well, you'd make yourself rich. Incredible."

"You don't know what 'incredible' means!"

"So? Nothing astonishes me. I've always heard worse."

He snorted again. "Want to bet the rest of the bottle?"

"I'll bet a full bottle." I placed one on the bar.

"Well—" I signaled my other bartender to handle the trade. We were at the far end, a single-stool space that I kept private by loading the bar top by it with jars of pickled eggs and other clutter. A few were at the other end watching the fights and somebody was playing the juke box—private as a bed where we were. "Okay," he began, "to start with, I'm a bastard."

"No distinction around here," I said.

"I mean it," he snapped. "My parents weren't married."

"Still no distinction," I insisted. "Neither were mine."

"When—" He stopped, gave me the first warm look I ever saw on him. "You mean that?"

"I do. A one-hundred-percent bastard. In fact," I added, "no one in my family ever marries. All bastards."

"Don't try to top me—*you're* married." He pointed at my ring.

"Oh, that." I showed it to him. "It just looks like a wedding ring; I wear it to keep women off." That ring is an antique I bought in 1985 from a fellow operative—he had fetched it from pre-Christian Crete. "The Worm Ouroboros … the World Snake that eats its own tail, forever without end. A symbol of the Great Paradox."

He barely glanced at it. "If you're really a bastard, you know how it feels. When I was a little girl—"

"Wups!" I said. "Did I hear you correctly?"

"Who's telling this story? When I was a little girl—Look, ever hear of Christine Jorgenson? Or Roberta Cowell?"

"Uh, sex change cases? You're trying to tell me—"

"Don't interrupt or swelp me, I won't talk. I was a foundling, left at an orphanage in Cleveland in 1945 when I was a month old. When I was a little girl, I envied kids with parents. Then, when I learned about sex—and, believe me, Pop, you learn fast in an orphanage—"

"I know."

"—I made a solemn vow that any kid of mine would have both a pop and a mom. It kept me 'pure,' quite a feat in that vicinity—I had to learn to fight to manage it. Then I got older and realized I stood darned little chance of getting married—for the same reason I hadn't been adopted." He scowled. "I was horse-faced and buck-toothed, flat-chested and straight-haired."

"You don't look any worse than I do."

"Who cares how a barkeep looks? Or a writer? But people wanting to adopt pick little blue-eyed golden-haired morons. Later on, the boys want bulging breasts, a cute face, and an Oh-you-wonderful-male manner." He shrugged. "I couldn't compete. So I decided to join the W.E.N.C.H.E.S."

"Eh?"

"Women's Emergency National Corps, Hospitality & Entertainment Section, what they now call 'Space Angels'—Auxiliary Nursing Group, Extra-terrestrial Legions."

I knew both terms, once I had them chronized. Although we now use still a third name; it's that elite military service corps: Women's Hospitality Order Refortifying & Encouraging Spacemen. Vocabulary shift is the worst hurdle in time-jumps—did you know that "service station" once meant a dispensary for petroleum fractions? Once on an assignment in the Churchill Era a woman said to me, "Meet me at the service station next door"—which is *not* what it sounds; a "service station" (then) wouldn't have a bed in it.

He went on: "It was when they first admitted you can't send men into space for months and years and not relieve the tension. You remember how the wowsers screamed?—that improved my chances, volunteers were scarce. A gal had to be respectable, preferably virgin (they liked to train them from scratch), above average mentally, and stable emotionally. But most volunteers were old hookers, or neurotics who would crack up ten days off Earth. So I didn't need looks; if they accepted me, they would fix my buck teeth, put a wave in my hair, teach me to walk and dance and how to listen to a man pleasingly, and everything else—plus training for the prime duties. They would even use plastic surgery if it would help—nothing too good for Our Boys.

"Best yet, they made sure you didn't get pregnant during your enlistment—and you were almost certain to marry at the end of your hitch. Same way today, A.N.G.E.L.S. marry spacers—they talk the language.

"When I was eighteen I was placed as a 'mother's helper.' This family simply wanted a cheap servant but I didn't mind as I couldn't enlist till I was twenty-one. I did housework and went to night school—pretending to continue my high school typing and shorthand but going to a charm class instead, to better my chances for enlistment.

"Then I met this city slicker with his hundred dollar bills." He scowled. "The no-good actually did have a wad of hundred dollar bills. He showed me one night, told me to help myself.

"But I didn't. I liked him. He was the first man I ever met who was nice to me without trying to take my pants off. I quit night school to see him oftener. It was the happiest time of my life.

"Then one night in the park my pants did come off."

He stopped. I said, "And then?"

"And then *nothing!* I never saw him again. He walked me home and told me he loved me—and kissed me good-night and never came back." He looked grim. "If I could find him, I'd kill him!"

"Well," I sympathized, "I know how you feel. But killing him—just for doing what comes naturally—hmm … Did you struggle?"

"Huh? What's that got to do with it?"

"Quite a bit. Maybe he deserves a couple of broken arms for running out on you, but—"

"He deserves worse than that! Wait till you hear. Somehow I kept anyone from suspecting and decided it was all for the best. I hadn't really loved him and probably would never love anybody—and I was more eager to join the W.E.N.C.H.E.S. than ever. I wasn't disqualified, they didn't insist on virgins. I cheered up.

"It wasn't until my skirts got tight that I realized."

"Pregnant?"

"The bastard had me higher 'n a kite! Those skinflints I lived with ignored it as long as I could work—then kicked me out and the orphanage wouldn't take me back. I landed in a charity ward surrounded by other big bellies and trotted bedpans until my time came.

"One night I found myself on an operating table, with a nurse saying, 'Relax. Now breathe deeply.'

"I woke up in bed, numb from the chest down. My surgeon came in. 'How do you feel?' he says cheerfully.

"'Like a mummy.'

"'Naturally. You're wrapped like one and full of dope to keep you numb. You'll get well—but a Caesarian isn't a hangnail.'

"'"Caesarian?"' I said. "Doc—*did I lose the baby?*"

"'Oh, no. Your baby's fine.'

"'Oh. Boy or girl?'

"'A healthy little girl. Five pounds, three ounces.'

"I relaxed. It's something, to have made a baby. I told myself I would go somewhere and tack 'Mrs.' on my name and let the kid think her papa was dead—no orphanage for my kid!

"But the surgeon was talking. 'Tell me, uh—' He avoided my name. '—did you ever think your glandular setup was odd?'

"I said, 'Huh? Of course not. What are you driving at?'

"He hesitated. 'I'll give you this in one dose, then a hypo to let you sleep off your jitters. You'll have 'em.'

"'Why?' I demanded.

"'Ever hear of that Scottish physician who was female until she was thirty-five?—then had surgery and became legally and medically a man? Got married. All okay.'

"'What's that got to do with me?'

"'That's what I'm saying. You're a man.'

"I tried to sit up. '*What?*'

"'Take it easy. When I opened you, I found a mess. I sent for the Chief of Surgery while I got the baby out, then we held a consultation with you on the table—and worked for hours to salvage what we could. You had two full sets of organs, both immature, but with the female set well enough developed that you had a baby. They could never be any use to you again, so we took them out and rearranged things so that you can develop properly as a man.' He put a hand on me. 'Don't worry. You're young, your bones will readjust, we'll watch your glandular balance—and make a fine young man out of you.'

"I started to cry. 'What about my *baby*?'

"'Well, you can't nurse her, you haven't milk enough for a kitten. If I were you, I wouldn't see her—put her up for adoption.'

"'*No!*'

"He shrugged. 'The choice is yours; you're her mother—well, her parent. But don't worry now; we'll get you well first.'

"Next day they let me see the kid and I saw her daily—trying to get used to her. I had never seen a brand-new baby and had no idea how awful they look—my daughter looked like an orange monkey. My feeling changed to cold determination to do right by her. But four weeks later that didn't mean anything."

"Eh?"

"She was snatched."

"'Snatched'?"

The Unmarried Mother almost knocked over the bottle we had bet. "Kidnapped—stolen from the hospital nursery!" He breathed hard. "How's that for taking the last thing a man's got to live for?"

"A bad deal," I agreed. "Let's pour you another. No clues?"

"Nothing the police could trace. Somebody came to see her, claimed to be her uncle. While the nurse had her back turned, he walked out with her."

"Description?"

"Just a man, with a face-shaped face, like yours or mine." He frowned. "I think it was the baby's father. The nurse swore it was an older man but he probably used makeup. Who else would swipe my baby? Childless women pull such stunts—but whoever heard of a man doing it?"

"What happened to you then?"

"Eleven more months of that grim place and three operations. In four months I started to grow a beard; before I was out I was shaving regularly … and no longer doubted that I was male." He grinned wryly. "I was staring down nurses' necklines."

"Well," I said, "seems to me you came through okay. Here you are, a normal man, making good money, no real troubles. And the life of a female is not an easy one."

He glared at me. "A lot you know about it!"

"So?"

"Ever hear the expression 'a ruined woman'?"

"Mmm, years ago. Doesn't mean much today."

"I was as ruined as a woman can be; that bastard *really* ruined me—I was no longer a woman … and I didn't know *how* to be a man."

"Takes getting used to, I suppose."

"You have no idea. I don't mean learning how to dress, or not walking into the wrong restroom; I learned those in the hospital. But how could I *live*? What job could I get? Hell, I couldn't even drive a car. I didn't know a trade; I couldn't do manual labor—too much scar tissue, too tender.

"I hated him for having ruined me for the W.E.N.C.H.E.S., too, but I didn't know how much until I tried to join the Space Corps instead. One look at my belly and I was marked unfit for military service. The medical officer spent time on me just from curiosity; he had read about my case.

"So I changed my name and came to New York. I got by as a fry cook, then rented a typewriter and set myself up as a public stenographer—what a laugh! In four months I typed four letters and one manuscript. The manuscript was for *Real Life Tales* and a waste of paper, but the goof who wrote it, sold it. Which gave me an idea; I bought a stack of confession magazines and studied them." He looked cynical. "Now you know how I get the authentic woman's angle on an unmarried-mother story … through

the only version I haven't sold—the true one. Do I win the bottle?"

I pushed it toward him. I was upset myself, but there was work to do. I said, "Son, you still want to lay hands on that so-and-so?"

His eyes lighted up—a feral gleam.

"Hold it!" I said. "You wouldn't kill him?"

He chuckled nastily. "Try me."

"Take it easy. I know more about it than you think I do. I can help you. I know where he is."

He reached across the bar. "*Where is he?*"

I said softly, "Let go my shirt, sonny—or you'll land in the alley and we'll tell the cops you fainted." I showed him the sap.

He let go. "Sorry. But where is he?" He looked at me. "And how do you know so much?"

"All in good time. There are records—hospital records, orphanage records, medical records. The matron of your orphanage was Mrs. Fetherage—right? She was followed by Mrs. Gruenstein—right? Your name, as a girl, was 'Jane' right? And you didn't tell me any of this—right?"

I had him baffled and a bit scared. "What's this? You trying to make trouble for me?"

"No indeed. I've your welfare at heart. I can put this character in your lap. You do to him as you see fit—and I guarantee that you'll get away with it. But I don't think you'll kill him. You'd be nuts to—and you aren't nuts. Not quite."

He brushed it aside. "Cut the noise. *Where is he?*"

I poured him a short one; he was drunk but anger was offsetting it. "Not so fast. I do something for you—you do something for me."

"Uh … what?"

"You don't like your work. What would you say to high pay, steady work, unlimited expense account, your own boss on the job, and lots of variety and adventure?"

He stared. "I'd say, 'Get those goddam reindeer off my roof!' Shove it, Pop—there's no such job."

"Okay, put it this way: I hand him to you, you settle with him, then try my job. If it's not all I claim—well, I can't hold you."

He was wavering; the last drink did it. "When d'yuh d'liver 'im?" he said thickly.

"If it's a deal—*right now!*"

He shoved out his hand. "It's a deal!"

I nodded to my assistant to watch both ends, noted the time—2300—started to duck through the gate under the bar—when the juke box blared out: "*I'm My Own Granpaw!*" The service man had orders to load it with old Americana and classics because I couldn't stomach the "music" of 1970, but I hadn't known that tape was in it. I called out, "Shut that off! Give the customer his money back." I added, "Storeroom, back in a moment," and headed there with my Unmarried Mother following.

It was down the passage across from the johns, a steel door to which no one but my day manager and myself had a key; inside was a door to an inner room to which only I had a key. We went there.

He looked blearily around at windowless walls. "Where is 'e?"

"Right away." I opened a case, the only thing in the room; it was a U.S.F.F. Coordinates Transformer Field Kit, series 1992, Mod. II—a beauty, no moving parts, weight twenty-three kilos fully charged, and shaped to pass as a suitcase. I had adjusted it precisely earlier that day; all I had to do was to shake out the metal net which limits the transformation field.

Which I did. "Wha's that?" he demanded.

"Time machine," I said and tossed the net over us.

"Hey!" he yelled and stepped back. There is a technique to this; the net has to be thrown so that the subject will instinctively step back *onto* the metal mesh, then you close the net with both of you inside completely—else you might leave shoe soles behind or a piece of foot, or scoop up a slice of floor. But that's all the skill it takes. Some agents con a subject into the net; I tell the truth and use that instant of utter astonishment to flip the switch. Which I did.

✿

1030 V—3 April 1963—Cleveland, Ohio—Apex Bldg.: "Hey!" he repeated. "Take this damn thing off!"

"Sorry," I apologized and did so, stuffed the net into the case, closed it. "You said you wanted to find him."

"But—You said that was a time machine!"

I pointed out a window. "Does that look like November? Or New York?" While he was gawking at new buds and spring weather, I reopened the case, took out a packet of hundred dollar bills, checked that the numbers and signatures were compatible

with 1963. The Temporal Bureau doesn't care how much you spend (it costs nothing) but they don't like unnecessary anachronisms. Too many mistakes and a general court martial will exile you for a year in a nasty period, say 1974 with its strict rationing and forced labor. I never make such mistakes, the money was okay. He turned around and said, "What happened?"

"He's here. Go outside and take him. Here's expense money." I shoved it at him and added, "Settle him, then I'll pick you up."

Hundred dollar bills have a hypnotic effect on a person not used to them. He was thumbing them unbelievingly as I eased him into the hall, locked him out. The next jump was easy, a small shift in era.

✿

1700 V—10 March 1964—Cleveland—Apex Bldg.: There was a notice under the door saying that my lease expired next week; otherwise the room looked as it had a moment before. Outside, trees were bare and snow threatened; I hurried, stopping only for contemporary money and a coat, hat and topcoat I had left there when I leased the room. I hired a car, went to the hospital. It took twenty minutes to bore the nursery attendant to the point where I could swipe the baby without being noticed; we went back to the Apex Building. This dial setting was more involved as the building did not yet exist in 1945. But I had precalculated it.

✿

0100 V—20 Sept 1945—Cleveland—Skyview Motel: Field kit, baby, and I arrived in a motel outside town. Earlier I had registered as "Gregory Johnson, Warren, Ohio," so we arrived in a room with curtains closed, windows locked, and doors bolted, and the floor cleared to allow for waver as the machine hunts. You can get a nasty bruise from a chair where it shouldn't be—not the chair of course, but backlash from the field.

No trouble. Jane was sleeping soundly; I carried her out, put her in a grocery box on the seat of a car I had provided earlier, drove to the orphanage, put her on the steps, drove two blocks to a "service station" (the petroleum products sort) and phoned the orphanage, drove back in time to see them taking the box inside, kept going and abandoned the car near the motel—walked to it and jumped forward to the Apex Building in 1963.

✪

2200 V—24 April 1963—Cleveland—Apex Bldg.: I had cut the time rather fine—temporal accuracy depends on span, except on return to zero. If I had it right, Jane was discovering, out in the park this balmy spring night, that she wasn't quite as "nice" a girl as she had thought. I grabbed a taxi to the home of those skinflints, had the hackie wait around a corner while I lurked in shadows.

Presently I spotted them down the street, arms around each other. He took her up on the porch and made a long job of kissing her good-night—longer than I had thought. Then she went in and he came down the walk, turned away. I slid into step and hooked an arm in his. "That's all, son," I announced quietly. "I'm back to pick you up."

"*You!*" He gasped and caught his breath.

"Me. Now you know who *he* is—and after you think it over you'll know who *you* are … and if you think hard enough, you'll figure out who the baby is … and who *I* am."

He didn't answer, he was badly shaken. It's a shock to have it proved to you that you can't resist seducing yourself. I took him to the Apex Building and we jumped again.

✪

2300 VII—12 Aug 1985—Sub Rockies Base: I woke the duty sergeant, showed my I.D., told the sergeant to bed him down with a happy pill and recruit him in the morning. The sergeant looked sour but rank is rank, regardless of era; he did what I said—thinking, no doubt, that the next time we met he might be the colonel and I the sergeant. Which can happen in our corps. "What name?" he asked.

I wrote it out. He raised his eyebrows. "Like so, eh? *Hmm—*"

"You just do your job, Sergeant." I turned to my companion. "Son, your troubles are over. You're about to start the best job a man ever held—and you'll do well. I *know.*"

"But—"

"'But' nothing. Get a night's sleep, then look over the proposition. You'll like it."

"That you will!" agreed the sergeant. "Look at me—born in 1917—still around, still young, still enjoying life." I went back to the jump room, set everything on preselected zero.

✪

2301 V—7 Nov 1970—NYC—"Pop's Place": I came out of the storeroom carrying a fifth of Drambuie to account for the minute I had been gone. My assistant was arguing with the customer who had been playing "*I'm My Own Granpaw!*" I said, "Oh, let him play it, then unplug it." I was very tired.

It's rough, but somebody must do it and it's very hard to recruit anyone in the later years, since the Mistake of 1972. Can you think of a better source than to pick people all fouled up where they are and give them well-paid, interesting (even though dangerous) work in a necessary cause? Everybody knows now why the Fizzle War of 1963 fizzled. The bomb with New York's number on it didn't go off, a hundred other things didn't go as planned—all arranged by the likes of me.

But not the Mistake of '72; that one is not our fault—and can't be undone; there's no paradox to resolve. A thing either is, or it isn't, now and forever amen. But there won't be another like it; an order dated "1992" takes precedence any year.

I closed five minutes early, leaving a letter in the cash register telling my day manager that I was accepting his offer, so see my lawyer as I was leaving on a long vacation. The Bureau might or might not pick up his payments, but they want things left tidy. I went to the room back of the storeroom and forward to 1993.

✪

2200 VII—12 Jan 1993—Sub Rockies Annex—HQ Temporal DOL: I checked in with the duty officer and went to my quarters, intending to sleep for a week. I had fetched the bottle we bet (after all, I won it) and took a drink before I wrote my report. It tasted foul and I wondered why I had ever liked Old Underwear. But it was better than nothing; I don't like to be cold sober, I think too much. But I don't really hit the bottle either; other people have snakes—*I* have people.

I dictated my report: forty recruitments all okayed by the Psych Bureau—counting my own, which I knew would be okayed. I was here, wasn't I? Then I taped a request for assignment to operations; I was sick of recruiting. I dropped both in the slot and headed for bed.

My eye fell on "The By-Laws of Time," over my bed:

Never Do Yesterday What Should Be Done Tomorrow.
If At Last You Do Succeed, Never Try Again.
A Stitch in Time Saves Nine Billion.
A Paradox May be Paradoctored.
It is Earlier When You Think.
Ancestors Are Just People.
Even Jove Nods.

They didn't inspire me the way they had when I was a recruit; thirty subjective-years of time-jumping wears you down. I undressed and when I got down to the hide I looked at my belly. A Caesarian leaves a big scar but I'm so hairy now that I don't notice it unless I look for it.

Then I glanced at the ring on my finger.

The Snake That Eats Its Own Tail, Forever and Ever … I *know* where *I* came from—but *where did all you zombies come from?*

I felt a headache coming on, but a headache powder is one thing I do not take. I did once—and you all went away.

So I crawled into bed and whistled out the light.

You aren't really there at all. There isn't anybody but me—Jane—here alone in the dark.

I miss you dreadfully!

Zaslow Crane was a major contributor to www. Smoke-and-Mirrors.us for 2½ years, and has sold stories and articles on everything ranging from science fiction to humor to cooking. He lives in a Central California town with a parrot, a dog, and a wife.

THE BOOK OF ALEXANDER

by Zaslow Crane

I stand at the banks of the Niagara River just a scant few hundred feet above the famous Falls. The water rushes by as in a never-ending flood, and I marvel, standing on one of the Three Sisters islands, how *easy* it would be to walk out into the current until I was swept away, swept over the edge, into the mist, the wet, the tumult and, ultimately, onto the rocks below.

There are no fences, no guards. No cameras would alert the authorities. I find this unusual. This American society has become so coddled, so watched and cosseted, so … protected, protected not to their benefit I think, that I marvel at how easy it would be to jump into a national monument and … *befoul it* with a suicide. Indeed, I'm led to believe that this very act happens with a good deal of regularity. So, I'll admit to thinking of throwing myself over the falls. Would I die? I think so, but I've no way to know for certain. But what if I lived? I'd be famous. And, I would still be alive. That would never do. Surely, the one-hundred-and-sixty-foot fall would kill me. Surely …

I took a deep breath. A seagull wheeled in the sky above me, crying out for something he or she wanted. Perhaps I was supposed to bring food. Who knows the desires of animals? Except for one, my love, people's desires have always been beyond me; animals are even further removed. The river beckoned. I resisted … for now.

I'd arrived almost a month ago. For some reason I can't explain, I've been drawn to this spot. Somehow needing to be here, to see this, and perhaps use this river toward an end that was many years in the making … in my case, much more than two millennia. Two millennia of unhappiness and loneliness. I'm tired, so tired. So *done*.

I watched the water for a time. I watched it rush by as if it was a businessman late for an appointment. The time that elapses … It really doesn't matter that much … Not to me, especially not now. I sat on a rock that might very well be as old as myself. I watched some more. I wondered what the tourists from all over the world would think. Might they even notice a middle-aged-looking man sitting on a boulder, watching the river? Or would I escape their notice altogether? Would I be … *could* I be so invisible? Could the scene I found myself in be so prosaic as to be beneath their consideration?

For so long, long ago, I was exactly the opposite. I was the focus, the cynosure, when I was young. Consequently, for reasons I will explain, I eschew notice these days whenever possible. Though with the ever more intrusive eye of the internet peering, delving ever more deeply into items that heretofore had been at least secret, if not beyond the purview of all but the initiated very few, I wonder how much longer I will be able to retain any sort of anonymity. Ah, but that's a care for another day, or perhaps not, if this idea that is coalescing in my mind works. The idea is as a half-remembered dream.

Sometimes I do dream. When I'm lucky enough to sleep deeply, I dream of days gone by. Days of campaigns … conquest … battles, camaraderie. Blood. Lots of blood. Other times, I dream of shadows, of a menace unseen and misunderstood … something even worse, something hard to believe, impossible to live with.

✿

There was a time, long, long ago, when I commanded an army, oversaw a burgeoning empire. It was an empire that spanned almost all of the known world at the time. And it was mine. Melancholy was the last thing on my mind, and those were heady times. I conquered Macedonia, then the rest of the Balkans. Then I set my sights on the Persian Empire and the addled satrap who ruled Egypt on behalf of Darius the Great. I was revered as a great leader, feared as an enemy!

If a city surrendered to me without making me waste time and the lives of my soldiers, I spared them all but a hefty tribute; if they wasted my time, I was more business-like. And I use this word purposefully. This was a business, and expended assets once used were never available again. Once we finally breached a recalcitrant city's walls, the men were put to death and the women and children sold into slavery.

Upon arriving in Egypt, I had thrown off the oppressive Persian yoke, and I was welcomed amid cheering and flowers thrown in my path. I led my armies through what would later be known as Alexandria. My army was efficient and dangerous, but we welcomed the adulation as our due. All of Alexandria flowed with wine that night and for many nights after. I'm certain that many good-looking babies were born in Egypt nine months later.

In time, the entire Levant was mine. I decided to take a break. My army was tired and in need of some recreation, and I had decided to attempt to learn from this, the oldest culture in the world. In addition, I needed to allow my spies to do their work of seeking out dissidents in other Persian possessions, and to catalogue troop movements and strengths in Persia. I'd instructed them to shave their heads once inside a city. And to then apply a tattoo of a given city's defenses upon their head. After their hair had regrown, they could easily walk out with plans, garrison numbers, muster requirements simply written on their no-longer-bald pates. Once they returned, we would carefully shave their heads and reveal all the information they'd gleaned from spying for their Master.

It was at this point, while I was waiting, that a group priests approached me. I'm certain that they hoped to ingratiate themselves to the new conqueror. And, in order to do so, they offered knowledge. I already knew that knowledge often conferred power. I had no idea what sort of power was in the offing. No idea at all. In time, I was shaken to my very soul. The Book of Thoth is a series of "books" … scrolls … hundreds of them, a certain number of books or scrolls for every day of the year. The Egyptians had apparently built the pyramids with the most rudimentary of tools. Yet build them they did, with knowledge, and with slave labor, inexpensive but exceedingly "low tech" to use modern parlance. The fitting between one stone and the next is so precise that one could not shove a single piece of paper into the gap between them. I held the very parchment in my hands. The knowledge they offered was staggering.

Now, how did a civilization that had fallen so far as to be conquered by the fat and lazy Persians accomplish this? And where was that knowledge? Surely, it was never truly lost. Only awaiting another great soul to utilize it properly. I'd hoped for such knowledge from the grateful and unctuous priests. Think of what a powerful person, such as myself, might do with the knowledge of moving huge stones easily, understanding the cosmos intimately. That knowledge has been … *misplaced*. I did glean one true thing from these priests: the cosmos dictates all. Of this the mathematicians assure me: alignment is locked into the stars, locked into the very gods themselves. If only that was *all* they offered me.

Once I was initiated into the most secret of secrets … my blood froze. This was not the knowledge I'd expected. Then, after absorbing what I'd been given, I was exultant! Egypt's civilization was impossibly old before mine had arisen from thatched-roof huts. There were texts that only a precious few had been taught to read, they were so old; the knowledge was passed down painstakingly from generation to generation over a thousand years. I accepted their offering, as was my due as conqueror. Well, then, once that celestial wall had been battered down … I was no longer a prisoner to my humanity.

They had conferred knowledge upon me which would allow me to consort with … the gods themselves. This knowledge, of course, in essence made *me* a sort of god. It made me a person who was no longer a slave to old age, decrepitude and disease. I felt a change in me, felt a sort of *inner singing*. It sounded so good at the time. I wonder at their wisdom, now; I certainly have a jaundiced view of my own past. However, I was in the flower of my youth … vibrant, virile and lord of millions who already fawned over my slightest whim to the point of something far beyond obedience. It was a very short step to then proclaiming that I was indeed a god. And who would call me a liar? So, in time, now a *god*, I set out to subdue the rest of the region, crossing the desert and losing many of my host in the process.

The desert, of course, was eventually crossed. Central Asia was lying open to me like a bride on our first night, though the charms of women were not as compelling as other nighttime activities … I was privy to the World, and of celestial designs, but I'd done nothing yet to evoke the changes that would conclusively show the populace and those awaiting my arrival that I was *a deity*.

In time, and I'm certain to the disbelief of those I encountered, I'd "subdued" Asia Minor, and much of India and the near Orient. All was rubble and submission beneath my sandal; all was under my control. Some fought, others realized the futility of resistance. We are mighty and I deserved all this adulation.

My armies were tired but exultant. And now that I'd conquered all the lands I'd set out to subjugate, I was faced with a quandary: Should I turn back and enjoy the adulation that I had earned? Or should I continue to the fabled East?

Oh, those questions seemed so simple then, as I was without the benefits of two thousand years' experience. The spices and riches of the Orient were a powerful attractant. Well, for me they were. For others … there was more than a bit of indecision. I called for a conference with all my generals. I explained the riches and glory that awaited us in the land called China. At this thought, my generals quailed. So I was then faced with another decision: Shall I listen to them? They say that all this time away from home and hearth has made the troops animals, without the comforts and improved sensibilities normally attributed to the nearness of women. Oh, certainly there were the attendant army whores, both female and young males; but, they explained, there is nothing like the love of your woman to make a man more … civilized.

And, I thought, *there is nothing like the love of your woman to make you want to go home and plant vegetables, never to campaign again, to be content to sit in a tavern and tell war stories to friends.*

I considered further. Shall I return the triumphant hero? And then what? Administrate? All of a sudden, I realized what I hadn't considered before. That is, fighting a battle is easy, conquering a people; a civilization is, was and will always be, straightforward, but administration, and governing? I think better to face the enemy who comes at you eyes flashing, sword all bloody, than the knife slipped in between your ribs by a *friend*. Ruling was tedious and difficult. I'd realized that fact simply by setting up caretaker governments as I continued on my quest to conquer the World.

Then, a tragedy struck. My lover died. Bagous was my first love, my reason to go forward: to see the love returned and the admiration in his eyes. His passing shook me to my soul, and there will never be his like in my mind. I looked deeply into myself and discovered that, while I might live forever, I would not, could not, bear the tedium of being a king ruling a distant land, particularly not without him by my side. Even if he were not also immortal, I'd have had his love and counsel for many more years had Fate not stepped in. My one love, now gone. *Damnable Fate.*

In the early morning hours, I lay awake pondering what I might do: Go forward, conquer China, or return to Macedonia, or even set up my government in Egypt, since it was relatively central and stable … I was stuck. Then an idea stole into my brain and I couldn't let it go, much as a small dog with a toy or a bone: I would leave, disappear, evaporate into the world at large rather than face this same world without Bagous. The empire I'd created be damned. I could create another if I chose. Without my lover … All was tedium.

There were many devotees who were in my retinue and I found one who looked like me, and sent him on as if he *were* me. My armor fit and I coached him regarding my speeches to the troops. I gave him detailed battle plans outlining the next phase of my campaign. I didn't care if my ruse lasted very long. I needed only days to away.

I later heard a story from traveling merchants: My other self was drinking wine with Nearchus, one of my admirals. No doubt my admiral saw through the ruse, but as to why he reacted the way he did, I am, to this day, still puzzled. My stand-in was poisoned. A fate I accidentally avoided and, until the last fifty or sixty years or so, was glad of it! I had no desire to really find out if I could live forever … if I were truly immortal. I could never think of a test that would not kill me if I were wrong. Unfortunately, the priests were a bit vague on this point, and I was overwhelmed by the ideas and potential, to the

point of distraction. I am chagrined to admit that I didn't press the point with them, so happy was I to receive this tribute.

Again, I spent time in the desert. This time I was alone. The heat turned my saliva to sand, burned my lips until I learned the trick of smearing camel fat on them, and it addled my brain until I learned the depth and breadth of this sort of heat. While on my "pilgrimage," I again consulted my notes on the Book of Thoth. I spent a month fasting in a cave, enduring the crushing heat and improving my understanding.

In time, I discovered that, with concentration, I could subtly change my face, my features and, of course, my demeanor. I *also* discovered that while traveling I was adept at languages. Being born where and how I had been, that part was not much of a surprise, I suppose. This, I felt, was also a manifestation of the knowledge I'd gained from the Egyptian priests. And while still missing him, I felt that my lover was looking over me, assisting where and when he could. I'd often imagine him whispering in my ear just as I drifted off to sleep, my bond with him still strong.

I slowly traveled East and North, hoping to at least see the Orient I'd longed to conquer. I moved slowly, avoiding contact as much as I was able and living simply. Hundreds of years passed. Many wives and lovers came and went, with them dying and me mourning my losses. I discovered that I'd arouse less interest if I took a female mate, and so I did. I'd learned a great deal as the Conqueror Alexander. I eventually settled in Uzbekistan and began yet another family, though *she* could never replace *him*.

In time, it became obvious that there was needed a man of action to set things right. I recalled with a certain fondness my campaigns, and retained a certain aptitude for organizing armies. In what seemed like no time, I was riding with the horde, killing (and, truth be told, reveling in the excitement again!), conquering and plundering. I used my tactical skills learned at the knee of Aristotle himself in battle, to mold this new mobile army into an efficient killing machine. No one could best our horsemen. Riding, shooting arrows and running down foot soldiers with a sword swung to sever important leg tendons was our strong suit. A warrior thus crippled can be killed at one's leisure. For me it was as if I'd rediscovered the use of a withered limb! I felt alive again. And shocking as it might sound to your ears, I was having fun! I reveled in the crash of sword on shield and the dying gasp of a conquered foe!

However, administration after the fact was not such a success. Conquering was a simple task: overwhelm, kill if and when necessary. Sell the rest into slavery, to plump the army's coffers; raid the stores for food and move on. Assigning a suzerain, or in my case a dozen of such obsequious overseers, was a daunting and unfulfilling task. In retrospect, I suppose that I should have learned, but Time moves quickly and only in one direction. So I hope that I might be forgiven having repeated this one mistake, after another triumph.

Looking back, I should not have been surprised … after the conquest, I became bored and unwilling to stay around to see how things turned out. I discovered that I was only interested in the building—well, building and fighting. I tired easily when thinking about the upkeep of what I'd designed and fought for. It was the campaign that was interesting, not sitting on a throne listening to petty squabbles and settling them. Seeing the hopeful faces of these supplicants was actually depressing, because I couldn't really help them, couldn't really make their lives better. Their lives were shit. And as powerful a ruler as I was … again … I couldn't find a way to remove the shit. All a ruler can do is work on the big items. The daily shit will always be the daily shit. I quickly realized that all I could do was take away this one source of pain that they would inevitably bring before me. Not the entire problem. The entire problem was the gods'—or at least well within the gods' dominion. It was clearly beyond my resources, despite how vast they must seem to these peasants before me. It was time to leave, I decided. Again, I found a pawn, trained him. And in time, he was assassinated and my empire crumbled under squabbling and assassinations.

Years passed; this time, I drifted West. Spain seemed as though it was an up-and-coming country, with an abundance of opportunity. It suited me. Also, there were events happening in the New World that offered a chance to make a name and a fortune. The New World. It was the first thing on everyone's lips, in those days. By then, I was known as Coronado: Francisco Vasquez de Coronado. I'd seen a lot by then, and it was easy to convince the crown that it was in their interest to send me to seek the fabled seven Cities of Cibola. The cities made of gold. There were many credible accounts of the Amerinds' cities, roads paved with gold because it was so plentiful and so beautiful. Advanced explorers … or spies … were summoned to describe what they'd seen and it was easy to imagine how Philip, our king, might have salivated over the potential of such wealth. The king and queen had many wars to finance, and if I could find and plunder such a golden city, I would stand to earn a fabulous estate in Andalucia, and a knighthood at least.

The search didn't go so well. After debarking in what is now Texas, I wandered through the featureless tract of the Midwest for eighteen months, without so much as a landmark or a stand of trees. This was my only defeat on a campaign. And I wasn't defeated by an enemy. Oh no. Not unless you consider an endless land capable of fighting back against an invader. Which it did!

I confess this desert of green nothingness came close to breaking my mind. I couldn't conceive of a place so flat and featureless, that one might ride all day in one direction and never see anything but the flat earth, and grasses. No trees. No mountains. No other features whatsoever, and few people. Even in the Egyptian deserts there were landmarks: mountains, oases, a stand of trees at an oasis … In the Midwest, there was nothing but flat land and grasses that waved in the breeze. Even the tracks we made in passing disappeared almost immediately.

It sounds odd now, knowing that there probably are five hundred McDonald's in the Midwest, but then, it was something beyond, far … far beyond my ken. Half of my contingent committed suicide or wandered off at night, into the trackless wilderness (which is, I suppose, the same thing). The rest of us took to wearing what the Red Amerinds wore most of the time—that is, a breechclout, boots and nothing else.

We traded when we were able, killed when the people we met were bellicose. If we killed them, it was wholesale, except for a few females to help keep our soldiers … sane—and here I'll insert an uncomfortable laugh. We had no use for slaves or more mouths to feed and no desire to leave behind someone bent on revenge. So Death was the only option, in my opinion.

Picture an Army of the *Spanish Empire* riding flea-bitten and exhausted horses, searching; carrying but not wearing armor, nor related equipment. Instead, picture this same Army dressed as New World Savages, our skin burning and peeling, and wearing next to nothing. This was my World; *my expedition*. I dared not return without gold. I dared not disappoint my liege. I dared not fail. Just the same, we were lost. Not simply lost without something as prosaic as a AAA map; we were lost in the most profound sense. Still searching for the seven Cities of Cibola, but after a year and a half searching, we'd found nothing. We'd experienced only undulating seas of grasses … for as far as the eye could see, and as far as a rider could ride. Truly, I wanted to die.

I quietly went insane; for as a leader, one must keep the gibbering, prancing idiot hidden so as to not alarm the lesser men under my command. But make no mistake. This expedition wrought changes I am, to this day, unable to explain to anyone, not even myself. Eventually, but nowhere soon enough, we again fetched up on the Southern Ocean, located a small fleet of Spanish ships bound for Madrid and a sympathetic admiral, who had heard of my quest.

Christ's blood! It took years to recover, if I ever really did. Who can truly say? Perhaps I still suffer from those days now. At any rate, I decided to find a quiet, out-of-the-way place where nothing happens. I'd mend my soul. I learned the new skill of mathematics as it applied to cannons, and I quietly prospered. It felt very good to be *alive again*, vital again. I felt as though the voyage to the New World had permanently dampened my spirits. It was … fun to learn about the math required to fire cannon effectively.

I'd lived in Corsica for quite some time, until things heated up again, and my *propensities* asserted themselves again. I'm told that history says that I was diminutive, but that is a lie. I was exactly average height for a Corsican in the late 1700s: five foot seven. Corsica was a backwater overseen, used and abused by France. And the situation in France was dire. The Reign of Terror after the revolution was mishandled and botched in too many ways to catalogue. It needed someone to step into the breach and control things—much like a military campaign, my area of expertise. I stepped into the strife. It was, after all, playing to my skill sets.

Many bad things happened, and events eventually spun out of my control, I'm not ashamed to say. The revolution that was supposed to set things right tipped the applecart over again and again, making things much worse. True to my nature, the campaign was The Thing. All of Europe trembled at the thought that my armies would be marching to their capitals. I did arrive at many of them. I was the monster who invaded my neighbors. No empire lasts forever; mine was more fleeting than most. After that, I laid low, and resolved to live a private life. I kept my own counsel and lived simply. I often wondered if I'd somehow become a pawn to Fate's designs. I felt as though I'd been used, and used roughly. Egypt was still a treasured memory … exotic … foreign. I moved to a new place every ten or twenty years, and in time, a couple hundred more years had passed. I no longer looked young and beautiful, but I was still healthy and virile. I could pass for a man of around thirty or thirty-five.

I found another backwater after the Great War, which I am proud to say I avoided. I needed a quiet place to contemplate and consider my Life. I learned to apply paint to people's houses, those few who still had the means to hire one such as I. I craved anonymity. I could manufacture a "past," if I chose; I certainly had the time. I had found Berlin. It was quiet; well, parts of it were after the Great War. However, the German economy was in shambles because they pretty much gave away the store after their defeat in what would later come to be known as World War One. All of Germany was having extreme economic difficulties. Hiding is such a place might seem ludicrous, but I assure you that hiding in a depressed and dysfunctional economy seemed to me to be the height of wisdom.

It gradually dawned on me that there was a fairly simple way to deal with the dire situation in which we found our selves in Germany, post-World War One. I realized, slowly, that I could actually *help* my fellow countrymen! I, hesitantly at first, embarked upon yet another *campaign*. Life had changed radically since my last foray into public life; but other things were remarkably similar. The onerous treaty of Versailles put all of Germany under an unlivable yoke of oppression, a yoke that was supposed to punish us for the recently fought and lost war; but what it really did was to sharpen our resolve.

Inflation was rampant. My poor neighbors needed a wheelbarrow full of cash to buy a loaf of bread. It was shameful that the government would or could do nothing to help. I said before that the daily shit was simply that: daily shit. It would take God to change things. I resolved that something must be done. I *am* a god after all. I tried to raise awareness and civic pride by emphasizing the very thing that we could be, as a nation, proud of: our noble heritage. I'd exhorted troops before going into battle. Addressing these hopeless souls was not so different. It was the beginning of another campaign. I could feel it. Speaking to the downtrodden, who were looking for a way out of the mess caused by their government … Common people … They needed Hope. I gave them that, and as my numbers of followers grew, I gave them so much more.

Then we needed a scapegoat, someone in our midst who we might point to and say: "Him … He and his ilk are what caused us to fall so low." Someone we might utilize to feel better even if only a quantum change.

You know my name.

Things spun out of control again. We got a bit carried away. Well, all right, *more than a bit*. I'm not proud of what I caused, but honestly, as I relate this, it's not as though I have any real regrets. A leopard can't change his spots; a scorpion will as soon sting you as say hello. I do what I do. I am Alexander, conqueror of the World. I started with a good idea and it twisted, and in twisting it became something else, something evil and terrible. I might never have become the person the world has known and reviled had I not been rendered alone and destitute by Fate. They say I committed suicide rather than stand trial for my crimes. Bullshit. Again, the judicious use of one of many stand-ins I kept as a safety against assassinations gave me the opportunity to disappear.

After this, and heartsick, I resolved never to become embroiled in any business like this ever again. I promised myself that no matter what, no matter what provocation or opportunity may present itself, I *will* remain forevermore anonymous and quiet. I've kept that promise to myself for a great many years. I'm proud of keeping my word to myself, but I've seen all these problems before, and not being able to step in and take charge has taken a heavy toll on me. What good is life if it is not lived? What good is the gift of eternal life if it is simply to be, and not do? Hence my ennui, my distress. Do you know that my last name has become synonymous with bad conduct and dictatorial behavior? It is another word for Satan to some, merely shorthand for evil on the internet. Before the development of modern culture, one might escape his reputation. Even I am appalled. My eyes have finally been opened.

I was sitting in a Tim Horton's in Niagara Falls, New York, eating breakfast and thinking. Tim Horton's coffee … I don't know what they put in it, but it certainly is addictive. I've only been here for a few weeks and I've already come to crave it. And, it's not as though it is anything exotic, no rare blend, nor is the food any better than, say, a McDonalds's or any other restaurant of their kind, but this coffee, steaming in front of me, helped me hatch my idea: *my escape.* Somewhere in the steam rising from the disposable cup, I saw or imagined I saw the mist rising from all that magnificent falling of water, so close by.

I finished my coffee and went to see if it might work, if I might throw myself over the falls and end all of this. I wondered what Bagous would think of all this. Might all those who suffered at my hands after his death … might they somehow have been saved or might I have steered away from ordering their destruction? He was wonderful counsel and better company. I wonder … if my life would have turned out differently, if I'd had him with me until he was old. Or would he say: "Jump, Alexander!" Would he have another idea? Oh … It's far too late to worry about that now.

I went to see if in this over-protected and spoiled society there might be a chance, a chance to use the Falls to do my bidding: *to kill an immortal.* Even if you've never visited it, you've seen pictures. It is a monstrous cascade, throwing a million gallons of water over a precipice every minute. It is impressive, massive and hopefully … deadly.

This might be considered my final campaign. If I can kill myself, it would accomplish three things: First, an end to this listless and purposeless way of life, and second and much more importantly, I am nothing less than a loaded gun left lying around for Fate to find and use, a horrible cycle that I'm trying to break. It hasn't been easy: staying aloof. Not easy at all. Finally, I'm lost without Bagous. I've been lost for almost all my life. Unhappily lost, to tell the truth. I've kept my word for seventy years, but how much longer can I resist the pull, the allure of the campaign? How long can I repel the desire, the beckoning of opportunity, which I already know will again lead to War? This is what I do, what I do well. How can I repudiate my most seminal nature?

✿

Well, I've walked out in the early morning's half-light, and that hundred feet has turned out to be more … three hundred at least. There are birds in the trees. They sing to the dawn or to each other, oblivious to a giant in their midst. The water is surprisingly cold, but no matter. I dig deeply into my stores of resolve and plod onward. I need to find a deeper place where the pull will be strongest; even this close to the Falls' edge, it is not sufficient. The river swirls insistently around my knees, but as powerful as this river is, it is not yet deep enough to take me away with it. I slog further. Eventually, I see a channel before me that is deeper, and once I step into that I will have achieved my aims.

I could simply stride into it. The water rushes all around me but all the more intensely right here. I'm certain that someone has noticed me by now, but at this juncture of this river, even if I am noticed, what could anyone do besides shout at me? I am alone with my thoughts. There's nothing more to be done anyway. Will the fall kill me? I can only hope.

Rather than step into the channel and allow myself to be carried away, I feel that it might be more fitting, more embracing, if I face my fate head-on. So rather than stepping into the river … I dive in, accepting—no, yearning—for this fate.

I'm tugged along inexorably, moving ever faster, until at last I am, at least for a moment, *a god*, airborne, excited, cured of sorrow and … ennui.

Original (First) Publication
Copyright © 2014 by Zaslow Crane

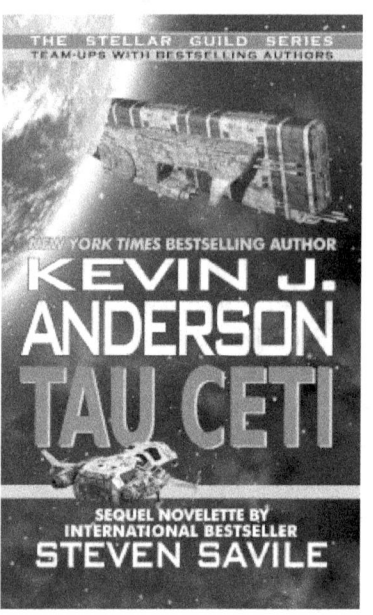

Jack McDevitt is a Nebula winner (and 16-time Nebula nominee) as well as a multiple Hugo nominee. He is the author of 21 novels, 5 collections, and 80 short stories.

NOTHING EVER HAPPENS IN ROCK CITY

by Jack McDevitt

Sorry I'm late tonight, Peg. Had to make a trip up to the observatory at closing time. They're having some kind of party up there and they needed a quick delivery. Ordinarily I would of sent Harry but Virginia hasn't been feeling good so I told him to go home and I went up myself.

No, not much was happening. They all seemed pretty loud, but other than that it wasn't very much. Nothing much ever happens in Rock City.

Oh, yeah, Jamie's home. Got his degree but no job. Bill tells me he's decided to be a lawyer. He wants to send him to one of those eastern schools but he's not really convinced that Jamie's serious. You know how that's been going. Me, I think it'd be just as well. We got enough lawyers around here as it is.

What else? I heard today that Doris is expecting again. Now there's a woman doesn't know when to quit. Frank said he's been trying to talk her into getting her tubes tied. But she's kind of skittish. Women are like that, I guess.

No offense.

Oh yeah, it was a pretty good day. We moved a lot of the malt. That new stuff I thought we'd never get rid of. There was a family get-together over at Clyde's. You know how they are. Must be sixty, seventy people over there for the weekend. All Germans. Putting it down by the barrel.

Jake was in today. They're getting complaints about underage kids again. I told him it ain't happening in our place. And it ain't. We're careful about that. Don't allow it. Not only because it ain't legal, either. I told him, it's not right for kids to be drinking and they can count on us to do what we can.

We had people in and out all day today. We sold as much stuff off the whiskey aisle as we did all week. We won't have any trouble making the mortgage this month.

What else? Nothing I can think of. This is a quiet town. Janet was in. Ticketed somebody doing ninety on the state road. Took his license, she said. Guy's wife had to drive him home. I'd've liked to of been there.

She told me there was a murder over in Castle County. I'm not sure about the details. Another one of those things where somebody's boy friend got tired of a crying kid. That ought to be death penalty. Automatic.

What's that? What was going on at the observatory?

I don't know. They had some VIP's visiting. We sold a couple bottles of rum to one of them this morning. Old guy, gray hair, stooped, kind of slow. Looked like he was always thinking about something else. Talked funny too. You know, foreign. Maybe Brit. Aussie. Something like that.

They're doing some kind of convention up there. Some of them are staying over at the hotel, according to Hap. Anyhow, we get this call about a quarter to nine, you know, just before we lock the doors. It's Harvey. They want eight bottles of our best champagne. Cold. Can we deliver?

Harvey told me once they always keep a bottle in the refrigerator up there. But with all these people in town I guess one bottle wasn't enough.

Well, to start with, we don't have eight bottles of our best champagne on ice. Or off. I mean how much of that stuff do we sell? But sure, I tell him. I'll bring it up as soon as we close.

I mean, you know Harvey. He won't know the difference. And I can hear all this noise in the background. The paper said they were supposed to be doing some kind of business meeting but all I can hear is screaming and laughing. And I swear somebody was shooting off a noisemaker.

Oh, by the way, did I tell you Ag was by today? She wants to get together for a little pinochle next week. I figure Sunday works pretty good. When you get a chance, give her a call, okay?

And Morrie's moping around. He won't talk about it but I guess Mary's ditched him again. You think he'd get tired taking all that from that crazy woman. Don't know what he wants. Ain't happy when he's with her and miserable when he isn't.

Oh, here's something you'll be interested in. Axel dropped a bottle of chianti today. I mean it went off in the back of the store like an explosion. I felt sorry for him except that it made a hell of a mess. He's getting more wobbly every day. I'm not sure we should be selling him anything now. At his age. But I don't have the heart to stop him. I've thought about talking to Janet. But that only puts it on her. I don't know what I'm going to do about that. Eventually I guess I'll have to do *something*.

What about the observatory? Oh yeah. Well, there's really nothing to tell. I took some Hebert's and some Coela Valley. Four of each. Packed 'em in ice and put 'em in the cooler.

So when I get there all these lights are on inside and people are yelling and carrying on. I never saw anything like it. It was like they'd already been into something. I mean Harvey and his friends are not people who know how to have a good time. But this other crew—.

Anyway Harvey said thanks and I wiped his card and he said do I want to stay a while? I mean they were into the bubbly before I could set it down.

So I say no thanks I have to drive back down the mountain and the last thing I need is a couple drinks. But I ask what's all the fuss and he takes me over to a computer screen which has graphics, big spikes and cones and God knows what else, all over it, but you can't begin to tell what it is, and he says *Look at that.*

I look and I don't see nothing except spikes and cones. So then he shows me how one pattern repeats itself. He says how it's one-point-something seconds long and it shows up three or four different places on the screen. Then he brings up another series and we do the same thing again. None of it means anything, as far as I can see.

So Harvey sees I'm not very impressed and he tells me we've got neighbors. He mentions someplace I never heard of. *Al-Car* or *Al-Chop* or something like that. He says it like it's a big deal. And then it dawns on me what he's talking about, that they've found the signal they're always looking for.

"How far away are they?" I ask.

He laughs again and says, "A long way."

So I say, "How far's that?"

"Mack," he tells me, "you wouldn't want to walk it."

For a minute I wonder if the people on the other end are going to come this way but he says no that could never happen. Don't worry. Ha ha ha.

Well, I say, tell them hello for me. Ha ha. And he offers me a three buck tip, which was kind of cheap considering how late it was and that I had to drive up and down that goofy road. I mean, I'm not going to take his money anyway. But three bucks?

Ran into Clay outside town, by the way. He was over at Howie's getting his speed trap set up. Says he picks off a few every Friday. Says he had to go over to Ham's place earlier because Ham was screaming at Dora again. I used to think she would pack up and leave one of these days but I guess not.

Yeah.

Anyway, that's why I was late. I'm sorry it upset you. I'll call next time, if you want. But you don't need to worry. I mean, nothing ever happens in Rock City.

Copyright © 2001 by LRC Publications

Andrea G. Stewart is a 2013 Writers of the Future finalist, and has recently sold stories to When the Hero Comes Home 2, *and* Beneath Ceaseless Skies. *This is her third appearance in* Galaxy's Edge.

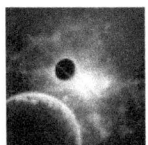

a

Sargasso Containment

story

www.SargassoLegacy.com

IN SECRETS, ABSOLUTION

by Andrea G. Stewart

Rat couldn't remember the smell of money. She used to have a lot of it, always cash, but now she had nothing. The only thing she truly owned was this: a small, unsharpened pencil. She turned it over and over in her hands, rolling her fingers over the ridges, remembering what it felt like to be free.

"Gonna take a hit?" Pam, her bunkmate, mimed snorting something, and then her eyes rolled back in her head, her narrow face relaxing into an expression of bliss.

"Shut up," Rat said, "or I'll tell them you smuggle extra food from the mess hall. Get myself a reduction in my sentence, yanno?"

"I've got a fast metabolism," Pam said with a shrug. "And sometimes, it gets me high—eating." She reached beneath her pillow and pulled out a nutri-biscuit.

Rat leaned her head against the wall and grimaced. Food on Ceres, fifteen light-minutes from Earth, didn't taste very good. They had their own farming operation here in the domes, but couldn't get the same results as back home. It seemed everything in the prison was tainted by the taste of metal or that printed, polymer plastic. She was damned near sure she owned the only scrap of wood in the entire place. "Don't know how you can keep eating that shit."

"Don't know how you can keep sniffing that pencil like it's the ass end of the warden. Do rats do that too, or is it only dogs? Huh, Rat? Do they?"

Rat said nothing. Better "Rat" as a nickname than "Narc" or "Snitch." Rats were quiet, quick, and clever. Rats survived.

She rubbed a thumb along the grain of the wood, brushed it over the lead, embedded inside. "Doesn't bother you then? The visions? Not knowing why they're happening?"

Pam waved a hand, encompassing the prison, the dwarf planet Ceres, the space beyond it. "Mine the asteroids. Sit in here. Mine the asteroids again. Thought I was getting a good deal, coming out here, shortening my sentence," Pam said. "Boring as hell. Least the visions are interesting." She took a defiant bite from her biscuit, the crunch echoing off the walls, too loud in this too-small room.

Pam was right. The visions always crept up, sooner or later. Might as well help them along, get it over with. Rat lifted the pencil to her nose and sniffed.

It smelled of old libraries, of classrooms, of moss-covered forests and pubic hair.

Blink. Gone.

"Aiyah!" Her mother was holding Rat's cheeks, warm, between her two palms. "Your face. So wide, so flat. Like someone stepped on it. You need to eat less."

The vision made her fifteen again, standing in the tiny tiled flat in Shanghai. "It's not fat. It's muscle." The words felt rehearsed, worn.

Her mother released her, turned back to the tablet on the counter, and swiped the screen, her fingers quick and agitated. "Your uncle says he's got muscle too, but I've never seen muscle jiggle when a person walks."

Rat's father strode down the hall, briefcase in one hand, jacket draped over the other arm. "Listen to your mother," was all he said. His expression was distant, as though he'd not heard any of the prior conversation at all.

She knew how this played out, how things had happened. She had said nothing. Had gone to school, had come home, had struggled through her homework like a good daughter. An obedient daughter.

"Can you keep a secret?" Twelve years old, walking in on her father and his coworker in an embrace far too intimate for casual acquaintance.

She was good at keeping secrets. She'd been doing it her whole life.

Not anymore.

"Baba doesn't stay late at the office to do work." Rat whirled on her mother. "He stays so he can have an affair with his co-worker. He's a cheater and a liar."

Her mother's face went pale, her hand hovered over the tablet. And then she strode over to Rat's father and struck him, hard, across the face.

Shouts, screams, denials, explanations.

And Rat slung her book bag from her shoulder, dropped it to the kitchen floor, and left. No one paid her any attention. The euphoria rose within her, a tidal wave, a tsunami—washing everything away. Leaving her clean.

✿

She woke in the dark, her back against the wall, the concrete floor cold beneath her. Mattress springs creaked as Pam spasmed in her bed, still caught in the throes of her own vision. Sometimes she paced, swinging at the empty air.

The door clicked open.

"Rat?" a voice whispered. "Rat, are you there?"

Marcus.

"The hell do you want, Marcus? I'm busy, yanno?"

"Busy." His voice was flat. "Sitting on the floor in your cell, in a power outage. While your friend's just sprung your door open."

"Where we gonna go? You want to put on a space-suit, run into the wilds of Ceres, live off the land?"

"Ha ha, very funny. I need your help."

That was all it took. She pushed herself to her feet. She owed Marcus. He probably didn't even remember, but she owed him.

With a hum and a click, the emergency lighting came on—tiny LED lights embedded in the seams between wall and ceiling. They illuminated the back of Marcus' head, the close-cut brown hair, the long, lean neck. He disappeared into the hallway.

"Hey," Rat called after him as she moved to follow. "Hey, where you think you're going?"

"We need to keep quiet," Marcus said when she caught up to him. The narrow hallway curved, the lights disappearing around the bend, reflecting from the metal walls. "Most of the guards should be

sealed in the mess hall or the break room, but there may be one or two out and about."

"You gonna tell me what's this about?" She hadn't seen him in the mess hall, in the mining tugboats, or on any of the asteroids—for nearly two weeks now.

He glanced back at her. "I think we're in the middle of an epidemic," he said. "We just don't know it yet."

Fear prickled up her spine. She shrugged her shoulders, trying to shake it off. "You're crazy, you know that? Doc says it's just solar sickness. Too long away from the sun. He looked at me yesterday, Pam the day before. Where you been?"

"In my cell, eliminating potential stimuli. I want to figure out what's causing the hallucinations before things get any worse."

He stopped at a door on the outer curve of the wall, with *Infirmary* engraved into the metal frame.

They'd get time added to both their sentences if they got caught in there. Rat lingered a little way behind Marcus as he pulled a plastic and metal card from his pocket and waved it in front of the reader. Wires hung from the ends, looped over once, twice.

"What's it to you? We're criminals, not superheroes. Leave it to someone else."

He turned to face her, and the spaces below his cheekbones looked like they'd been cleaned out with a spoon. "Doc's incompetent, Rat. If this really *is* an epidemic, it'll spread to other colonies. Maybe even Earth."

She shrugged a shoulder. "Not my problem."

The door clicked open, revealing a second set—sliding pressure doors. "You've been having the visions?"

Rat nodded and tucked the tiny pencil into her bra.

"That's how it starts. Here, get the left side. If we pull at the same time, we can open them manually."

She did as he asked. A rush of air poured from the infirmary as the doors opened, assaulting Rat with the smell of antiseptic and latex.

Blink.

✿

She stood in the embrace of a young man, his hands caressing the small of her back. "I want to be with you," he was saying, "I really do, but for now can you keep a secret? No one has to know we're seeing one another."

"Okay," she said. So stupid. How could she have believed this shabi? He was sweet to her in private, and pretended he didn't know her in public. She'd had so little self-respect.

But when he drew away, she lifted her head and kissed him anyway. Why the hell not? It still felt nice.

This time, when she slipped from the stairwell, she didn't skulk back to her parents' apartment. She waited just outside the door for him to emerge.

She should have done things this way the first time. What good did keeping secrets do? It had never ended well for her before. The first time she'd blurted out the truth was the first time she'd ever gotten something good; ratting out her boss got her this gig in Ceres instead of thirty-to-life in a penitentiary on Earth.

Kai Xiang stepped from the stairwell.

"Hey," she called out to the few classmates of hers still wandering the halls. All gazes snapped to Rat. "Kai Xiang likes to make out with me. Sometimes we hold hands and he cries about how his baba left their family."

A couple girls laughed from behind upraised hands. Everyone started whispering. Kai Xiang just stood there, rooted to the spot, his eyes wide.

Rat strode away, her head held high, pride swelling in her chest. She was walking on clouds, her legs tingling, the sun warm on her face. Nothing could stop her. No one.

✿

"Rat." Marcus leaned in close, his brow low over his eyes. He waved a hand in front of her face. "You there?"

She pushed his hand away, annoyed. "Just had another one. I'm fine."

He kept staring at her, like he didn't believe her, like he thought she was going to keel over and die at any second.

"Leave off. You got what you came for?"

Marcus turned away, finally. "I found some notes. Most of the prisoners have complained about the visions. Only a few of the guards. It might be the food supply."

"Or it might be the Other, trying to get through to all us sinners, just like those crazies at the edge of the Sargasso Grid keep saying. Repent, yanno?"

He kept talking, like he hadn't heard her. "The guards get some of their food shipped in. We eat mostly home-grown."

She threw her head back. "Home-grown. Hah! Like it's tasty and wholesome."

He put a finger to his lips and Rat quieted. "We have to get back now. I want to check the agricultural domes, but we'll do it another time."

"We? Who is this 'we'?" she said as she followed him down the hall. "You say you need my help, I help. One time. I got my own problems, like getting off this rock." She stopped outside her cell, but Marcus kept on walking. "Marcus," she hissed. "Marcus!"

He pivoted, pointing at the metal wall. "Prisoners die out there. We sign our waivers, we suit up, we mine. I've been out on the asteroids for over nine hundred hours. What if I'm the next one to get a busted suit? I want to at least be safe in here, on the ground. If I'm not, what's the point of being on Ceres in the first place?"

She didn't have an answer for that. "Idiot!" she tossed at his departing back. "So stupid!"

He let her insults pass without comment, and she ducked inside her cell, sealing the door shut behind her. The blue-tinged emergency lights gave the room an eerie glow, reflecting like tiny moons off each metallic surface. Pam still lay on the bottom bunk.

The mattress springs didn't squeak.

"Pam? Hey Pam, you awake?"

Rat's voice bounced from the walls, each iteration fainter, mingled with the harshness of her breathing. And as she listened, she realized: the only breath she could hear was her own.

✿

The power came on just as the emergency team responded. Two medics rushed in, as if they actually cared if Pam lived or died. They did CPR on her scrawny, wiry body, got her tortured heart beating again, her breathing regular.

And sometimes it gets me high—eating. It didn't mean anything, it couldn't. Pam had never been the

73

picture of health anyway. She'd done too many drugs back on Earth, messed herself up.

But as they wheeled her out to the infirmary, Pam's words ran through Rat's mind, circulating, like the refrain on an overplayed song. She'd know if the food was contaminated, wouldn't she? Wouldn't it taste different, feel different? It all tasted like shit—could shit taste shittier?

She'd gotten a month earned time for ratting out the newbie who'd tried to smuggle in heroin. Two weeks for snitching on the guy who'd bragged of sharpening his toothbrush into a shiv. She had six months left on her sentence now, and she'd have to find someone doing something really out-of-line in order to have the rest commuted. No way could she work off enough time to get released any earlier than four or five months.

Narcing on someone—that was the way to go.

She climbed onto the upper bunk, settled in, pulled the pencil from her bra. She'd found it on the sidewalk, as they'd been transported from the prison to the spaceport. Just a dirty little unsharpened pencil, and she'd picked it up because she'd needed *something*. Something from Earth, from home.

Of course they'd caught her. She hadn't taken precautions, hidden it inside her body like the rest of them had. Marcus had been there, next in the search line.

"You're confiscating a little unsharpened library pencil?" he'd said. "Well, you'll have a hell of a lot of paperwork to do. Wait 'til you see what the rest of these guys have."

The guard had handed it back to her. "Prisoners are allowed one to two small, personal items. Should have filled out the forms before you boarded. You'll have to do it on Ceres."

She hadn't, and no one had badgered or hounded her to make sure she had.

It was hers.

☼

The doors unlocked, a clang sounding over the speakers, harsh and unwelcome as the wrong-answer buzzer on a game show. Rat liked to imagine it that way sometimes. "The largest animal on Earth is … a potato?" *Bzzzzt.* "Wrong answer. Instead of going home, you get to eat bad food!"

The other prisoners on her time schedule filtered out of their cells, putting their hands on the wall, trailing along it toward the mess hall. Keeping a hand on the wall meant that they all walked in a line, just the way the guards liked it. Rat followed the others, the metal smooth beneath her fingertips. They all smelled of the same soap, the same shampoo.

The line broke up once they reached the mess hall. She lingered at the entrance, reluctant to make her way to the dispenser. She hadn't eaten very much over these past six days. Pam was still in the infirmary, comatose. What if Marcus was right?

Her stomach no longer grumbled; it felt tight, like the skin stretched over the surface of a drum. Nutri-biscuits, simulated meat, and a small pat of fresh greens. Which part of it was safe, and which part would make her sick?

"What's the matter, Rat?" one of the prisoners called, already seated at his metal-and-plastic table. "You on a diet? You need it."

Jason. She'd ratted on him once before, for sneaking a female prisoner into his cell, but only got herself eight days' earned time. She didn't reply to him—rats were quiet, they were clever. She needed to find someone else acting out, breaking rules, and it was better if she didn't draw attention to herself.

She took a tray, got in line, and watched the others. The woman two spaces in front of her—Loretta—fidgeted, picking at her baggy pants with red-tipped fingers, the nails bitten and raw. She was hopped up on something, Rat was sure of it. The dispenser slid a plate onto her tray, and she followed Loretta as she made her way to a table. If she found Loretta's supplier, she could get at least a month of her time commuted.

"Hey!" Marcus appeared beside her, a tray in his hands, the plate already scraped clean of food.

Her tray tilted as she jumped, and she struggled to keep her spork from jumping ship. "You always like to sneak up on people like that?"

He took a quick glance from side to side before sliding something onto her tray. A granola bar—not one of those disgusting nutri-biscuits—but a real granola bar, sticky with honey, smelling strongly of peanut butter.

She didn't bother thanking him; she shoved it in her mouth before anyone saw. It was cloyingly sweet, pieces of baked oats wedging between her teeth. "Why?" she managed around it.

"We're friends. Thought you might be hungry."

She chewed and swallowed as the other inmates made their way to the tables, trays in hand. "Come on, really?"

He shrugged. "I can't get to the ag domes without applying for a work permit. But I got someone to lend me their kitchen card. Will you come with me? I can get the power down again. I just need someone to watch my back."

She snorted. *Friends*. Could any two people in a prison be friends? He should have waited to give her the granola bar. She owed him, sure, but probably not this much. "What's the point? So both of us can get caught?"

"I'll be eligible for parole in a week. If I figure out what's happening, if I get out, I can warn everyone else."

"Parole already? Damn!" They'd arrived at the same time, and her sentence had been only a little longer than his. She moved toward the nearest table. Loretta's table was now full. He was already causing her trouble, and she hadn't even agreed to help. "Why's it matter so much to you, yanno?"

He followed on her heels. "I've got people I care about, back home. I made promises, and I mean to keep them. I can't make anyone listen to me without proof."

"Who cares about them? Worry about you."

He set his tray on the table next to hers with a clatter, though she glared at him. "Have you had any visions lately, Rat?"

"Not since the last time I saw you," she said. "Why—?"

Two tables down, Loretta shot to her feet. "Don't!" she cried out. "No, I didn't mean it, please!" Her eyes were glazed, her hands held in front of her, fingers curved like claws. Whatever she was seeing, no one else could, but all eyes snapped to her anyway. Just as suddenly as she'd arisen, she collapsed. The table was bolted down, but plates and trays scattered, flipped as Loretta fell to the floor, convulsing, her knees still draped over the bench.

Rat scanned the room. There, and there too. Two of the other prisoners hadn't reacted at all, because they stared straight ahead at nothing, muscles twitching, caught in their own visions. The two guards by the entrance rushed toward Loretta, shoving other prisoners out of the way.

"Now!" Marcus whispered to her. "We can go now!"

She should have just pretended she couldn't hear him, but if what was happening to Loretta was going to happen to all of them, then it didn't matter much if she got caught. "Fine," she hissed between her teeth. As the other prisoners rose from their seats to huddle around the spectacle, Rat followed Marcus to the kitchen door. Stupid, acting like this, but she didn't have much choice.

The door opened with a click, and then they were inside.

It was past prep time, so the place was empty—no inmates checking the machines or throwing corn into the hopper for processing. "So this is where the magic happens, huh?" she said. She put a hand on one of the metal funnels. "Nutri-biscuits, made with love and care."

Marcus didn't respond; he went to rifle through the cabinets. No fun, this man.

She strolled past the hopper to one of the plastic bins used to transport the corn from the ag domes to the kitchen. A few ears still lay in the bottom. She picked one up, peeled back the husk to reveal small, shriveled kernels. Dark orange spots marked the insides of the leaves. "Marcus!" She waved him over. She'd seen this sort of thing before, on some of her mother's potted garlic. Rust. You could still eat the garlic; it just grew smaller than normal. She ran a hand over the rust, the spots like Braille beneath her fingertips. "Do you think this might be it?"

He passed her, reached into the bin, and pulled back the husks on the other two ears. They both looked the same as the first. "It's something," he said. "It's worth looking into." He ripped off an edge of the husk and tucked it into the waistband of his pants. "Let's get out of here, before someone notices."

At the door, he stopped, opening it just a crack to peer out.

Rat sighed and reached up to scratch her nose. Her hand brought with it the green scent of plant sap, the sweetness of the corn, and something below that she couldn't define—something metallic and sour.

Blink.

✿

She was in a darkened hallway, the door in front of her limned with light. The sound of laughter and the clicking of mahjong tiles seeped from the corners, the thick scent of cigar smoke and sweat.

Ah, she knew this place. Her uncle's home—where she'd been sent for two weeks during the summer she turned seventeen. She walked forward, her footsteps one in front of the other, as though set on a track. The doorknob turned easily.

Her uncle sat facing away from her, the back of his chair pressing into his wide shoulders like fingers into risen dough. Black hair clung to the nape of his neck, damp with sweat. Three others hunched at the table around him; Rat only recognized one—because he'd been the one she'd snitched on to get to Ceres.

Cheng Gong. A connected man, in both government and in crime, though he would only become more connected as the years passed.

Beneath the table, Rat caught the flicker of fingers across a dim, hand-held screen. Each man sat behind his row of mahjong tiles, like kings behind the walls of their castles. And each had a camera trained on his tiles.

Her uncle never did play fair.

This time, she did not open the door only a little further; she flung it wide. "Jiu jiu," she said to him. "Where do you keep the strainer? I wanted to make noodles."

"Hey," one of the men said, his gaze barely lifting from his tiles, cigar held loosely between his teeth. "Who's this?"

It took a moment for her uncle to answer. The little screen was gone, but he knew she'd seen it. She read it in the wrinkled brow, the flared nostrils, the slightly parted lips, as though he teetered on the edge of begging. "Jingfei," he said finally. "My sister's daughter."

The first time this had happened, she'd said nothing. She'd kept his secret, and he'd given her a cut of his winnings—the first transaction of many. Her jiu jiu was on the bottom rung of the criminal ladder, and she'd clung to him for years before she'd worked her way up. And he hadn't always been kind.

"He cheats." Rat spoke directly to Cheng Gong. "Cameras, trained on all your tiles."

It happened quickly—her uncle on the floor, blood on his face, two of the men beating him. Cheng Gong stood from his seat, the lamp shining off his bald pate. "Girl," he said, "how would you like to work for me?"

She drifted to the table, picked up one of the discarded cigars, and drew in a mouthful. It tasted bitter and sweet, like chocolate and cream. "Yes," she said. "I'd like that."

And then she was joining the other men in beating her uncle, kicking and hitting.

✿

She woke in a place she didn't recognize. Metal and plastic prep tables stood in front of her, a stack of trays in the corner. She was in some part of the kitchen, still.

Marcus was gone.

Something heavy covered her right foot. "Ah, shit," she said when she glanced down. "Shit shit shit."

One of the guards, blood leaking from beneath dark brown hair, sprawled across the floor. Pam used to swing at invisible enemies when she was high; Rat supposed she'd done the same. "Marcus," she hissed. Her voice echoed off the walls. No answer.

He'd had his own ass to save, and once she'd started in on her vision, there couldn't have been much he could have done.

Something prickled in the back of her mind, like carbonation, floating to the surface. She fumbled at the guard's belt for his tablet. A few quick swipes, typing, and she had it. Marcus Jones: 1285 hours. Every muscle in her body seemed to seize up at once, her breathing gone shallow. Why tell her he'd worked over nine hundred hours when the system said he'd worked over twelve hundred? Every prisoner on this rock knew the hours they'd worked. And Marcus getting out so much sooner than she?

With shaking fingers, she hooked the tablet back onto the guard's belt, just as two more guards burst into the kitchen.

✿

A month. They added a month to her time. She told them it was the visions that made her attack the guard, but they didn't care. They took the pencil, and her world shrank: just metal and plastic and water and rock.

The bunk below her squeaked as Maya, her new roommate, shifted. Pam had passed away two days prior. "We must accept the Other, let the visions wash over us," she muttered.

Rat hit the corner of the bunk bed frame with her palm. "Shut up."

The opposition only increased Maya's fervor. "Victor Carvalho had visions," she said, her voice tremulous. "He had visions at the edge of the Grid and he survived. He accepted the visions, accepted the Other. He was the only one to live, to bring back his message of hope …"

Rat ground her teeth. She never thought she'd actually miss Pam. Now she was stuck with some crazy who thought the impassible space surrounding the solar system was some sign from God. Machines malfunctioned and people went nuts out there, but she'd never believed the cult's assertions. She swung her legs over the side of the bunk. "I'd love to stay and chat about the Other, but I got work, yanno?"

She'd taken on all the extra time she could. She wasn't going to die on this rock. Not like Pam.

The door clanged open. She trailed down the hallway with the others in her shift, all the way to the tugboat bay. She suited up, grabbed the tag designating her assignment. Tugboat number eight.

The tugboats were a mishmash of old ships, partially stripped and retrofitted so they could bring asteroids into orbit around Ceres. Tugboat number eight hunched in the bay, looking like nothing so much as a giant metal toad. She circled round to the entry ramp.

Marcus was inside, strapped into his seat. She'd recognize that close-clipped hair and lean neck anywhere. She clambered inside the ship and dropped into the seat beside him. "You ditched me," she said, as the other prisoners began to filter in.

"I didn't have a choice." He kept his gaze straight ahead, all business.

"It wasn't the first time." She paused, let that sink in. "How many hours have you really worked, Marcus? Nine hundred or twelve hundred?"

His shoulders stiffened; his fingers tightened around his helmet.

"Got enough dirt on you to get myself off this rock, yanno?" She owed him nothing anymore, not a goddamned thing.

Marcus turned to her then, his eyes darting about, his voice low. "I didn't know you back then. I bribed one of the guards as soon as I got on Ceres to get access to the prison mainframe. And then I uploaded a little program that adds extra time to my work hours. If I'd known we were going to be friends, I'd have done the same for you." His face went still. "I need to get out, Rat. I'll take samples with me, find a cure."

She shifted in her seat, and the pencil didn't jab into her ribs as it usually did. "The pencil," she said. "You remember that?"

His mouth gaped for a moment, and then shut. He nodded.

"You did that for me?"

The other prisoners found their seats, buckled themselves in. He waited until the ramp to the ship began to rise, and then he spoke again. "I was smuggling in a diamond necklace, an heirloom. I didn't want the guards to check me so carefully. It bought me my access to the mainframe."

She narrowed her eyes at him. Why this? It didn't make him sound any better, didn't make her feel more kindly toward him. Why not lie, tell her he did it to help her?

As if he could read her thoughts, he leaned away from her, shouting to be heard over the roar of the tugboat's engines. "Friends don't lie to each other." He shook his head as he said it, a slight smile on his face, as though chastising her for the mere thought.

Friends. Stupid man, trying to make friends with a rat.

So stupid.

✿

So many people, so many secrets. Rat curled her knees to her chest on the upper bunk, her hair brushing the ceiling. Better to blurt them out, to sell those secrets for her freedom, for her dignity, for her own advancement.

It was who she was.

Jingfei kept her mouth shut. Rat never did. Rat was cleverer than Jingfei. Rat got what she wanted.

But what if Marcus was right, about all of it?

Didn't matter. She had to get off of Ceres. She had to survive.

A clang sounded and her door opened. A guard stood in the doorway. "The warden will see you now, Jingfei."

She slipped from her bunk.

"It won't save you," Maya said. She peered out from her bunk like an animal from the depths of a cave. "You must go to the Grid. You must accept the Other."

Rat flipped her off behind her back as she left the cell.

The walk to the warden's office was a long one, through three cellblocks and past the ag domes. She couldn't see the cornfield through the glass and the distance, but she wondered if it was all infected, the way the ears in the kitchen had been.

The warden sat behind her desk, fingers laced together beneath her chin, an absent look on her face. She was whip-thin, her cheekbones like mountains on the landscape of her face. Silvering hair fell just below her chin.

"Warden," the guard said. "This is the prisoner that requested to see you."

The warden didn't move.

"Warden?" the guard said again.

She blinked, waking from her reverie. "Yes?"

The guard jerked a thumb at Rat.

"Of course." She glanced down at her desk, and then back up. "Jingfei, yes."

Rat, she corrected the warden in her head.

"You have information for me?"

A few words, and Marcus would get so much time added to his sentence that he wouldn't get off this rock 'til he was old and gray. They'd make an example of him.

Marcus hadn't begged, hadn't pleaded, hadn't even given her that look like her uncle had—all white-faced and wide-eyed. Why? She held his life on the tip of her tongue. Her gut twisted as her mouth moved. "Really good information. You're gonna piss yourselves when you hear it."

The warden merely raised her eyebrows and spread her hands, palms up, inviting Rat to continue.

To continue ratting out her friend. Godammit, was she thinking of him as her friend now? She gritted her teeth. This was her ticket off of Ceres; it

didn't matter whose expense it came at. Yet Marcus hadn't been worried. He'd given her all the information and left the decision up to her. He *trusted* her, trusted her judgment.

She didn't.

"Are you going to tell me, or are we just going to stare at one another all day?" the warden asked.

If Marcus trusted her judgment, why didn't she? She didn't have to only keep her mouth shut, or to only blurt out everyone's secrets. She could choose.

She chose. "You're a bunch of assholes," Rat said. "The prison system is broken."

The warden rolled her eyes and waved a hand at the waiting guard. He took Rat by the arm. "Waste my time again, and I'll add two weeks to your sentence, Rat," the warden called after her.

Jingfei, she corrected the warden in her head. She didn't have to snitch on anyone anymore. She didn't have to be Rat. She had a name, and Jingfei wasn't always stupid. "Yeah, yeah, I'm going," she said as she wrenched her arm free from the guard.

She was passing the ag domes when she realized what she'd seen in the warden's office. The distant look, the slowness to respond.

The warden had been in the midst of a vision.

☼

Marcus's ship was the last to leave before things got bad. Jingfei didn't see him, but she didn't need to. He'd given her enough of a goodbye on the tugboat. She wondered if he was breathing a sigh of relief, or if he'd known what she would choose all along.

They'd been shut inside their cells for two days now with no food, as the infection took root inside the prison, as Jingfei's visions grew more and more frequent. Once in a while, she heard a shout, or a scream, or someone pounding on the metal doors.

"We're going to die, we're going to die, we're going to die!" Maya crouched in a corner of the cell, her arms wrapped around her torso.

"Shut up!" Jingfei snarled.

A clang sounded and all the doors on the cell block clicked open at once. Maya pushed past her, into the quickly flooding hallway. No one trailed their hands on the wall this time; they all ran toward the mess hall, a mass of shouting, pressing bodies.

Jingfei suppressed a laugh—rushing to the kitchen so they could eat more of that contaminated food? She waited until the flood died to a trickle, then dashed toward the tugboat bay. She might have let her ticket off this planet fly away, but she wasn't going to die on this rock.

Her rubber-soled shoes slapped against the concrete floor as she ran, the sound echoing from the walls, mingling with the faint sound of shouts in the distance. She caught a whiff of her own sweat.

Blink.

Running down the sidewalk in Shanghai, jostling other people, curses following in her wake. Her heart filled with anger and pain from her mother's words.

The vision faded, and she nearly ran head-first into a guard. He was walking in circles, muttering to himself, hands twitching at his sides. "I don't know how to make it up to her," he said. "There's nothing I can do."

Jingfei caught herself on the wall, her breathing heavy. She reached out and pulled the guard's tablet free from his belt. Careful not to get too close, she leaned in a little. "You can do something. Authorize a launch. Tugboat number eight."

The man's brow furrowed. "How will that help?"

She racked her brain. "She wants to see the stars," a quick check to his nametag, "Chandra."

He fumbled at the proffered tablet as Jingfei prayed to all the gods she knew the name of, to all the ancestors she was familiar with. She didn't have time. She kept running.

A panel had been torn loose from the wall, wires hanging out. One of them sparked, sending the scent of burning plastic into her nostrils. Blink.

Venting her anger on her first victim, being thankful for her meaty fists instead of shamed. Dim lamplight from the corner, the tinny sound of Chinese opera through the wall as he capitulated.

She stumbled when she came to, struggling to re-orient herself, wondering what she'd been doing. *The tugboat bay.*

She wasn't sure how long it actually took to get there, her world a haze of visions and light. Any moment she'd seize up like Pam or Loretta. Any moment she'd descend into a coma and then die.

Tugboat number eight was one of three ships left in the bay.

She worked between visions—hauling herself into the ship, shoving a dying guard from the pilot seat, pressing buttons. She set a course for the station at the edge of the Grid; she wasn't sure why.

And then the bay doors were opening, the ship was in the air. Stars, all the stars, like pinholes in a vast, ethereal blanket. At least she would die free.

Blink.

Nothing.

She woke with the taste of copper in her mouth. Alive.

The ship engine thrummed and the stench of rot crept into her nostrils. The guard she'd shoved to the side lay dead on the floor, his face stretched across his skull. The dry, sterile air in the tugboat had begun to mummify him.

Her slightest movement produced a loud rasp; it made her ears and head ache. It was just her clothes, rubbing against the seat. She smacked her lips, experimentally, and the sound was like an entire body hitting wet pavement.

Quiet, she had to stay quiet.

Her hands moved soundlessly over the controls as she checked the date. Twenty-eight days since she'd launched and fallen into a coma. She checked it again. How could she be alive? Twenty-eight days with no food and no water, and the infection racing through her veins.

And then she noticed her hands. Her fingers were stretched, elongated—a piano-player's hands, not a criminal's. The infection had done something to her. She felt off-balance, *changed*.

Jingfei searched the ship. The guard had possessed the presence of mind to bring aboard a crate of food. She cracked it open, suddenly ravenous, and peeled back the wrapper on a granola bar.

It made her think of Marcus. She hoped he'd made it, was searching for his cure, like he'd wanted. The scent of honey wafted from the bar. Blink.

No vision of the past this time. A station, floating in space, the stern face of a man she'd seen on telecasts back on earth—Victor Carvalho, survivor of the Grid. And at the back of her mind, a *presence*, an Other.

She snapped back to the present, her mouth dry. The euphoria that always came at the end of her visions rose within her, prompting a laugh at the back of her throat.

She was Jingfei, but she was also Rat, through and through. Rats were quiet, quick, and clever.

Rats survived.

Tina Gower is the winner of the 2013 Writers of the Future $5,000 Gold Prize, as well as the 2013 Daphne du Maurier Award for Best Mystery/Suspense. This is her fourth appearance in Galaxy's Edge.

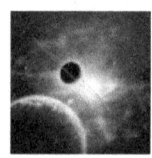

a
Sargasso Containment
story
www.SargassoLegacy.com

CALMING THE TEMPEST

by Tina Gower

True, Lily had been absent-minded lately. She'd misplaced her com-tablet. She'd thought she left her microscope on her desk in the office, but found it in the lab the next morning. She even did the whole accidental swap of the milk and her mold samples, barely stopping herself before taking a swig.

But she'd never leave research samples in disarray. That was too far-fetched to believe. Her slides were lined in neat two-inch rows. She slid the fungi section out sample by sample. It was subtle, but she always organized the samples by domain, then kingdom, phylum, class, order, family, genus, species. The pathogenic fungi section, particularly the *pucciniales* order, had been alphabetized.

She held up one slide to the artificial night-light. A thumbprint, larger than her own, hovered like a ghost, smack in the center.

"*Mamãe?*" Mateo's voice croaked through the intercom from his bedroom. "Where'd you go?"

"I'm right here, *filho*," Lily called. She set the mystery aside for another time. Mateo needed her. Lately, his needs came before work.

Had it really been two weeks since Mateo had first collapsed? She forced an easy smile and deliberately appeared calm when she entered the room. Sure, it was difficult to ignore the flickering machines and the vibrations sent to her tablet on her hip—his half-hour updates. An hour ago the specialist teleconferenced the latest results. The lead on a similar case in the penal colonies came back a bust. The assigned doctor recorded it as space sickness, possibly meningitis. Dr. Adal didn't trust the report and vowed to research the case further, but Lily didn't want to chase a remote possibility. She wanted to find an answer now.

She ran the tests again. After all, she was Lucky Lily. Even though she hated the nickname and implication that she didn't work hard for what she earned. Every time a door closed three more opened for her. Rejected from the top school for biochemistry? She got into the second-best school, and within a year of attending, it became the number-one. Collide with a stranger at a station stop, dropping her tablet and destroying the device? The stranger turned out to be the funding behind the Sargasso Exploration Initiative and within days she got her team on the *Basilisk* a bid for a second official attempt to break the Sargasso Grid Barrier. Then she got pregnant and it looked like she'd miss her huge opportunity, only to land a better position at the Mars Space Station as Lead Biologist. And the *Basilisk* met a tragic end. It turned her childhood friend, Victor, the sole survivor, into a complete mental mess. Maybe she was lucky, but not the people around her.

Her tablet vibrated, a soft hum against the tense silence.

"What is that, *Mamãe*?" Mateo's eyes opened to slits, focused on her fingers scrolling through the results.

"It's nothing, *filho*."

And it was a whole-lot-of-nothing.

Meningitis test. Negative.

CT. Normal.

Full body MRI and PET. No mass detected.

Viral load. Normal.

A stream of negative and normal all down the row, until she hit kidney function, which was elevated. He was entering the beginning stages of organ failure.

She placed a request to speak with the specialist again to see what could be done. Although, the doctor had warned her this was coming. She crawled next to Mateo on the bed and curled next to him. She'd never wanted a test to come back with something, anything, but now she begged for it. Please

let him have something that they could identify and then they'd have a disease to treat.

To keep her mind off the medical stuff she sent a security report to Avery.

I think someone's been going through my lab samples from the Mars surface.

Avery: *Matty entertaining himself?*

Lily dug her fingernails into the screen and bit down on her lower lip hard. Idiot. Mateo was awake for only a few hours a day and usually only minutes at a time. He hadn't left his bed all week. And if he did, he knew the rules about not messing with the samples.

No. I don't think, so. I'd like someone to come down and take a look.

Avery: *Sure thing, Lil. I'll send a guy in a few hours. We've got an important shipment coming through the station right now.*

She didn't want to wait a few hours and her name was Lily *not* Lil. Someone had broken into her lab and there were only thirty or so staff on the space station. If Mars eased up their regulations on unapproved species she could have set up on the surface. They would have taken a breach or possible contamination seriously. Avery treated her like an afterthought. They were a science station, a cargo hold, a pit stop, not a military base. But they could still be a little more professional.

If Mateo got better … she stopped herself. She stiffened with guilt over her mistake. Of course he'd get better. It wasn't an "if," it was a "when"—When he got better she'd start the process again to get her lab transferred to the surface. She rubbed small circles on her son's back. "I love you, *filho*. You're going to get better. Maybe tomorrow."

She almost believed herself.

Mateo floated off back into dreamland, but Lily stared at the ceiling, preparing for another sleepless night.

Lily snatched the nutri-biscuit and ripped at the packaging. The corn-plastic crinkled loudly. "Mateo, you have to eat. This will help your body fight this bug."

"No, *Mamãe*! Marcus says not to eat that. He says it will make me sicker!"

Lily squeezed her eyes shut, breathing deeply, willing her patience to step forward. "I've told you that your invisible friend doesn't know what will make you better. He's not a doctor."

"He's not invisible! He is real."

"Is he a doctor?"

Mateo broke eye contact and suddenly became very interested in the fold of his sheets. His face flamed with anger, his lips pressed in a line.

"It's called a hallucination …" How did she explain it to an eight-year-old? At first she missed the early signs of the disease because she'd thought having invisible friends and vivid daydreams was part of childhood.

"He's real," Mateo mumbled under his breath.

Lily let out a heavy sigh and propped her butt on the edge of his bed. "Well, according to Marcus, what can you have?"

Mateo's brows furrowed, stubbornly holding on to his irritation. "Broth," he bit out. "Rice or fruit if it's from Earth or Mars. Nothing from Ceres."

Lily made the order. "Ceres doesn't grow fruit trees. The penal colony is limited on what they can grow. Remember how we talked about the solar and gravity limitations in the ag domes?"

She tapped through the food selections for items Mateo might try. She had thought she'd never have to deal with food pickiness. Mateo was always good about trying anything. "What about carrots? Fresh from Mars this morning." Well, as fresh as flash-frozen-carted-through-space could get.

No answer. He'd fallen asleep again. Lily eased him back into a more comfortable position and watched his chest rise and fall. She unwrapped the nutri-biscuit, but couldn't bring herself to eat it. The taste reminded her of cardboard, metal and plastic with vanilla flavoring. Mateo used to eat several a day, and being one of the only few on this floating box who could stomach them, he had a lifetime supply. She held the bar between her fingers while she stewed.

It was the silence she hated. The moments where the what-ifs crept in. She'd called down to the Mars surface again. No cases reported. On the space station, Mateo was the only one showing symptoms. There were around thirty inhabitants on the station and they'd not taken many precautions at first, so she'd have expected at least one other illness, if not her own.

A zing of anxiety shot through her. If she were to get sick, she wouldn't be able to care for Mateo. She brought the protein biscuit to her lips, paused, remembered Mateo insisting it would make him sicker, then tossed it on the counter to test. Nobody else who'd eaten them had shown symptoms. Yet.

Might as well not take any chances.

The room chimed, alerting her that someone was requesting access. She scanned her tablet to see and a "maintenance" symbol appeared, but no picture of who had been sent. Not exactly protocol, but not unheard of in the small station, where things were a bit more lax.

She tucked a can of sanitization spray into her pocket, keeping her fingers touching the seam where it hid, and clicked "allow."

The door opened. The man stood in the entry for a minute, observing the room with a slow scan of his gaze, and tilted his head as if he were used to smaller spaces. He flicked his eyes to Mateo's room before landing on Lily. "You had a break-in?"

Lily nodded. Unable to speak for a minute, she didn't recognize the man. And on a station where there were only thirty or so staff, that raised her awareness to be cautious. Some of the men circulated to the surface for some duties and he might be new to the rotation. However, he had a badge, an ID number clearly printed, and his name reflected off the holographic display as "M. Jones."

She swallowed. "Yes. My files were out of order. I left them as I found them." She motioned to the rack where she kept her bio-samples from the surface.

He scratched at his close-cropped hair, scanning the rows of samples. "Any particular ones?"

Lily pulled out the tray of fungi in question.

He pulled out several granola bars from his pocket, setting them on the counter, and produced a pair of latex gloves from a sealed bag. "You have an impressive collection of rust, Mrs. Silva."

Her lips twitched at his correct fungus identification, layman as it was. "Just the ones we can grow on Mars. Unfortunately, most are banned now for obvious reasons of wreaking havoc on the crops, hence my lab being on the space station. I monitor the samples they send me from here."

"Could someone have opened the cases and exposed the station?"

"No, they're sealed tight. It would have compromised the sample and obvious signs of tampering would be evident."

"So they just reorganized?" He held up the sample with the thumbprint. He frowned as if he saw something he didn't like.

"Are you saying this is unimportant? Someone—unauthorized—entered my lab. My quarters are attached. My son—"

"Mrs. Silva," the man held a hand out to calm her. "I take the break-in very seriously."

"Do you—" Lily pressed her lips together, keeping her frustration in check. It would do her no good to argue further. The man had convinced her he was sincere in his concern, but Avery had sent some new guy. Obviously he didn't feel it was important enough to come himself.

The man placed the sample in a plastic bag and set it in his pocket. "I'm going to run this through the data systems. In the meantime don't open this door for anyone until I get back."

Lily crossed her arms at the sudden seriousness of the man's tone of voice.

"For anyone," he reiterated and backed away from her to the entry.

She slammed her flat hand against the wall when he left. Damn him. Damn people who ordered her around. She wasn't some staff member, she didn't have an army rank, she was her own boss. She could leave her own quarters if she wished.

She felt the feather-light brush against her hand. "I heard yelling."

Lily looked down into the widened amber eyes of her son. She squeezed her eyes shut and massaged her forehead. "You're not supposed to be walking around, Mateo." She sighed, patted his hand, noting the improved color. "It was just a maintenance worker. He's gone now." She absently checked his numbers; they'd improved slightly. She tamped down the relief, not wanting to hope.

"Oh." The little boy's faced scrunched up in confusion. "I didn't mean him. I meant the ones in my dream. They say to stay away."

If it wasn't imaginary friends, it was imaginary aliens. She wondered for a moment if she'd followed

Brandon and forced him to be more of a participant in their son's life, if she'd be dealing with this now. It was a brief, very brief, moment of guilt and she dashed it away just as quickly. That asshole Brandon didn't do much beyond the first few unsatisfying moments of conception and sending money when he docked from expeditions. Weren't scientists supposed to be stable nerdy types who made wonderful partners? Brandon's charming personality and addiction to danger should have been her first clue he'd make a horrible husband.

Thankfully she'd avoided that and Brandon was more than willing to adhere to her idea of how they should proceed after the accidental pregnancy.

"Marcus brought more granola bars!" Mateo snatched the bars the man had left from the counter.

"No, those are the service worker's. Don't touch."

She gently pulled them from his grip. Mateo's face reddened and scrunched into the horrifying mask of a child about to succumb to the fits of a tantrum. Always, when he was sick he'd regress. Her normally easygoing child was replaced with a stubborn, emotional hellion.

She sent a note to Avery. *I think your worker left his granola bars on my counter. I'd like to get them out of sight before Mateo eats them.*

The worker? I'm sorry, it must be Mateo's granola stash or he took some from the kitchens and didn't tell you. I've been tied up on another emergency. We'll get someone down there soon.

A chill started from her neck, ran down her spine, and settled in her gut. She set the controls on the room to monitor and turned on every camera, set the alarm on her door. Nobody would enter without setting off every bell and whistle in this corridor. She hoped to be back before Mateo's nurse came on duty in fifteen minutes.

"Mommy is going to run an errand. Do not leave the room, Mateo, do you hear me?"

The little boy nodded solemnly, the seriousness of her tone jerking him out of his would-be fit. He flipped a tablet onto his lap. She heard the soft sounds of a cartoon in progress. Good boy.

First she checked the security office and didn't see the man who'd been in her room. The other officers gave her a passing glance.

Avery pushed aside his sandwich. "Can I help you, Lil?"

A number of smart replies came to mind, for one that lunch was less important than her security concern, but instead she narrowed her eyes and said, "It's *Lily*."

He brushed his hands on his pants, a half-grin on his face while he glanced at the younger officer in the room. "Anderson, go run a check on Lily's room. And stick around until she gets back. The kid will get scared if he wakes up and she's not there."

She moved sideways for Anderson to slide by.

Avery turned his full focus on her. "Yesterday it was a sound in the air ducts. Day before that, a loose grate in the hallway. And a dozen other complaints just in the last week. I know you've been keyed up lately …"

"Someone was in my room about ten minutes ago. He said he was from Maintenance and I didn't recognize him."

Avery dismissed her concern with a wave and bit into his sandwich. "They get new people rotating in all the time," he said around the hunk of food in his mouth. "This is a station orbiting Mars. We're not a place for frequent stopovers and our crew is small. It would be difficult for an unauthorized person to sneak on board."

"Difficult, but not impossible. Can you at least check into it? His badge read 'M. Jones.' That shouldn't be too hard to look up."

He blew out an exasperated breath. "Sure, Lil— Lily." He stretched out her name to make a point. "Look,"—his tone softened—"I can tell we're rubbing each other wrong right now. And you coming in while I'm in the middle of lunch, makes it look like I didn't take your concerns seriously, but I do. We're all worried about Mateo. We got clearance for another doctor from the surface to come up and take a look. Nobody's going to stop until we figure this out."

Lily nodded. As much as Avery's personality grated her, he was concerned about Mateo as much as anyone else. "I should get back."

"I'll have that name check for you in a few."

She doubted it, but left without stating her skepticism.

The worker had said he was going to run a data check on the thumbprint. The only system capable of scanning prints was located in the security room, but Avery didn't have the slide on his desk or seem to be aware of the order. Where else on the station was there an open computer? One hidden in a place where nobody from the station would disturb the man's work?

She jogged down the corridor until she came to a T, and on a hunch she headed toward the storage unit. On the way she peeked into the maintenance quarters and didn't see the man who'd been in her room. Lily glanced at her tablet, checking the security controls on her room. Nothing. And the camera positioned in Mateo's room showed him back in bed sleeping.

The storage section hummed. This area of the station boasted the largest square footage, but little manpower. Cargo units were lined along the walls and middle of the room. A maze of plastic boxes, rejected shipments yet to be returned to their home. Mars enforced strict regulations on what items could enter its borders. As a small but independently run entity, they flexed what little power they had, especially against Earth's continued attempts to open the borders and allow more aggressive colonization. Bottom line: Mars' developing ecosystem couldn't handle the increase in population. It currently housed a number of ag domes run by various science interest groups. A scientist's heaven.

Lily moved along the aisles, creeping forward with careful steps. The faint hiss of the air pressure gauge and the steady vibration from the gravity ring were her only company. The computer station was empty. It hovered in the corner, pulled from the wall where someone had forgotten to put it back, but the screen was black, indicating it hadn't been used recently. Her mystery man wasn't here. Lily backed away from the cargo, retracing her steps to the nearest entry.

She was nearly to the door when she saw a wrapper trapped in the vent. She bent, inspecting the foil packaging. Granola bar.

She shivered, and not because the environmental controls had been set too low. She twisted, backing against the wall. Every hair follicle on her body tingled with that someone's-behind-you feeling. This time she made her rounds along the passageway with a different eye for detail. The unlatched panel exposing the air conditioner ducts, the whiff of recently warmed bean and cheese burrito (Mateo's staple dinner), and the off-kilter, oversized freight container in one of the walkways.

Lily stepped away from the freight and fumbled in her pocket for the sanitization spray. She needed a better defense.

She held it with both hands pointed at the container. "Come out. Hands where I can see them." In a zing of anxiety she realized she should have called security, but if Avery wouldn't take her real break-in seriously, then he wouldn't come running on a hunch.

There was a cough in the container, a short throat-clearing sound. "All right. I'm coming out. I don't have any weapons."

"I'm supposed to believe that?"

The freight door squeaked and the cropped mousy brown hair of the man who'd been in her room a few moments ago crawled out. When he was clear of the opening, he stayed on his knees and held up his hands.

"What would a maintenance worker be doing in a freight container?"

"I'm legit—" he said. Lily could see the sweat dotted around his forehead and mouth.

"Right."

"You can look me up, but I'd rather you not, because it will alert the wrong people that I'm still on board."

"That doesn't sound legit at all." Lily readjusted her spray and tugged on her tablet.

"I'd rather you not do that." The man motioned to his side. Lily snapped her hands back to the spray. "Whoa! Hey, I'm not armed. I told you the truth. I've got a little cut on my side. My patch is coming off."

Lily lowered the spray. "Keep your hands up. I'll look at the patch." She gave him a level look. "I'm a fourth-degree black belt."

"I won't hurt you."

His gaze was so sincere she believed him. The way he spoke slowly and quietly, the way he held himself. He didn't show any signs of danger.

The guy remained still, a small smile hung on his lips. Lily lifted his shirt, revealing the clear, pocked silicone patch over a three-inch wound just below his left rib. "It looks a little red. Did you get some antibiotic on it?"

"Right after it happened, but not when it reopened. I jammed the patch back in place. I didn't get a chance before you found me."

Lily gently pulled the patch off and the man was good on his word. He didn't budge. "This reopen while you were in my room?"

"Right after."

"Being a burglar has its disadvantages." She applied the antibiotic cream and slapped on a new patch.

"I wasn't the one who broke into your room, but I'll find out who did."

Lily grabbed her tablet, hesitating over the call button. The guy's smooth talking had convinced her to trust him, even for a moment longer while she got some answers.

"What does the 'M' stand for? Marcus?"

"I didn't enter the room. I was crawling through the vents when I heard your kid calling out. He'd seen me going by the panel in his room. It's right above his bed. I was cleaning out the ducts. The robot broke down and we had to send someone to do it by hand. We had a few conversations. I was curious when I'd heard he was sick."

"You gave him medical advice."

His expression became more solemn. "How's he doing?"

"Same."

"How frequent are his blackouts?"

"I'm not going to talk about him with you." Lily kept the sanitization spray close. "Tell me what you were doing in my room and why you're hiding here. I'm calling Avery in five minutes." Lily didn't mention she wasn't about to turn him over until she found out why he told her son to stay away from food from Ceres and if it was connected to his numbers improving. She didn't like coincidences, but first she wanted to know if he was a threat.

His shoulders dropped. "I came on the station two weeks ago from the belt. They had an opening in Maintenance and I took it." He lowered his eyelids long and slow. Something about what he was saying wasn't right.

"Two weeks ago." There was one memorable dock from a few weeks back. A ship that limped in from Ceres carrying a paroled prisoner. "What day?"

He paused, his fingers absently going to the cut on his side. "The reason I ask about Mateo is because where I came from we had a similar outbreak. I think I can help." He motioned behind him and Lily gave a small chin jerk, letting him know she was willing to listen.

He reached behind him and pulled out a plastic-wrapped cornhusk. "It's from Ceres. Rust infection as far as I can tell, unlike any I can identify." He handed it over. "But you can. If I'm right, the answer to Mateo's illness is right there."

Lily secured the husk under her jacket. He had to know that a sure way to get her to listen was to promise her son's returned health. "How do I know you aren't trying to get rid of me?"

"I don't need to get rid of you. My time is limited either way. I'd like to help Mateo before the time's up."

Lily reserved her concern. He could be playing on her sympathy, but she had to see if what he was claiming was true. "If what you tell me is a lie, any of it, if this sample is just some average *pucciniales*, then no duct on this station will hide you."

"I swear on my sister's life." And the intense look he shot her made her stumble as she turned to run from the cargo hold.

✿

Dr. Adal shook her head in disbelief. So far the conversation had consisted mostly of brow-raising and hesitant optimism.

"A fungal infection would explain why we had trouble pinning down the diagnosis."

"Exactly." Lily lined up the samples on her lab counter. "It was in the nutri-biscuit from Ceres. I put in a recall order. I've already got a culture responding to an amphotericin mixture. It's stopped the reproduction and is killing the fungus."

"We can't give it to Mateo, not until—"

Lily slammed the door to her freezer unit. "We don't have time for a full trial. I have a sick kid in my home now!"

"Lily—"

"Don't 'Lily' me!" Her body shook, and she took a deep breath to rein in her temper. "I have reason to believe that the outbreak was caused by contamination in the food supply on Ceres. We'll need to alert the trade commission on Earth."

"I've done that, but we don't want to cause a panic."

"You want me to conduct a clinical trial first? Fine. Call up the penal colony. I'm betting that outbreak you mentioned yesterday will have a few subjects who'll volunteer."

"I didn't get an update on that lead. But we did receive word—"

"Great. Tell them I've got a prototype ready to go."

"The penal colony is under quarantine. Complete pandemic. We don't have any word on survivors. Chances are there are none."

Lily stopped then. Dr. Adal couldn't have smacked her across the face any more than with those words. Lily dropped onto the lab stool. "How long?"

Dr. Adal's gaze dropped. "There's some evidence that some of the victims had been suffering for months, others only a few days. It seems to affect each person differently. There is a drug on the underground market that seems to have cropped up with similar effects, not as severe though."

"Who'd take this willingly? Mateo is a kid. His body mass and immune system …" Lily's cheeks prickled with the lack of blood, her pulse hammered in the vein of her neck. Mateo was just a little guy. He didn't stand a chance. She had to do something.

"There's no way to know if we can develop a working cure in time."

"*Mamãe?*"

Lily shot up from her seat. "I have to go." She didn't wait for the doctor to respond; she flipped off the telecom.

Mateo sat up in his bed, the side of his face heavy with red creases and his hair standing straight up on one side.

Lily swallowed hard. "Are you hungry? I have some broth." She tested the liquid she'd set aside in anticipation of him waking. It had cooled, meaning more time had passed since she'd met Marcus this morning.

"They don't want me to stay away anymore." Mateo's eyes were glassy and unfocused. "They said I have to come. *Mamãe*, I have to go."

Her door chimed. Lily checked her tablet. Avery. She released the locks on her door.

"I need you to describe the Maintenance worker to me. I ran a check. M. Jones is scheduled to return to the Mars surface, but he hasn't checked in."

Lily hesitated. "Don't you have video surveillance?"

"We don't have enough storage to keep video from all areas of the station. What do you remember about him?"

Marcus had told her the truth about the fungus. What if it were true that he was also in danger if he were found? She needed to contact him again to be sure. She needed more information about the fungus, how it spread, what other symptoms to expect. The more she could gather the faster and more efficiently she could help Mateo and any others.

She scratched her forehead, attempting what she hoped was a thoughtful expression. "I don't really recall. I remember he was average height, medium brown hair. It could have been light blond." She shrugged as if that was all she could recall.

"So he's average height, and has the same color hair as the majority of the people on the station." Avery gripped the lab counter. "Can you give me anything else to go off of?"

She glared. "I don't know, Ave, maybe if you'd asked me after it happened I'd have remembered more."

He blew out a breath. "Okay, that's fair. I almost deserved that. You call me right away if you find this guy. It looks like he's an ex-con, possibly dangerous. If you see him, send an alert on your tablet directly to me."

"I will." She smiled, forcing herself to relax and appear as though she'd forgiven him.

He left. She gathered her samples to start another test, twirling around to just barely miss Mateo at her heel. She let out a squeak.

"Marcus is in trouble." The rings around his eyes made them appear as huge as sand dollars. "You have to help him."

"Honey, those are hallucinations. The people talking to you are not real."

"Marcus is real. He needs help." He grabbed her arm and pulled her to his room.

She looked around, half expecting the man to pop out of a corner. The room was empty. She sighed.

"Why don't you get some rest, I'm working on a medicine—"

A rustle from above cut her off. "Keep looking at Mateo." Marcus' voice whispered through the vent. "Don't look up. Pretend to be talking to the kid."

"Don't hurt him. Whatever you want, I'll—"

"—The thumbprint was Avery's."

"I—what?"

"I don't think you're in danger. The rust you have in your lab isn't the same rust that's growing on Ceres. I have reason to believe he's working for the people who are after me."

"And who is that?" She fussed with Mateo's pirate jammies, willing her fists to unclench. "Never mind, you're a thug, of course you have people after you."

"I didn't commit any crime. Well,"—she detected humor laced in his voice—"at least not the one I was sent to prison for. It was a deal. My brother-in-law owed a large sum of money to the local mob. The mob boss's son had committed a minor crime they wanted me to confess to and serve his time. It was a clean deal. They just didn't expect for me to get out so soon; they think I ratted them out."

"Did you?"

"No …" There was a creak and light tapping sound, as though he were adjusting his position. "I hacked the penal colony's system and tacked on work hours to get released sooner."

"Right." Lily resisted the temptation to scowl; she was looking right at Mateo who stood still as a deer listening to the conversation between them. "And the prisons are always full of innocent people."

He chuckled. "Not on Ceres. As far as I could tell."

"How am I supposed to believe you?" Although she did. Damn him.

"You don't need to. I just need your help to make sure a shuttle is docked in the loading bay. I have to get back to my sister. They've already found me here and on Mars. You've already got the word out about the rust. I need to go back to her." His voice changed to pleading, and from the sound of stifled desperation and loathing he didn't do it often.

Lily had just gotten a glimpse of hope that Mateo would get better. Now Marcus was implying that Avery worked for the mob in some way. Did he really expect that she and Mateo would be safe if they stayed here? Did he really expect her to risk her own career if she were caught helping him?

"*Mamãe*, you're hurting me." Mateo whimpered.

She released her tight grip on her son's arms and pulled him into a hug. "It's okay, *filho*. I'm sorry." She scooped him into his bed, his body going limp. She ran the back of her hand down his face when his eyes rolled back in his head, another attack coming on. She swallowed the lump in her throat from keeping the tears held at bay. When Mateo's spasms slowed, she kissed his forehead.

All at once the choice was clear. Marcus offered hope of a cure. She'd get him a goddamn shuttle.

"One hour." She shot a gaze to the vent and caught his nod before he crawled away.

☼

Lily wrapped her son with the grey wool blanket her mother had given her, tucking the ends with care. She'd rolled him like this as a baby when he'd wake in the night, fussing and hungry, but he didn't fuss or squirm now. She only had a small window of time. She didn't have to fake the blotchy skin, the bags under her eyes, or sticky tracks where her tears had streaked her face.

She'd hefted her son in both arms, cradling his body close to hers as the small bag of luggage she'd packed in haste rolled behind them. She kept her head down through the silent gasp of disbelief. She averted her eyes when the close-knit staff stopped their work to watch her walk by. Their expressions of grief and sorrow and pity because of her small lie were too much to bear.

It was Amil, the chemist she worked closely with on projects for the surface, who broke the ranks and rushed to her side. "When?" The older man rested a shaky hand on the blanket that covered Mateo's face.

Her chin wobbled. She couldn't do it, she couldn't lie to the degree she'd planned. "Not yet." Her voice cracked with emotion. "But soon. I want to take him to my mother in Brazil." The tears came freely, following the familiar trail along her cheeks. "She's never met him." And, god, she *should* have taken him sooner. That was not a lie. After her son had gotten sick she realized how pointless her job had become. It was not what she'd imagined when she'd signed on.

"I'll call down to the surface,"—Amil backed away, not looking her in the eye this time—"make the arrangements for the project, let them know you'll be gone."

"Thank you." Lily set Mateo into the shuttle next to the bag of medical supplies that would last them the trip.

Amil peeked into the hatch. "We heard about the fungus. There was nothing that could be done?" The blinking eyes of the crew gathered behind him; it seemed Amil was serving as their voice. Nobody was sure of what to say to the woman who was about to lose her child. And she would if they didn't let her go soon. She was doing a terrible job of creating a distraction.

She drew the group away from the shuttle, pretending concern for the paperwork. A service worker rushed to her side, grabbing the tablet. "I'll take care of this for you."

"Then, I …" Lily fumbled for her luggage and another man swooped in and took it from her. She caught the handle as the luggage was lifted away, clutching it hard, not letting it go. Inside were the medical supplies she needed for Mateo.

"Ma'am?" the man angled his face and she recognized Marcus at once. Fake ID tags, but his service uniform helped him blend into the crowd gathering.

Not wanting to draw attention to him, she released her hold. "I'm sorry. I'm a little distraught."

Marcus faded into the shuttle with her luggage. She turned to the group. "I don't know what to say. I, uh …" she stuttered over her real inability to come up with a sufficient and believable good-bye and allowing for Marcus to hide himself in the shuttle before they took off.

Those whom she'd been friendly with over the year reached in for hugs. Others stood a distance away, their expressions hollow.

"I should go." Her muscles felt thick as though she were walking through mud. The stress of the past weeks had caught up to her. At least she didn't have to fake that. The hatch closed with a hiss.

"This was not the plan," Marcus whispered from the corner near Mateo's makeshift bed. "You only had to make sure the shuttle was in place. I would have done the rest."

"And how did you expect to fly it out of here? How would you have convinced the dock control to open the doors?"

"I'd have hacked my way in. I got out of Ceres; this would have been a cakewalk."

She spun to the controls, typing in the flight plan. "And leave me here with Avery. I don't think you thought through what a risk you put me in." She finished with the computer. "I don't want to be here anyway. I should have left a long time ago."

"You were not at risk. He was only looking for the rust—"

"You mean the rust that is pumping through my son as we speak?"

"He was looking for something he could make into a drug, not the contaminated nutri-biscuits or the infection." Marcus gently unwrapped the wool blanket from Mateo's face. "What did you give him?"

"I put him in an induced coma." She snapped from the control panel and slid next to her son, untangling his wrist from the blanket, and injected another drug into his IV. "What's going on? The doors should be opening?"

The shuttle buzzed and a voice came in through the speaker. "Lily, I need to inspect the shuttle. Security measure."

Avery. "Shit."

Marcus removed a panel from under the bed and folded himself inside, draping the wool blanket over the opening when he couldn't get the panel back in place.

Lily flung the hatch open. "Avery, are you serious. *My* son is dying."

His lips pressed together in a line. He kept his voice low, so no one would overhear. "I saw the security videos of you in the cargo hold. Lily, this is a dangerous man."

"One I hope you find soon, but it has nothing to do with me."

"Then let me in. Don't make this hard. Everyone is watching."

"Exactly. You should have been paying closer attention. What were you doing in my room?"

He glared. "I can enter the room of any resident—"

"Shove it. If you don't let me go right here and now, I'll report you for an investigation." She was going to anyway, but he didn't need to know. She had him

and he could do nothing. She had it all set up. As soon as she was scheduled to be far enough away from the station the investigation message would be sent. Avery was on borrowed time.

"You'll regret this. You don't know who you're messing with." He stepped away from the hatch. "I hope you arrive on Earth safely, Mrs. Silva."

She locked the hatch back into place and the bay doors slid open.

"They won't talk to me anymore." Mateo frowned, kicking the blanket from his legs. "I'm hot." He rolled to his side away from Lily and Marcus. "Leave me alone."

"At least he's feeling better." Marcus pulled the blanket over her son when his even breathing had indicated he'd fallen back asleep.

Lily shook her head, rechecking the flight information. "We're headed the wrong direction."

"My sister lives near Jupiter. I let you enter the coordinates for Earth to throw them off. I've made contact with a Nikki Dark; she works with the Space Patrol. I think we can help them get the rust situation under control. What about Avery?"

"He's not going to be a problem anymore. In fact, he's probably being arrested as we speak." She'd also found other evidence that pointed to Avery being in contact with the mob to seal the deal. She rubbed her forehead. "I'm not good at this." Then she laughed. "Oh my god. It's finally happened."

Marcus shot her a look. "What?"

"My son hates me, I'm running from the mob, I don't know if I have a job anymore, and my travel mate is a convicted felon who I probably shouldn't have trusted. I think my luck may have finally run out."

She crossed her arms and stared at the corner of the shuttle, nowhere to go. She'd really gotten herself into a fine situation.

Mateo stirred in his sleep, turning so she could see his oval face and pixie features, his brown hair a twisted mess. The color of his skin had been restored, no signs of infection in his system; her treatment had worked. She'd found a means to ward off a possible epidemic. And she had information that could potentially bring down a drug ring. She'd probably have her pick of jobs anywhere she wanted.

Marcus tipped an eyebrow at her, noticing her change in posture.

"Damn." Her grin spread wide. "I'm still freakin' Lucky Lily."

Joy Ward is the author of one novel. She has several stories in press, at magazines and in anthologies, and has also done interviews, both written and video, for other publications.

Michael and Peter Spierig adapted "All You Zombies—" to the screen—they both wrote the screenplay and directed the movie. And discussed it with Joy Ward for this issue's interview.

THE *GALAXY'S EDGE* INTERVIEW

Joy Ward interviews
Michael and Peter Spierig

Robert Heinlein's gender-bending short story "All You Zombies" has been turned into the exciting new movie Predestination that hits wide release January 9th in the United States. I got the chance to chat with the visionary directors, Michael and Peter Spierig. The Australian twins directed and wrote the screenplay for Predestination, which stars Ethan Hawke as a temporal agent and Sarah Snook in a role that stretches across gender lines. The Spierig brothers have made several other notable movies, including Undead and Daybreakers.

Joy Ward: *How did you get "All You Zombies"?*

Peter Spierig: I read the story and gave it to Michael and we both said we have to make this into a movie.

It's one of the most original things I've ever read. You know when you read something and you say "I can't let this go; I have to make this." It really is a completely original time-travel story and there aren't that many out there.

JW: *It was very forward-thinking in the Fifties. How does that carry forward to the present?*

Peter: Our version of it is kind of like what the original author's is. The amazing thing about it is, his story, which was written in the Fifties, is still very present, modern and original today which is really a testament to how clever the guy was.

JW: Michael, what did you see that made you want to turn this into a movie?

Michael Spierig: What I saw in the short story was the same thing as Peter saw in it. I think I had to read it three or four times to see what Peter saw in it. I've been a fan of Heinlein for a long time but I had never read that one. The thing that excited me so much about that story was that while the short story was written in the late Fifties it was unlike anything I've read before and I still think it's unlike anything that's out today. So it was an honor that we could make such an interesting story that has had such a history and is revered as one of the great time-travel short stories.

JW: What do you want the viewers to come away with after they have watched your movie?

Peter: Well, I think if people think they have seen something new and different in the genre then that's great. I hope it's a total mindbender for people. It has a lot of twists and turns and really interesting characters and really unique characters. It is always hard to talk about this without giving too much away. But my hope is they have seen something new and different and it sticks with them after the credits are rolling.

JW: This is such a unique piece of work. What were the challenges in bringing this to the screen?

Michael: There are a lot of challenges when dealing with this subject matter. The challenges were first of all the physical aspects of making the film. The biggest challenge was how we were going to deal with the transgender character in this film. We went back and forth constantly about the technique. Are we going to get a male actor for the male part and a female actor to play the female part? Or should we be bold and do the more interesting approach which is just to find an actor to play both parts? If that doesn't work, obviously the whole movie disintegrates. We found this incredible actress, Sarah Snook, who proved to us that this approach could work. Also, we had a relationship with Ethan (Hawke) prior. He was the first person we sent the script to. So for Ethan to come on board and say yes, changed the trajectory of the film. It helped considerably to get financed. Usually, first you get financed. It's a difficult process but it's such a thrill that comes with it.

JW: When you are looking for source material in general, what are you looking for?

Michael: Peter and I are always looking for something that is hopefully a little different in the genre.

Peter: You can either read a piece of material and you hope it's unique and understand in that genre that it is something really interesting. That's what we look for. We didn't specifically say we made a zombie movie, we made a vampire movie or we want to go and do a werewolf film. It's not that sort of specific. It's more an idea we have or an idea we love that we want to get made.

JW: Is there any more Heinlein in your future?

Michael: Possibly. He has a catalogue of fantastic work. I'm not saying we are going to make any of these but I've always been a big fan of *The Moon is a Harsh Mistress*, *Stranger in a Strange Land*, the list goes on and on. His books can be very difficult to adapt. *Stranger in a Strange Land*, which is so loved, is so much about concepts that can be very difficult to translate to the large screen. Everybody knows what has been adapted, *The Puppet Masters* and *Starship Troopers*. But yeah, I love his work. He's really subversive, really interesting; one of the greatest sci-fi writers of all time.

JW: What is your approach to directing? How do you handle the directing with the two of you?

Peter: It's something we've done for so long now it's kind of an organic thing. It starts with the screenplay, when we talk through every aspect of the story and the script and what we're trying to achieve. So by the time we get into pre-production, Michael and I have really worked it out in tremendous detail already. Then we very rarely argue so we have a clear idea on how we want to do something. That goes for interacting with the actors. We can look at a take and both almost immediately say yeah that's the one we've got it, let's move on. I think that's just tremendous amounts of preparation and spending way too much time with each other.

JW: What other writers are you looking at, that you would like to use as source material?

Peter: There are lots. It's tricky too because there are so many pieces of work that have already been optioned that people have. So it's hard to find something that somebody doesn't already have, especially the classic sci-fi gurus.

Michael: There are countless names. There's Arthur C. Clarke. *Childhood's End* is awesome. Heinlein's *The Moon is a Harsh Mistress* is another awesome tale. I always thought that Asimov's *Foundation* Series, either as a movie or HBO or something like that. It would be great to see *Foundation* come to life. So there are endless novels out there. I just don't have time to read them all.

JW: Do you read a lot of science fiction?

Peter: Yeah.

JW: Who are you reading?

Michael: I'm reading *The Divine Invasion* by Philip K. Dick, which is quite interesting. I like Philip K. Dick. I think Hollywood has sort of romanticized him over the years. His work is quite difficult to adapt because it is such a head trip. He's very interesting. I love his paranoia.

Peter: I've actually got a Heinlein book sitting on my desk. Michael mentioned it before: *The Moon is a Harsh Mistress*, which I've never read. There just are not enough hours in the day.

JW: So both of you are really into the science fiction classics?

Michael: Sometimes. Sometimes the classics become about the technologies. It becomes fun to imagine what we could do with the technologies and how antiquated some of the ideas seem. At the core there are so many fantastic ideas.

JW: What does it do for you to be able to address these ideas?

Michael: It's a balance. Isn't it? If you're into science and into technology, as a lot of those authors were, especially someone like Arthur C. Clarke, if you're into that type of work, it's often hard to find a human element in some of these conceptual stories. The trick is to find a balance between emotion and character interaction and sort of the science and the ideas behind the stories. That's the real trick. And to hopefully create material that people will go and see. Hopefully you're not being too abstract, too scientific. To actually create stories with a heart and soul that people will want to go and see. That's the real tricky thing.

JW: Who are your influences?

Peter: There are plenty. Maybe we're children of the Eighties but there's a lot. It was a great time for film. Obviously George Lucas, Stephen Spielberg, James Cameron, people like that. But there are people from our country, too. Back in Australia they had guys like George Miller when he did Mad Max and things like that. There's Peter Jackson, especially when he was starting the films that he made with no money and just a lot of passion. So there's a long list but there's people who have nothing to do with our art specifically, our genre of films, like Peter Weir, another Aussie. Obviously we are huge fans of Stanley Kubrick as well.

There are people right now doing amazing things, like Christopher Nolan. Someone like Sam Raimi as well, is really interesting especially where he came from that sort of low-budget world and now he's one of the biggest filmmakers around. It's amazing because there's quite a few of those people who started out in that low-budget world and now they make these huge tent-pole movies nowadays.

JW: Where do you see your careers going? Where do you want them to go?

Peter: There have been opportunities to do some big movies and things like that. It always comes back to are we excited about the story, can we get really passionate about this and do the best job we can with the material? Sure, we'd love to do some of those bigger movies. We would also, if there's a small movie that's also interesting and exciting we would jump on that too. It always comes back to the story. If the story is solid that's what we're attracted to.

JW: *What has been the high point of your career so far?*

Peter: There's been quite a few. Just being able to walk into a movie theater and see the movie playing and the audience watching it is a huge thrill. And you know we came from Brisbane, Australia, where the success rate of feature film directors at the time when we started was zero. To walk into a theater in America or, just recently we were in a film festival in Shanghai, and to see people watching our films is pretty great.

JW: *What goes through your mind as you're watching people watch your films?*

Peter: It's a mixture of things, I guess. The fact that it's here and in a theater and people are watching it is pretty major and exciting. On top of that you have what most creative people do while someone is watching their work, which is gee, I hope people like it. I hope I haven't created something that is a disaster. You always watch those things and say, gee, I wish I could have had another take. I don't know why. That's just the way a lot of creative people are.

JW: *How did that make you feel?*

Peter: It was great. The first time we actually saw it with an audience we had a test screening and those are always, those can be incredibly nerve-wracking. The fate of your movie can be not entirely but it can have a—the 200 or so people in that theatre can have a pretty big influence over your movie. That's always really nerve-wracking.

JW: *Did they make changes based on the test screening?*

Peter: When we had our test screening we were only six weeks into the edits so we weren't even a completed film at that point. It was sort of close but we had a lot of work to do anyway and we were going to do. But the test went extremely well, which is always really encouraging. Those tests can be really hard because you don't have a lot of things in the film and you have all this temporary stuff in there and no visual effects and the actors' voices aren't there for all the placing of stuff. So it can take you out of the movie. But the thing is it tested really well.

JW: *Are you going to be coming through the US for the release?*

Peter: We're in the US at the moment and we're in the US a lot, especially when we're working on other things at the moment. We just have to be here so we definitely come to the US quite a lot.

JW: *Are you going to start hitting the science fiction convention circuit like San Diego Comic-Con? Are they going to put you on tour?*

Michael: I don't think they will for this movie. We've got a number of other things I expect will be perfect for Comic-Con.

JW: *How do you want to be remembered? A hundred, two hundred years down the line when film historians are talking about your movies, what do you want them to say?*

Michael: As long as our films are somehow relevant and our films are out there and people watch them and enjoy them, and get the same enjoyment out of them that Peter and I did, then I'm thrilled. Then we've succeeded. If your "art" sticks around through time and generations I think you've succeeded and that's all we can hope for.

Peter: I agree completely.

JW: *Is there anything else you would like to tell the readers, especially coming from a science fiction background?*

Peter: I would just say that these types of films, *Predestination*, they are and can be hard to get made and they need people to support them and go out to see them and talk about them because as a viewer, as a science fiction fan, I want to see more of these kinds of movies. But the audience has to go out there and see them, so I just hope we get the support and people like what we do.

That then tells the studios, tells the financiers that people want to see more of this interesting science fiction material and there's an audience for it.

Paul Cook is the author of eight books of science fiction, and is currently both a college instructor and the editor of the Phoenix Pick Science Fiction Classics line.

BOOK REVIEWS

by Paul Cook

The Martian
by Andy Weir
Crown - 2014
ISBN: 978-0804139021 (Hardcover)

Imagine the *Mars* novels of Ben Bova (but not those of Kim Stanley Robinson) merged with Tom Godwin's classic story, "The Cold Equations", and you'd have a good sense of what Andy Weir's first novel, *The Martian*, is about.

Botanist/engineer Mark Watney gets left behind on Mars when the rest of his crew has to abandon their habitat in the face of a monstrous dust storm. Those who have reached the MAV (Martian Ascent Vehicle) have to leave immediately because the storm threatens to topple it. The last anyone has seen of Mark Watney is that he's been impaled by a loose antenna and lost in the storm. Reluctantly, the crew leaves Mars without him. They assume he is dead and buried in the sands of Mars. Watney, though, has survived. The blood of his wound froze instantly in the bleak Martian atmosphere and he makes it back to what remains of the habitat and does everything he can to survive.

The novel goes back and forth between Watney's first-person journal entries and the narratives of the various engineers, bureaucrats, and astronauts back on the earth who mount an attempt at rescuing Watney, once they have learned that he's alive. There are satellites left in orbit and the whole world sparks with interest in his plight.

The writing in *The Martian* is crisp, clean, and precise. Weir knows his science, and through Watney's cleverness we learn just how much oxygen and hydrogen can be gotten from human waste. We learn of the mechanics of heating and how to water potatoes by harvesting the habitat's own humidity—and spreading soil inside the habitat on every square inch of floor-space. We learn how the "cold equations" of physical laws can be depended upon to turn a bad situation into something manageable.

The Martian is fast-moving and engaging, told in a style typical of the "can-do" spirit that has defined hard science fiction since John W. Campbell Jr. took over *Astounding* in 1937. Weir's Mars is not as mundane as Bova's and he's successfully avoided the politics and endless rhapsodizing of the Mars books by Kim Stanley Robinson. Andy Weir finds himself in a nice middle place between Bova and Robinson. To quote Goldilocks: *The Martian* is just right.

Twenty-First Century Science Fiction
David G. Hartwell and Patrick Nielsen Hayden, editors
Tor - 2013
ISBN-13: 978-0765326003 (Hardcover)

I'd love to be around one hundred years from now to see a collection of the major science fiction stories of the 21st century. Right now we'll have to settle for David Hartwell's and Patrick Nielsen Hayden's *Twenty-First Century Science Fiction* from Tor, which only includes entries from the last thirteen years. The title is a bit coy and Hartwell and Nielsen know this. I think they want to suggest that stories in this century might not look like stories from the last century. If that was their intent, I think they come very close.

This is a superior collection of science fiction, by any standard. Among the stories that excel here are "Strood" by Neal Asher, wherein aliens help human beings in a very odd and very funny way; "Eros, Philia, Agape" by Rachel Swirsky, about a robot that leaves his human wife to "find himself"; "The Tale of the *Wicked*" by John Scalzi, a homage-of-sorts to Asimov's Three Laws of Robotics, this time applied to a "smart" space ship that takes over its human crew; "The Calculus Plague" by Marissa Lingen that posits a world where memories, as viruses, are turned loose (much in the same manner as the nanobots in Greg Bear's "Blood Music"); "Finisterra" by David Moles, an engaging adventure of a human culture that lives on the backs of giant balloon creatures in the atmosphere of a Jupiter-sized world; "The Algorithms For Love" by Ken Liu, a clear masterpiece that explores ideas about artificial intelligence and the nature of the "self" in a way no other science fiction author has done before.

Many writers are new to me and they have excellent stories as well: "The Albian Message" by Oliver Morton is a truly superb first-contact story; "Second Person, Present Tense" by Daryl Gregory, about a drug that evokes hyper-clarity and its consequences in human beings, especially when you take too much of it—a true "hard science" science fiction story. Another "hard science" story here is "Balancing Accounts" by James L. Cambias, about robots on Saturn. Cambias seems to be emerging as one of the major writers of Campbellian "hard" science fiction. Which is all to the good.

I would say that my favorite story in the anthology is by Yoon Ha Lee: "A Vector Alphabet Of Interstellar Travel." It's a Stapletonian description of space-faring alien cultures. It's a short, clever story and it defies all the "rules" about what a short story is, what it's supposed to look like, what it's supposed to accomplish. It's charming and sweet, and should not be missed.

If I have any criticism of this book, it lies in the introductions the editors provide for each story. They're often filled with spoilers or give away too much of the story before the reader has time to enjoy it and make up their own mind. If you skip them, you'll be fine.

Afterparty
by Daryl Gregory
Tor - 2014
ISBN-13: 978-0765336927 (Hardbound)

Afterparty is a near-apocalyptic novel about bio-tech-future-out-of-control. Everyone with a chem-jet printer or a desk-top lab can mix and match all kinds of mind-altering drugs, and society is a ruin because of it. A chemical called Numinous has caused a young girl to kill herself (a New Age church might be part of the reason why) and the chemical's inventor, Lyda Rose, herself a chemically damaged person, decides that she owes it to the girl—and humanity—to figure out why. Someone has appropriated the formula and is making it on his (or her) own and Lyda Rose, along with the other members of the test group at Little Sprout, which manufactured it, race across Canada to stop them. Along the way they encounter a world filled with churches presided over by chemical visionaries, an assassin who raises miniature buffalo in his apartment, and a group of old women who are out for their own brand of justice.

Afterparty will undoubtedly make the Nebula and Hugo short lists in 2015. Reviews elsewhere have praised the novel's inventiveness, its excellent writing, and its fast pace. But while many of the novel's ideas do seem fresh (I did like the miniature bison), the novel has a basic flaw that I couldn't get past.

Lately, many novels and short stories are being published where the narrative goes from first-person to third, and this is very annoying. Gregory tells *Afterparty* in this same fashion, sometimes even adding parables that seem to come from himself. At no time was I ever fully absorbed in the narrative or what the characters needed to do. These "jolts" in perspective constantly told me that the story wasn't as important as the *way* the story was told. (This is the attraction of the French to a writer such as Alain Robbe-Grillet or, closer to home, to the novels of David Foster Wallace. It's not *story* that matters; it's the delivery system.) At no time was I *not* aware that I was reading a book, something written by a person, something published by a publishing company—an artifact. I never got "lost" in the story, which, to me, has always been the sign of a good tale. (This is why Elmore Leonard and Lee Child are bestselling writers. The reader *never* is aware of the writing or the writer or the vehicle itself.) After a while, I didn't care about the characters in *Afterparty* and the reading of it became a chore.

I know I'm in the minority here. But if history is to judge, editors and publishers will publish more of these broken, disjointed narratives and audiences will accept them (because they are published). If these shifts don't bother you, then I think you'll find a lot to enjoy in *Afterparty*.

☼

The Very Best of Fantasy and Science Fiction – Volume Two

Gordon Van Gelder, editor
Tachyon - 2014
ISBN: 978-1616961633 (Trade paperback)

Gordon Van Gelder is the current editor of *The Magazine of Fantasy and Science Fiction*, and as with his earlier volume of this series, has put together a killer anthology of the very best from *F&SF*. Of course, he has a wealth of stories to draw from, going all the way back to 1949 when Anthony Boucher and Francis McComas were its editors. Like the previous volume, this collection ranges in stories published in the early 1950s to the present day. There are stories of the fantastic as well as a few satires. What's missing here are stories of outright hard science fiction—but Mr. Van Gelder can be forgiven that.

The early satires here are "The Cosmic Expense Account" by C.M. Kornbluth, "The Country of the Kind" by Damon Knight, and "The Attack of the Giant Baby" by Kit Reed. Irony and humor abound with classics such as "The Third Level" by Jack Finney and "—All You Zombies—" by Robert A. Heinlein, "The Aliens Who Knew, I Mean, *Everything*," by George Alec Effinger and the more contemporary "*The New York Times* at Special Bargain Rates" by Stephen King. The anthology is also made strong by recent stories by Maureen F. McHugh, Bruce Sterling, M. John Harrison, Geoff Ryman, Paolo Bacigalupi, Robert Reed, and Ken Liu, the one writer here who has the most potential to revolutionize both science fiction and fantasy with both his lyrical writing style and his fabulist imagination. Speaking of which (or whom), we can't leave out our greatest fabulist, R.A. Lafferty, whose wonderful, funny, scary, and thoroughly delightful story "Narrow Valley" is here and should be read by everybody on the planet. The straight-on science fiction stories here are all classics in the field: "Salvador" by Lucius Shepard, "Rat" by James Patrick Kelly, "Sundance" by Robert Silverberg, "Jeffty is Five" by Harlan Ellison.

This anthology is a healthy mix of both fantasy and science fiction. The emphasis, as Van Gelder says, is on the quality of story-telling across the decades, and some of our best story-tellers are here. My guess is that you'll find something here you hadn't read before (I did) and stories that are worth rereading.

The Best of Connie Willis: Award-Winning Stories
Del Rey - 2013
ISBN: 978-0-354-54066-9 (Trade paperback)

Here is a collection that belongs in everyone's science fiction library. Connie Willis has been writing science fiction since 1978, in both the novel format as well as short fiction, and compiled here in one neat volume are her ten stories that have won either the Hugo or the Nebula Award—and sometimes both. The classics included here are "A Letter From The Clearys," "At The Rialto," "Fire Watch," and the wistful "The Last of the Winnebagos." "Fire Watch" and "The Winds of Marble Arch" are part of Willis' novels about the London Blitz and you can see how her ideas have evolved over time.

What stands out in Willis' writing is her sense of humor, something that is missing in science fiction today. We aren't talking about outright satire here, although "At the Rialto" comes close. "At the Rialto" is a hilarious send-up of academia, but it's also a great primer in quantum physics and alternate universe theory. Willis really writes with a sense of kindness that I find refreshing. Even when she writes about bleak futures ("A Letter from the Clearys" and "The Last of the Winnebagos"), she treats the lives of her characters gently and respectfully. Like Nancy Kress, Connie Willis understands that her characters are members of families and often these families matter more than the world at large. (This feature is what makes "A Letter From the Clearys" so poignant and heartbreaking.)

The other characteristic that stands out in her writing is her actual prose style. Like Stephen King, Willis has been able to capture in writing the way Americans actually think and speak. Her stories, even the longest of them, seem to move right along in a casual, easy-going way, even if the circumstances within are truly harrowing as in "Fire Watch" and "The Winds of Marble Arch."

Because of her writing style, her stories tend to be longer rather than shorter. This allows Ms. Willis to flesh out her characters and paint the "universe" of each story in a clearer fashion. I highly recommend this book to you, especially if you've kept up with her novels, especially *Blackout/All Clear*, which won the Hugo for Best Novel in 2010 and the Nebula Award for Best Novel in 2011.

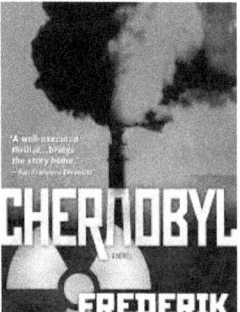

FROM THE VAULT:
Reprints, Reissues and Re-releases of Note
Chernobyl
by Frederik Pohl
Tor - 2014
ISBN-13: 978-0765375964 (Paperback)

Frederik Pohl, who passed away in 2013, was one of science fiction's major luminaries. His career spanned five decades. He was a fan, an author, an editor, SFWA president. His fiction has won him every major award the field has to offer. His novels (*Jem, Gateway, Man Plus, The Space Merchants*—with C.M. Kornbluth, among them) are classics in the field. He did it all.

With *Chernobyl* he did something different, and this time it was personal.

Pohl's people came from the western regions of the Soviet Union, most of whom lived in the Ukraine which was a part of the world no one had been paying any attention to until 1986 when a valve in the cooling system stuck and blew up Reactor #4 and heavily damaged Reactor #3 at a nuclear plant in a little village called Chernobyl. Tons of radioactive debris shot thousands of feet into the air, and eventually the disaster killed over a thousand people. It killed *all* of the people who immediately responded to the disaster. The others came later. Much of the region around Chernobyl is now a wasteland, even though Reactors #1 and #2 are still operating.

Pohl's novel *Chernobyl* originally appeared in 1987. It's a brilliant retelling of the story in fictional form, and is clearly a masterpiece even though it isn't science fiction. In *Chernobyl*, Pohl skillfully recreates the event, including some of the technical data that was made available to him when he went to the Soviet Union to do research. He writes about the villages whose houses are destroyed; he writes of the first responders who know they're already dead; he writes about the politicians who don't want to tell the world what's just happened. One scene still gives me shivers. One of the main characters, using scuba gear, has to swim *underneath* Reactor #3 as it's raging out of control. The reactor sits in a gigantic pool of tepid water, but it's the only way to reach the other side of the building where the controls are for cooling that reactor down. No scene in all of literature is as harrowing as this.

This is a work of fiction, but Pohl's genius is to make the disaster come alive, and portraying the heroes and victims with absolute humanity. I consider this one of the best books I've ever read and I'm glad it's back in print.

Copyright © 2014 by Paul Cook

Gregory Benford is a Nebula winner and a former Worldcon Guest of Honor. He is the author of more than 30 novels and 6 books of non-fiction, and has edited 10 anthologies.

MINING A GENRE
OR
SF LITE: STAR TREK

by Gregory Benford

Here's a backward look at the first true media giant use of science fiction: Trek. The short article below was written in 1996 for the *Los Angeles Times*. Then I add an after-comment.

1996:

A new series in the Star Trek franchise has begun: *Enterprise*. Set before the era of the original show, it reminds us of how this vision of the future, unremarkable even when it began, has come to stand for The Future it our world culture.

Indeed, the astonishing persistence of a television series, routinely launched with little fanfare over thirty years ago, calls for explanation and rumination. Those of us from inside the science fiction genre view Star Trek with oblique bemusement, cousins eyeing a rich relative.

Hollywood and TV have always methodically harvested ripened fruit from genre vineyards. Cowboys and detectives are easy for a broad audience to fathom, but true, hard-core science fiction seemed, well, downright eerie. Its density and strangeness had made TV's job far harder than Hollywood's scare-'em-with-science, giant-bug formula evolved in the 1950s.

Gene Roddenberry's ever-growing profit center began with a single insight, when he casually referred to Trek as "Wagon Train in space." He saw that the genre needed translation into human terms, and so evolved the fundamental strategy that opened sf (as it is known to insiders; outsiders call it "scifi").

Trek became a huge multimedia phenom by imagining a shared experience: Our Gang visits the future. The Enterprise crew had well-defined roles lead by an affable captain. William Shatner saw that humor and a calm, everyday air aboard would be crucial. Spock was Sherlock Holmes in space, the series' most original notion. The crew/family's often whimsical efforts to convert him to emotion provided an amusing leitmotif against a background blend of the mildly fantastic and reassuringly familiar. Manageable exoticism sold.

Trek taught a generation to seek the sci-fi experience in this associative way, far from the deliberate dislocations and strangeness sought by genre insiders.

Seldom did Trek challenge genre stereotypes. By harvesting fresh ideas and themes invented in print it loomed over most conventional TV. Several well-known genre sf writers wrote some of the best scripts in the first two seasons (Harlan Ellison, David Gerrold, Norman Spinrad, Theodore Sturgeon), only to be often rewritten and finally not invited back. The series now depends on writers who seem rather proud of their ignorance of written sf.

Roddenberry's favorite theme was flawed gods, usually alien superbeings or warped humans, often speaking to the problems of hubris. For genre insiders like me, Trek's greatest sins lay in its general scientific incoherence. In the very first show, an alien "salt vampire" preferred to kill people for a few grams of salt in their bodies, rather than simply steal galley stores.

As it spawned offspring series and films, quickie technical solutions threw into question the entire physics and technology of the series. The early shows opted for the "transporter" to avoid expensive shots of rockets landing and lifting off. Thereafter the series dodged the problems of what a society looks like where everything can be quickly duplicated. Worse, plots often relied on telepathy and "mind science" for motivation and twists.

Sf studies the collision between our humanity and an indifferent universe. Many modern anxieties stem from our broadening awareness of our chilly loneliness. Trek dodged this deeper issue, inventing SF Lite, the sci-fi option. In Trek, human emotion and gut feeling is forever superior to cold logic. The galaxy is user-friendly.

The show pivoted around a desire to please everyone, with a token Russian, Asian and black woman in the crew. This apparently forgave its air of earnest moralizing, a trait we still see today in the frequent oracular pronouncements delivered *ex cathedra* from

the Enterprise bridge. The films continued this; even in the perhaps-best, "Star Trek IV: The Voyage Home", the most adventurous position taken is Save The Whales.

Trek's dazzling successes inspired over a hundred novels, a gold mine for Pocket Books. Alas, the hoped-for transference of Trek book readers to mainline sf didn't happen. Perhaps this relates to the unusual popularity of older, Golden Age writers in sf—Heinlein, Asimov, Bradbury, Clarke, Herbert, with their time-honored approaches. Here, too, readers prefer to go to the strange future in the company of somebody they know; it's reassuring.

This suggests that whatever the medium, the way to reach this enormous audience is to find a shared, quasi-communal vehicle. Later, "Star Wars" made this strategy more explicit with an entire set of future family, its sons-and-fathers revelations played out over three films with three more in the pipeline.

It did take courage to show TV's first inter-racial kiss, to confront militarism during Vietnam on one hand and soon after to deplore counter-cultural excesses as well. Trek did and does assume a world that works, surely a reassuring fresh breeze to anyone reading the newspapers.

In Trek's future everyone cheerfully wears spandex and looks great, a remarkable prospect for a nation which, over the last three decades, has seen the average adult add a pound of weight in each passing year. Could this be the secret heart of our love for the show?

Comment in 2014:

I ended the above piece with a short bio note, adding "He has never written for *Star Trek*."

Today in 2014, not so. At the tail end of the *Enterprise* disaster, 9 months before the show got cancelled, the head director called me in to develop a story arc. That's right—the production never had a plan. In desperation, Brandon Braga realized maybe it should.

So I worked on how to tie *Enterprise* into what we now call Classic Trek (Hollywood actually talks that way). In my arc, the explorers discover why aliens are nearly always humanoid: because the galaxy has been sowed with similar genes in lower life forms, stimulating evolution of primates. I wrote up these ideas and delivered plot outlines for two shows to develop the method.

None of this got used. Instead, Braga began writing most of the scripts alone, approving them himself, and thus pocketing the maximum take from the dying series. He discarded all continuity with Classic Trek. The other writers on the show—who would've made considerable extra money if their scripts were used—got irked. Morale fell. *Enterprise* ended.

So this sad finish came from neglecting the basics of Classic Trek, a rather sour ending note. The show failed to recognize the magic Roddenberry had wrought.

Copyright © 1996, revised 2014 by Gregory Benford

Barry N. Malzberg is the winner of the very first Campbell Memorial Award, a multiple Hugo and Nebula winner, and the author of more than 90 books.

FROM THE HEART'S BASEMENT

by Barry N. Malzberg

LIFE-LINE

Special Robert A. Heinlein issue in conjunction with release of film based upon his 1959 novelette for *Fantasy & Science Fiction*, "All You Zombies."

Big noise from Winnetka and elsewhere surrounding the big-budget release of a property 55 years old. Heinlein himself (1907–1988) has been dead for over a quarter of a century. This is good news for the desperate and the disparate among us: his life was not short but his art has already lasted longer than the entirety of a career which lasted just under fifty years.

Heinlein had become, by the time he published "All You Zombies," a figure both iconic and isolated, and in the decades which followed its publication he became even more of both … the isolation and self-segregation of his last years is reminiscent of L. Ron Hubbard's, another old pal. Heinlein lived behind barbed wire, issued inflexible edicts to his editors, appeared at occasional conventions only through careful preparation and arrangement, and became ever more stubborn and (to his editors and fan base) infuriating. But there was no arguing with the work which justified his high self-evaluation. In the early forties he taught John W. Campbell—and through him everyone associated with the genre—how this stuff should be written. No long expository passages, minimal flashbacks if any, extrapolation embodied in intense if simple plot. Crudely drawn but identifiable principal characters, unshaded conflict, and above all a practicality as intense as his plots. His characters (unlike those of those contemporaneous influences, Kuttner and Moore) suffered not from ambivalence, recrimination, the torments of choice.

Heinlein like *his* influence Rudyard Kipling gave us the Competent Man, the Man Who Knew How Things Worked and who worked them, coolly in a crisis.

Science fiction for this most influential of its modern writers was a problem-solving device and through the clatter of the most dangerous century, he went about solving them. He took off three years for civilian war work (there is a famous photo of Heinlein, Sprague de Camp, and Asimov) in the laboratories of Philadelphia and he emerged from those years not flummoxed by the nuclear stalemate he had predicted five years earlier in "Solution Unsatisfactory" but enamored of it.

This problem would give competent men a satisfactory challenge. Of course much of his work transplanted the postwar situation to and beyond the solar system but Lazarus Long was always recognizable. Lazarus Long in fact was my Uncle, Herbert Finney (1898–1961), another alumnus of the United States Naval Academy (1920). In consequence, I never had much difficulty understanding and coming to terms with Heinlein (class of 1929). As I wrote in 1975 in a story introduction, "Heinlein had an absolute vision of how the world worked in 1946 … and then his vision froze."

So it all linked, and in the '50s through his nonjuvenile juveniles and novels like *Double Star* and *Citizen of the Galaxy* Heinlein became wholly identified with science fiction in its false Spring, in its pre-*Star Wars* period, waiting for the apocalypse. Damon Knight wrote in the early fifties (this is a close paraphrase), "Consider Heinlein in the early forties. He had discovered a new and interesting field of work in which, from the very beginning, he was manifestly superior to any of his competitors. He was able to sell as much as he could write, and he was regarded as far the best practitioner of this interesting field. What a good time he had!"

The William Patterson biography in two volumes, published in 2010 and 2014, shows us a somewhat different story. Considering Heinlein in the late 1930s is something like considering Marilyn Monroe in that early film *As Young As You Feel*, which I parsed in my previous essay. Here is Monroe the starlet at 25, still unknown, tottering on the precipice of a career or a fall, caught by circumstances she

found uncontrollable and facing oblivion at every moment. If she failed in Hollywood where would she go? Young (but not young enough for starlet roles soon), poorly educated, first marriage broken, orphaned young, what was there for her? Here was Heinlein—pensioned out of the Navy for poor health, possessing nothing other than nautical skills and what he hoped was a narrative talent, living on the margin as World War II loomed, knowing there would be no place for him there. An inept fling at politics, fantasies of public service, an unpublished and probably unpublishable novel, a Navy veteran in a peacetime society which had little use for the military or its veterans.

To *this* Heinlein, the Heinlein stripped of myth and shadow, it must have all been frightening. Last chance gulch, really. If he failed as a civilian, the Navy was not going to take him back, even in wartime. He could certainly write a little but so could a lot of people in that great pulp era. Science fiction was a good choice, most of its practitioners were far less skilled than Heinlein and the general level of talent was far less than existed in the mystery or *Argosy*. He had a reasonable chance, maybe, but a penny a word even in 1939 was no measure of security, and ability might not be either. Most of us are scared at the beginning and certainly "Life-Line" and "Blow-Ups Happen" and "The Roads Must Roll" (particularly "The Roads Must Roll") were written by a frightened man. These were hard times for an aspirant pulp writer, they were hard times for everyone (even Orson Welles and other princes) and Heinlein must have felt that his options were steadily disappearing. The nihilism took a while to emerge in the fiction (the pulps were no place for nihilism) but "All You Zombies" has been written by someone who has seen the void and seen himself and can see no distance between them.

We know how it all turned out and we know what Heinlein became, even through the sad withdrawal and monomania of his last years. History is written by and of the winners, and it all seems very clear now, in fact it seems inevitable: Heinlein's odyssey was that of a Heinlein protagonist. That protagonist, after much misdirection and side journeys, became the protagonist of "All You Zombies," already foreshadowed in "By His Bootstraps." Heinlein ran all of the matchless corridors of self, he ran through the doors, he ran through the prison, he ran to the fields where the rabbits could not go. And ultimately, as in those two novelettes, and as in The Great Lorenzo in his best novel, *Double Star*, Heinlein found himself torn and pressed into a mirror from which stared his own, his stricken, his utterly knowledgeable and utterly barren self. The man was science fiction. We are science fiction. Science fiction is the world.

November 2014: New Jersey

Copyright © 2014 by Barry N. Malzberg

SERIALIZATION
Melodies of the Heart *(novella)*

Part 1

"Melodies of the Heart" is the lead novella in the collection, CAPTIVE DREAMS.
by Michael Flynn
Phoenix Pick, 2012
Trade Paperback: 266 pages.
ISBN: 978-1-61242-059-2

"Melodies of the Heart," copyright © 1994 by Michael Flynn. Originally appeared in *Analog Science Fiction and Fact*, January 1994. Reprinted as part of *Captive Dreams* by Phoenix Pick, 2012.

MELODIES OF THE HEART
[serialization – Part 1 of 3]

Michael Flynn

I have never been to visit in the gardens of my youth. They are dim and faded memories, brittle with time: A small river town stretched across stony bluffs and hills. Cliffside stairs switchbacking to a downtown of marvels and magical stores. A little frame house nestled in a spot of green, with marigolds tracing its bounds. Men wore hats. Cars gleamed with chrome and sported tail-fins enough to take flight. Grown-ups were very tall and mysterious. Sometimes, if you were good, they gave you a nickel, which you could rush to the corner grocery and buy red hot dollars and jawbreakers and licorice whips.

I don't remember the music, though. I know I should; but I don't. I even know what the tunes must have been; I've heard them often enough on Classic Rock and Golden Oldy shows. But that is now; my memories are silent.

I don't go back; I have never gone back. The town would all be all different—grimier and dirtier and twenty years more run down. The house I grew up in was sold, and then sold again. Strangers live there now. The cliffside stairs have fallen into disrepair, and half the downtown stores are boarded up and silent. The corner groceries are gone, and a nickel won't buy you squat. Grown-ups are not so tall.

They are still a mystery, though. Some things never change.

> *The music is dreamy,*
> *It's peaches and creamy,*
> *Oh! don't let my feet touch the ground ...*

I remember her as I always remember her: sitting against the wall in the garden sunshine, eyes closed, humming to herself.

The first time I saw Mae Holloway was my first day at Sunny Dale. On a tour of the grounds, before being shown to my office, the director pointed out a shrunken and bent old woman shrouded in a shapeless, pale-hued gown. "Our Oldest Resident." I

smiled and acted as if I cared. What was she to me? Nothing, then.

The resident doctor program was new then. A conservative looking for a penny to pinch and a liberal looking for a middle-class professional to kick had gotten drunk together one night and come up with the notion that, if you misunderstood the tax code, your professional services could be extorted by the state. My sentence was to provide on-site medical care at the Home three days a week. Dr. Khan, who kept an office five miles away, remained the "primary care provider."

The Home had set aside a little room that I could use for a clinic. I had a metal desk, an old battered filing cabinet, a chair with a bad caster that caused the wheel to seize up—as if there were a Rule that the furniture there be as old and as worn as the inhabitants. For supplies, I had the usual medicines for aches and pains. Some digitalis. Ointments of one sort or another. Splints and bandages. Not much else. The residents were not ill, only old and tired. First aid and mortuaries covered most of their medical needs.

The second time I saw Mae Holloway was later that same first day. The knock on the door was so light and tentative that at first I was unsure I had heard it. I paused, glanced at the door, then bent again over my medical journal. A moment later, the knock came again. Loud! As if someone had attacked the door with a hammer. I turned the journal down open to the page I had been reading and called out an invitation.

The door opened and I waited patiently while she shuffled across the room. Hobble, hobble, hobble. You would think old folks would move faster. It wasn't as though they had a lot of time to waste.

When she had settled into the hard plastic seat opposite my desk, she leaned forward, cupping both her hands over the knob of an old blackthorn walking stick. Her face was as wrinkled as that East Tennessee hill country she had once called home. "You know," she said—loudly, as the slightly deaf often do, "you oughtn't leave your door shut like that. Folks see it, they think you have someone in here, so they jes' mosey on."

That notion had been in the back of my mind, too. I had thought to use this time to keep up with my professional reading. "What may I do for you, Mrs. Holloway?" I said.

She looked away momentarily. "I think—" Her jaw worked. She took a breath. "I think I am going insane."

I stared at her for a moment. Just my luck. A nut case right off the bat. Then I nodded. "I see. And why do you say that?"

"I hear music. In my head."

"Music?"

"Yes. You know. Like this." And she hummed a few bars of a nondescript tune.

"I see—"

"That was *One O'Clock Jump*!" she said, nearly shouting now. "I used to listen to Benny Goodman's band on *Let's Dance*! Of course, I was younger then!"

"I'm sure you were."

"What did you say?"

"I said, 'I'm sure you were'!" I shouted at her across the desk.

"Oh. Yes," she said in a slightly softer voice. "I'm sorry, but it's sometimes hard for me to hear over the music. It grows loud, then soft." The old woman puckered her face and her eyes drifted, becoming distanced. "Right now, it's *King Porter*. A few minutes ago it was—"

"Yes, I'm sure," I said. Old folks are slow and rambling and forgetful; a trial to talk with. I rose, hooking my stethoscope into my ears, and circled the desk. Might as well get it over with. Mrs. Holloway, recognizing the routine, unfastened the top buttons of her gown.

Old folks have a certain smell to them, like babies; only not so pleasant. It is a sour, dusty smell, like an attic in the summer heat. Their skin is dry, spotted parchment, repulsive to the touch. When I placed the diaphragm against her chest, she smiled nervously. "I don't think you'll hear my music that way," she said.

"Of course not," I told her. "Did you think I would?"

She rapped the floor with her walking stick. Once, very sharp. "I'm no child, Doctor Wilkes! I have not been a child for a long, long time; so, don't treat me like one." She waved her hand up and down her body. "How many children do you know who look like me?"

"Just one," I snapped back. And instantly regretted the remark. There was no point in being rude; and

it was none of her business anyway. "Tell me about your music," I said, unhooking my stethoscope and stepping away.

She worked her lips and glared at me for a while before she made up her mind to cooperate. Finally, she looked down at the floor. "It was one, two nights ago," she whispered. Her hands gripped her walking stick so tightly that the knuckles stood out large and white. She twisted it as if screwing it into the floor. "I dreamed I was dancing in the Roseland Ballroom, like I used to do years and years ago. Oh, I was once so light on my feet! I was dancing with Ben Wickham—he's dead now, of course; but he was one smooth apple and sure knew how to pitch woo. The band was a swing band—I was a swinger, did you know?—and they were playing Goodman tunes. *Sing, Sing, Sing. Stardust.* But it was so loud, I woke up. I thought I was still dreaming for a while, because I could still hear the music. Then I got riled. I thought, who could be playing their radio so loud in the middle of the night? So I took myself down the hall, room by room, and listened at each door. But the music stayed the same, no matter where I went. That's when I knowed …" She paused, swallowed hard, looked into the corner. "That's when I knowed, knew, it was all in my head."

I opened the sphygmomanometer on my desk. Mae Holloway was over a hundred years old, according to the Home's director; well past her time to shuffle off. If her mind was playing tricks on her in her last years, well, that's what old minds did. Yet, I had read of similar cases of "head" music. "There are several possibilities, Mrs. Holloway," I said, speaking loudly and distinctly while I fastened the pressure cuff to her arm, "but the best bet is that the music really *is* all in your head."

I smiled at the *bon mot*, but all the wire went out of her and she sagged shapelessly in her chair. Her right hand went to her forehead and squeezed. Her eyes twisted tight shut. "Oh, no," she muttered. "Oh, dear God, no. It's finally happened."

Mossbacks have no sense of humor. "Please, Mrs. Holloway! I didn't mean 'in your head' like that. I meant the fillings in your teeth. A pun. Fillings sometimes act like crystal radios and pick up broadcast signals, vibrating the small bones of the middle ear. You are most likely picking up a local radio station. Perhaps a dentist could …"

She looked up at me and her eyes burned. "That was a wicked joke to pull, boy. It was cruel."

"I didn't mean it that way—"

"And I know all about fillings and radios and such," she snapped. "Will Hickey had that problem here five years ago. But that can't be why I hear music." And she extruded a ghastly set of false teeth.

"Well, then—"

"And what sort of radio station could it be? Swing tunes all the time, and only those that I know? Over and over, all night long, with no interruptions. No commercials. No announcements of song titles or performers." She raised her free hand to block her ear, a futile gesture, because the music was on the other side.

On the other side of the ear …? I recalled certain case studies from medical school. Odd cases. "There are other possibilities," I said. "Neurological problems …" I pumped the bulb and she winced as the cuff tightened. She lowered her hand slowly and looked at me.

"Neuro …?" Her voice trembled.

"Fossil memories," I said.

She shook her head. "I ain't—I'm not rememberin'. I'm hearin'. I know the difference."

I let the air out of the cuff and unfastened it. "I will explain as simply as I can. Hearing occurs in the brain, not the ear. Sound waves vibrate certain bones in your middle ear. These vibrations are converted into neural impulses and conveyed to the auditory cortex by the eighth cranial nerve. It is the auditory cortex that creates 'sound.' If the nerve were connected to the brain's olfactory region, instead, you would 'smell' music."

She grunted. "Quite a bit of it smells, these days."

Hah, hah. "The point is that the sensory cortices can be stimulated without external input. Severe migraines, for example, often cause people to 'see' visions or 'hear' voices. And sometimes the stimulus reactivates so-called 'fossil' memories, which your mind interprets as contemporary. That may be what you are experiencing."

She looked a little to the side, not saying anything. I listened to her wheezy breath. Then she gave me a glance, quick, almost shy. "Then, you don't think I'm

… You know … Crazy?" Have you ever heard hope and fear fused into a single question? I don't know. At her age, I think I might prefer a pleasant fantasy world over the dingy real one.

"It's unlikely," I told her. "Such people usually hear voices, not music. If you were going insane, you wouldn't hear Benny Goodman tunes; you would hear Benny Goodman—probably giving you important instructions."

A smile twitched her lips and she seemed calmer, though still uneasy. "It's always been a bother to me," she said quietly, looking past me, "the notion that I might be—well, you know. All my life, it seems, as far back as I can remember."

Which was not that far, the director had told me that morning. "All your life. Why is that?"

She looked away and did not speak for a moment. When she did, she said, "I haven't had no, any, headaches, doc. And I don't have any now. If that's what did it, how come I can still hear the music?"

If she did not want to talk about her fears, that was fine with me. I was no psychiatrist, anyway. "I can't be sure without further tests, but a trigger event—possibly even a mild stroke—could have initiated the process." I had been carefully observing her motor functions, but I could detect none of the slackness or slurring of the voice typical of severe hemiplegia. "Dr. Wing is the resident neurologist at the hospital," I said. "I'll consult with him."

She looked suddenly alarmed, and shook her head. "No hospitals," she said firmly. "Folks go to hospitals, they die."

At her age, that was largely true. I sighed. "Perhaps at Khan's clinic, then. There really are some tests we should run."

That seemed to calm her somewhat, for she closed her eyes and her lips moved slightly.

"Have you experienced any loss of appetite, or episodes of drowsiness?" I asked. "Have you become irritable, forgetful, less alert?" Useless questions. What geezer did not have those symptoms? I would have to inquire among the staff to find out if there had been a recent change in her behavior.

And she wasn't listening anymore. At least, not to me. "Thank you, Doctor Wilkes. I was so afraid … That music … But only a stroke, only a stroke. It's such a relief. Thank you. Such a relief."

A relief? Compared to madness, I suppose it was. She struggled to her feet, still babbling. When she left my office, hobbling once more over her walking stick, she was humming to herself again. I didn't know the tune.

> *Even though we're drifting down life's stream apart,*
> *Your face I still can see in dream's domain;*
> *I know that it would ease my breaking heart*
> *To hold you in my arms just once again.*

✿

It was dark when I arrived home. As I turned into the driveway, I hit the dashboard remote, and the garage door rose up like a welcoming lover. I slid into the left-hand slot without slowing, easing the Lincoln to a halt just as the tennis ball, hanging by a string from the ceiling, touched the windshield. Brenda never understood that. Brenda always came to a complete stop in the driveway before raising the garage door.

I could see without looking that I had beaten her home again. And they said doctors kept long hours … When I stepped from the car, I turned my back on the empty slot.

I stood for some moments at the door to the kitchen, jiggling the car keys in my hand. Then, instead of entering the house, I turned and left the garage through the back-yard door. I had seen the second-story light on as I came down the street. Deirdre's room. Tonight, for some reason, I couldn't face going inside just yet.

The back yard was a gloom of emerald and jade. The house blocked the glare of the street lamps, conceding just enough light to tease shape from shadow. I walked slowly through the damp grass toward the back of the lot. Glowing clouds undulated in the water of the swimming pool, as if the ground had opened up and swallowed the night sky. Only a few stars poked through the overcast. Polaris? Sirius? I had no way of knowing. I doubted that half a dozen people in the township knew the stars by name; or perhaps even that they had names. We have become strangers to our skies.

At the back of the lot, the property met a patch of woodland—a bit of unofficial greenbelt, undeveloped because it was inaccessible from the road.

Squirrels lived there, and blue jays and cardinals. And possum and skunk, too. I listened to the rustle of the night dwellers passing through the carpet of dead leaves. Through the trees I could make out the lights of the house opposite. Distant music and muffled voices. Henry and Barbara Carter were throwing a party.

That damned old woman … Damn all of them. Shambling, crackling, brittle, dried-out old husks, clinging fingernail-tight to what was left of life …

I jammed my hands in my pockets and stood there. For how long, I do not know. It might have been five minutes or half an hour. Finally the light on the second floor went out. Then I turned back to the house and re-entered through the garage. The right-hand stall was still empty.

✿

Consuela sat at the kitchen table near the French doors, cradling a ceramic mug shaped like an Olmec head. Half the live-in nurses in the country are Latin; and half of those are named Consuela. The odor of cocoa filled the room, and the steam from the cup wreathed her broad, flat face, lending it a sheen. More *Indio* than *Ladino*, her complexion contrasted starkly with her nurse's whites. Her jet black hair was pulled severely back, and was held in place with a plain, wooden pin.

"Good evening, Nurse," I said. "Is Dee-dee down for the night?"

"Yes, Doctor. She is."

I glanced up at the ceiling. "I usually tuck her in."

She gave me an odd look. "Yes, you do."

"Well. I was running a little late today. Did she miss me?"

Consuela looked through the French doors at the back yard. "She did."

"I'll make it up to her tomorrow."

She nodded. "I'm sure she would like that."

I shed my coat and carried it to the hall closet. A dim night-light glowed at the top of the stairwell. "Has Mrs. Wilkes called?"

"An hour ago." Consuela's voice drifted down the hallway from the kitchen. "She has a big case to prepare for tomorrow. She will be late."

I hung the coat on the closet rack and stood quietly still for a moment before closing the door.

Another big case. I studied the stairs to the upper floor. Brenda had begun getting the big cases when Deirdre was eighteen months and alopecia had set in. Brenda never tucked Dee-dee into bed after that.

Consuela was washing her cup at the sink when I returned to the kitchen. She was short and dark and stocky. Not quite chubby, but with a roundness that scorned New York and Paris fashion. I rummaged in the freezer for a frozen dinner. Brenda had picked Consuela from among a dozen applicants. Brenda was tall and thin and blonde.

I put the dinner in the microwave and started the radiation. "I met an interesting woman today," I said.

Consuela dried her cup and hung it on the rack. "All women are interesting," she said.

"This one hears music in her head." I saw how that piqued her interest.

"We all do," she said, half-turned to go.

I carried my microwaved meal and sat at the table. "Not like this. Not like hearing a radio at top volume."

She hesitated a moment longer; then she shrugged and sat across the table from me. "Tell me of this woman."

I moved the macaroni and cheese around on my plate. "I spoke with Dr. Wing over the car phone. He believes it may be a case of 'incontinent nostalgia,' or Jackson's Syndrome."

I explained how trauma to the temporal lobe sometimes caused spontaneous upwellings of memory, often accompanied by "dreamy states" and feelings of profound and poignant joy. Oliver Sacks had written about it in one of his best sellers. "Shostakovich had a splinter in his left temporal lobe," I said. "When he cocked his head, he heard melodies. And there have been other cases. Stephen Foster, perhaps." I took a bite of my meal. "Odd, isn't it, how often the memories are musical."

Consuela nodded. "Sometimes the music is enough."

"Other memories may follow, though."

"Sometimes the music is enough," she repeated enigmatically.

"It should make the old lady happy, at least."

Consuela gave me a curious look. "Why should it make her happy?" she asked.

"She has forgotten her early years completely. This condition may help her remember." An old lady re-living her childhood. Suddenly there was bitterness in my mouth. I dropped my fork into the serving tray.

Consuela shook her head. "Why should it make her happy?" she asked again.

That little bird knew lots of things,
It did, upon my word ...

The universe balances. For every Consuela Montejo there is a Noor Khan.

Dr. Noor Khan was a crane, all bones and joints. She was tall, almost as tall as I, but thin to the point of gauntness. She cocked her head habitually from side to side. That, the bulging eyes, and the hooked nose accentuated her bird-like appearance. A good run, a flapping of the arms, and she might take squawking flight—and perhaps appear more graceful.

"Mae Holloway. Oh, my, yes. She is a feisty one, is she not?" Khan rooted in her filing cabinet, her head bobbing as she talked. "Does she have a problem?"

"Incontinent nostalgia, it's sometimes called," I said. "She is experiencing spontaneous, musical recollections, possibly triggered by a mild stroke to the temporal lobes." I told her about the music and Wing's theories.

She bobbed her head. "Curious. Like *déjà vu*, only different." Then, more sternly. "If she has had a stroke, even a mild one, I must see her at once."

"I've told her that, but she's stubborn. I thought since you knew her better ..."

Noor Khan sighed. "Yes. Well, the older we grow, the more set in our ways we become. Mae must be set in concrete."

It was a joke and I gave it a thin smile. *The older we grow ...*

The file she finally pulled was a thick one. I took the folder from her and carried it to her desk. I had nothing in particular in mind, just a review of Holloway's medical history. I began paging through the records. In addition to Dr. Khan's notes, there were copies of records from other doctors. I looked up at Khan. "Don't you have patients waiting?"

She raised an eyebrow. "My office hours start at ten, so I have no patients at the moment. You need not worry that I am neglecting them."

If it was a reproof, it was a mild one, and couched in face-saving Oriental terms. I hate it when people watch me read. I always feel as if they were reading over my shoulder. I wanted to tell Khan that I would call her if I needed her; but it was, after all, her office and I was sitting at her desk, so I don't know what I expected her to do. "Sorry," I said. "I didn't mean to ruffle your feathers."

✿

Holloway was in unusually good health for a woman her age. Her bones had grown brittle and her eyes nearsighted—but no glaucoma; and very little osteoporosis. She had gotten a hearing aid at an age when most people were already either stone deaf or stone dead. Clinical evidence showed that she had once given birth, and that an anciently broken leg had not healed entirely straight. What right had she to enjoy such good health?

Khan had been on the phone. "Mae has agreed to come in," she told me as she hung up. "I will send the van to pick her up on Tuesday. I wish I could do a CAT scan here. I would hate to force her into hospital."

"It's a waste, anyway," I muttered.

"What?"

I clamped my jaw shut. All that high technology, and for what? To add a few miserable months to lives already years too long? How many dollars per day of life was that? How much of it was productively returned? That governor, years ago. What was his name? Lamm? He said that the old had a duty to die and make room for the young. "Nothing," I said.

"What is wrong?" asked Khan.

"There's nothing wrong with me."

"That wasn't what I asked."

I turned my attention to the folder and squinted at the spidery, illegible handwriting on the oldest record: 1962, if the date was really what it looked like. Why did so many doctors have poor handwriting? Holloway's estimated age looked more like an 85 than a 65. I waved the sheet of stationery at her. "Look at the handwriting on this," I complained. "It's like reading Sanskrit."

Khan took the letter. "I can read Sanskrit, a little," she said with a smile. "It's Doctor Bench's memo, isn't it? Yes, I thought so. I found it when I assumed

Dr. Rosenblum's practice a few years ago. Dr. Bench promised he would send Mrs. Holloway's older records, but he never did, so Howard had to start a medical history almost from scratch, with only this capsule summary."

I took the sheet back from her. "Why didn't Bench follow through?"

She shrugged. "Who knows? He put it off. Then one of those California brush fires destroyed his office. Medically, Mae is a blank before 1962."

Just like her mind, I thought. Just like her mind.

> *For the joy of eye and ear*
> *For the heart and mind's delight*
> *For the mystic harmony*
> *Linking sense to sound and sight …*

✿

The third time I saw Mae Holloway, she was waiting by the clinic door when I arrived to open it. Eyes closed, propped against the wall by her walking stick, she hummed an obscure melody. "Good morning, Mrs. Holloway," I said. "Feeling better today?"

She opened her eyes and squeezed her face into a ghastly pucker. "Consarn music kept me awake again last night."

I gave her a pleasant smile. "Too bad you don't hear Easy Listening." I stepped through the door ahead of her. I heard her cane tap-tap-tapping behind me and wondered if a practiced ear could identify an oldster by her distinctive cane tap. I could imagine Tonto, ear pressed to the ground. "Many geezer come this way, *kemo sabe*."

Snapping open my briefcase, I extracted my journals and stacked them on the desk. Mae lowered herself into the visitor's chair. "Jimmy Kovacs will be coming in to see you later today. He threw his back out again."

I opened the issue of the *Brain* that Dr. Wing had lent me. "Never throw anything out that you might need again later," I said, running my eye down the table of contents.

"You do study on those books, doctor."

"I like to keep up on things."

I flipped the journal open to the article I had been seeking and began to read. After a few minutes, she spoke again. "If you spent half the time studying on people as you do studying on books, you'd be better at doctorin'."

I looked up scowling. Who was she to judge? A bent-up, shriveled old woman who had seen more years than she had a right to. "The body is an intricate machine," I told her. "The more thoroughly I understand its mechanisms, the better able I am to repair it."

"A machine," she repeated.

"Like an automobile."

"And you're jest an auto mechanic." She shook her head.

I smiled, but without humor. "Yes, I am. Maybe that's less glamorous than being a godlike healer, but I think it's closer to the truth." An auto mechanic. And some cars were old jalopies destined for the junk heap; so why put more work into them? I did not tell her that. And others were not built right to begin with. I did not tell her that, either. It was a cold vision, but in its way, comforting. Helplessness is greater solace than failure.

Mae grunted. "Mostly milk sours 'cause it's old."

I scowled again. More hillbilly philosophy? Or simply an addled mind unable to hold to a topic? "Does it," I said.

She studied me for a long while without speaking. Finally, she shook her head. "Most car accidents are caused by the driver."

"I'll pass that along to the National Transportation Safety Board."

"What I mean is, you might pay as much attention to the driver as to the automobile."

I sighed and laid the journal aside. "I take it that you want to tell me what is playing on your personal Top 40 today."

She snorted, but I could see that she really did. I leaned back in my chair and linked my hands behind my head. "So, tell me, Mrs. Holloway, what is 'shaking'?"

She made fish faces with her lips. Mentally, I had dubbed her Granny Guppy when she did that. It was as if she had to flex her lips first to ready them for the arduous task of flapping.

"*Does Your Mother Know You're Out, Cecelia?*"

"What?" It took a moment. Then I realized that it must have been a song title. Some popular ditty now thankfully forgotten by everyone save this one old lady. "Was that a favorite song of yours?" I asked.

She shook her head. "Oh, mercy, no; but there was a year when you couldn't hardly avoid it."

"I see."

"And, let's see …" She stopped and cocked her head. The Listening Look, I called it. "Now it's *The Red, Red Robin*—"

"Comes bob-bob-bobbing along?"

"Yes, that's the one. And already today I've heard *Don't Bring Lulu* and *Side by Side* and *Kitten on the Keys* and *Bye-bye Blackbird*." She made a pout with her lips. "I do wish the songs would play out entirely."

"You told me they weren't your favorite songs."

"Some are, some aren't. They're just songs I once heard. Sometimes they remind me of things. Sometimes it seems as if they *almost* remind me of things. Things long forgotten, but waiting for me, just around a corner somewhere." She shook herself suddenly. "Tin Pan Alley wasn't my favorite, though," she went on. "I was a sheba. I went for the wild stuff. The Charleston; the Black Bottom. All those side kicks … I was a little old for that, but … Those were wild days, I tell you. Hip flasks and stockings rolled down and toss away the corset." She gave me a wink.

This … *prune* had gone for the wild stuff? Though, grant her, she had had her youth once. It didn't seem fair that she should have it twice. "Sheba?" I asked.

"A sheba," she said. "A flapper. The men were sheiks. Because of that … What was his name?" She tapped her cane staccato on the floor. "Valentino, that was it. Valentino. Oh, those eyes of his! All the younger girls dreamed about having him; and I wouldn't have minded one bit, myself. He had It."

"It?"

"It. Valentino drove the girls wild, he did. And a few boys, too. Clara Bow had It, too."

"Sex appeal?"

"Pshaw. Sex appeal is for snugglepups. A gal didn't have It unless both sexes felt something. Women, too. Women were coming out back then. We could smoke, pet, put a bun on if we wanted to—least, 'til the dries put on the kabosh. We had the vote. Why we even had a governor, back in Wyoming, where I once lived. Nellie Taylor Ross. I met her once, did I tell you? Why I remember—"

✿

Her sudden silence piqued me. "You remember what?"

"Doc?" Her voice quavered and her eyes looked right past me, wide as tunnels.

"What is it?"

"Doc? I can see 'em. Plain as day."

"See whom, Mrs. Holloway?" Was the old biddy having a seizure right there in my office?

She looked to her left, then her right. "We're sitting in the gallery," she announced. "All of us wearing pants, too, 'stead o' dresses. And down there … Down there …" She aimed a shaking finger at a point somewhere below my desk. "That's Alice with the gavel. Law's sake! They're ghosts, Doc. They're ghosts all around me!"

"Mrs. Holloway," I said. "Mrs. Holloway, close your eyes."

She turned to me. "What?"

"Close your eyes."

She did. "I can still see 'em," she said, with a wonder that was close to terror. "I can still see 'em. Like my eyes were still open." She raised a shaking hand to her mouth. Her ragged breath slowly calmed and, more quietly, she repeated, "I can still see 'em." A heartbeat went by, then she sighed. "They're fading, now," she said. "Fading." Finally, she opened her eyes. She looked troubled. "Doc, what happened to me? Was it a hallucy-nation?"

I leaned back in my chair and folded my hands under my chin. "Not quite. Simply a non-musical memory."

"But … It was so *real*, like I done traveled back in time."

"You were here the whole time," I assured her with a grin.

She struck the floor with her cane. "I know that. I could see you just as plain as I could see Alice and the others."

I sighed. Her sense of humor had dried out along with the rest of her. "Patients with your condition sometimes fall into 'dreamy states,'" I explained. "They see or hear their present and their remembered surroundings simultaneously, like a film that has been double-exposed. Hughlings Jackson described the symptom in 1880. He called it a 'dou-

bling of consciousness.'" I smiled and tapped the journal Wing had given me. "Comes from studying on books," I said.

But she wasn't paying me attention. "I remember it all so clearly now. I'd forgotten. Alice Robertson of Oklahoma was the first woman to preside over the House of Representatives. June 20, 1921, it was. Temporary Speaker. Oh, those were a fine fifteen minutes, I tell you." She sighed and shook her head. "I wonder," she said. "I wonder if I might remember my Ma and Pa and my little brother. Zach …? Was that his name? It's always been a trouble to me that I've forgotten. It don't seem right to forget your own kin."

An inverse square law, I suppose. Memories dim and blur with age, their strength depending on distance and mass. Too many of Mae's memories were too distant. They had passed beyond the horizon of her mind, and had faded like an old photograph left too long in the sun. And yet sometimes, near the end, like ashes collapsing in a dying fire, the past can become brighter than the present.

"No," I said. "It don't seem right."

"And Mister … Haven't thought on that man in donkey's years," she said. "Green Holloway was my man. I always called him Mister. He called me his Lorena."

"Lorena?"

Mae shrugged. "I don't remember why. There was a song … He took the name from that. It was real popular, so I suppose I'll recollect it bye and bye. He was an older man, was Mister. I remember him striding up through Black's hell; gray and grizzled, but strong as splo. All brass and buckles in his state militia uniform. Company H, 5th Tennessee. Just that one scene has stayed with me all my life, like an old brown photograph. Dear Lord, but that man had arms like cooper's bands. I can close my eyes and feel them around me sometimes, even today." She shivered and looked down.

"Splo?" I prompted.

"Splo," she repeated in a distracted voice. Then, more strongly, as if shoving some memory aside, "Angel teat. We called it apple john back then. Mister kept a still out behind the joe. Whenever he run off a batch, he'd invite the spear-side over and we'd all get screwed."

I bet. Whatever she had said. "Apple john was moonshine?" *High tail it, Luke. The revenooers are a-coming.* What kind of Barney Google life had she led up in those Tennessee hills? "So when you say you got screwed, you mean you got drunk, not, uh …"

Mae sucked in her lips and gnawed on them. "It was good whilst we were together," she said at last. "Right good." Her lips thinned. "But Mister, he lit a shuck on me, just like all the others." She gave me a look, half angry, half wary; and I could almost see the shutter come down behind her eyes. "Ain't no use getting close to nobody," she said. "They're always gone when you need them. Why, I ain't, haven't seen Little Zach nigh unto …" She looked momentarily confused. "Not for years and years. I loved that boy like he was more'n a brother; but he yondered off and never come back." She creaked to her feet. "So, I'll just twenty-three skidoo, Jack. You got things to do; so do I."

I watched her go, thinking she was right about one thing. Old milk does go sour.

> *There will I find a settled rest*
> *While others go and come.*
> *No more a stranger or a guest*
> *But like a child at home.*

Brenda's silver Beemer was parked in the garage when I got home. I pulled up beside it and contemplated its shiny perfection as I turned my engine off. Brenda was home. How long had it been, now? Three weeks? Four? It was hard to remember. Leave early; back late. That was our life. A quick peck in the morning and no-time-for-breakfast-dear. Tiptoes late at night; and the sheets rustle and the mattress sags; and it was hardly enough even to ruffle your sleep. Always on the run; always working late. One of us would have to slow down, or we might never meet at all.

My first thought was that I might give Consuela the night off. It had been so long since Brenda and I had been alone together. My second thought was that she had gotten in trouble at the office and had lost her job.

Doctors make good money. Lawyers make good money. Doctors married to lawyers make *very* good money. It was not enough.

"Brenda?" I called as I entered the kitchen from the garage. "I'm home!" There was no one in the kitchen; though something tangy with orange and sage was baking in the oven. "Brenda?" I called again as I reached the hall closet.

A squeal from upstairs. "Daddy's home!"

I hung up my overcoat. "Hello, Dee-dee. Is Mommy with you?" Unlikely, but possible. Stranger things have happened.

"No." Followed by a long silence. "Connie is telling me a story, about a mule and an ox."

Another silence; then footsteps on the stairs. Consuela looked at me over the banister as she descended.

"The mule and the ox?" I said.

"Nothing," she replied curtly. "An old Mayan folk tale."

"Where's Brenda?" I asked her. "I know she's home; her car is in the garage." Maybe she was in the back yard; by the pool or in the woods.

No, she didn't like the woods; she was afraid of deer ticks.

"Mrs. Wilkes came home early," Consuela said, "and packed a bag—"

Mentally, I froze. Not *this*. Not *now*. Without Brenda's income … "Packed a bag? Why?"

"She said she must go to Washington for a few days, to assist in an argument before the Supreme Court."

"Oh." Sudden relief coupled with sudden irritation. She could have phoned. At the Home. In my car. I showed Consuela my teeth. "The Supreme Court, you say. Well. That's quite a feather in her cap."

"Were she an Indio, a feather in the cap might mean something."

"Consuela. A joke? Did Brenda say when she would be back?"

Consuela hesitated, then shook her head. "She came home; packed her bag; gave me instructions. When the car arrived, she left."

And never said good-bye to Dee-dee. Maybe a wave from the doorway, a crueler good-bye than none at all. "What sort of instructions?" That wasn't the question I wanted to ask. I wanted to ask whose car had picked her up. Whom she was assisting in Washington? Walther Crowe, the steel-eyed senior partner with the smooth, European mannerisms? FitzPatrick, the young comer who figured so often on the society pages? But Consuela would not know; or, if she did, she would not say. There were some places where an outsider did not deliberately set herself.

"The sort of instructions," she replied, "that are unnecessary to give a professional. But they were only to let me know that I was her employee."

"You're angry." I received no answer. Then I asked, "Have you and Dee-dee eaten yet?"

"No." A short answer, not quite a retort.

"I didn't pull rank on you. Brenda did."

She shrugged and looked up at me with her head cocked to the side. "You are a doctor; I am a nurse. We have a professional relationship. Mrs. Wilkes is only an employer."

She was in a bad mood. I had never seen her angry before. I wondered what patronizing tone Brenda had used with her. I always made the effort to treat Consuela as an equal; but Brenda seldom did. Sometimes I thought Brenda was half-afraid of our Deirdre's nurse; though for what reason, I could not say. I glanced at the overcoat in the closet. "Would you and Dee-dee like to go out to eat?"

She gave me a thoughtful look; then shook her head. "She will not leave the house."

I glanced at the stairs. "No, she'll not budge, will she?" It was an old argument, never won. "She can play outside. She can go to school with the other children. There is no medical reason to stay in her—"

"There is something wrong with her heart."

"No, it's too soon for—"

"There is something wrong with her heart," she repeated.

"Oh." I looked away. "But … We'll eat in the dining room today. The three of us. Whatever that is you have in the oven. I'll set the table with the good dinnerware."

"A special occasion?"

I shook my head. "No. Only maybe we each have a reason to be unhappy just now." I wondered if Brenda had left a message in the bedroom. Some hint as to when she'd return. I headed toward the dining room.

"The ox was weary of plowing," Consuela said.

"Eh?" I turned and looked back at her. "What was that?"

"The ox was weary of plowing. All day, up the field and down, while the farmer cracked the whip behind him. Each night in the barn, when the ox complained, the mule would laugh. 'If you detest the plowing so much, why do it?' 'It is my job, señor mule,' the ox would reply. 'Then do it and don't complain. Otherwise, refuse. Go on strike.' The ox thought about this and, several days later, when the farmer came to him with the harness, the ox would not budge. 'What is wrong, señor ox?' the farmer asked him. 'I am on strike,' the ox replied. 'All day I plow with no rest. I deserve a rest.' The farmer nodded. 'There is justice in what you say. You have worked hard. Yet the fields must be plowed before the rains come.' And so he hitched the mule to the plow and cracked the whip over him and worked him for many weeks until the plowing was done."

Consuela stopped and with a slight gesture of the head turned for the kitchen.

Although entitled to two evenings a week off, Consuela seldom took them, preferring the solitude of her own room. She lived there quietly, usually with the hall door closed; always with the connecting door to Dee-dee's room open. Once a month, she sent a check to Guatemala. She read books. Sometimes she played softly on a sort of flute: weird, serpentine melodies that she had brought with her from the jungle. More than once, the strange notes had caused Brenda to stop whatever she was doing, whether mending or reading law or even making love, and listen with her head cocked until the music stopped. Then she would shiver slightly, and resume whatever she had been doing as though nothing had happened.

Consuela had furnished her room with Meso-American bric-a-brac. Colorful, twisty things. Statuettes, wall hangings, a window treatment. Squat little figurines with secretive, knowing smiles. A garland of fabric flowers. An obsidian carving that suggested a panther in mid-leap. Brenda found it all vaguely disturbing, as if she expected chittering monkeys swinging from the bookshelves and curtains; as if Consuela had brought a part of the jungle with her into Brenda's clear, ordered, rational world. It wasn't proper, at all. It was somehow out of control.

"Did you like having dinner downstairs today?" I asked Dee-dee as I studied Consuela's room through the connecting door. The flute lay silent on Consuela's dresser top. It was the kind you blew straight into, with two rows of holes, one for each hand.

"It was okay, I guess." A weak voice, steady but faint.

I turned around. "Only okay?" There was an odd contrast here, a paradox. Although it was evening and Deirdre's room was shrouded in darkness, Consuela's room had seemed bright with rioting colors.

"Did I leave any toys downstairs?" A worried voice in the darkness. Anxious.

"No, I checked." I resolved to check again, just in case we had overlooked something that had rolled under the sofa. Brenda detested disorder. She did not like finding things out of place.

"Mommy won't mind, will she? That I ate downstairs."

I turned. "Not if we don't tell her. Mommy will be at the Supreme Court for a few days."

Dee-dee made a sound in her throat. No sorrow, no joy. Just acknowledgment. Mommy might never come home at all for all the difference it made in Dee-dee's life. "Ready to be tucked in?"

Dee-dee grinned a delicious smile and snuggled deeper into the sheets. It was a heartbreaking smile. I gave her back the best one I could muster, and took a long, slow step toward her bed. She shrieked and ducked under the covers. I waited until she peeked out and took another step. It was a game we played, every move as encrusted with ritual as a Roman Mass.

Hutchinson-Gilford Syndrome. Dee-dee's smile was snaggle-toothed. Her hair, sparse; her skin, thin and yellow.

Manifestations: Alopecia, onset at birth to eighteen months, with degeneration of hair follicles. Thin skin. Hypoplasia of the nails … I had read the entry in Smith's over and over, looking for the one item I had missed, the loophole I had overlooked. It was committed to memory now; like a mantra. *Periarticular fibrosis; stiff or partially flexed prominent joints. Skeletal hypoplasia, dysphasia and degeneration.*

Dee-dee had weighed 2.7 kilos at birth. Her fontanel had ossified late, but the slowness of her growth had not become apparent until seven months. She lagged the normal growth charts by one-third. When she lost hair, it did not grow back. Her skin had brownish-yellow "liver" spots.

Natural history: Deficit of growth becomes severe after one year. The tendency to fatigue easily may limit participation in childhood activities. Intelligence and brain development are unimpaired.

Deirdre Wilkes was an alert, active mind trapped in a body aging far too quickly. A shrunken little gnome of a ten-year-old. *Etiology: Unknown.* I hugged her and kissed her on the cheek. Then I tucked the sheets tightly under the mattress.

Prognosis: The life span is shortened by relentless arterial atheromatosis. Death usually occurs at puberty.

There were no papers delivered on Hutchinson-Gilford that I had not crawled through word after word, searching for the slightest whisper of a breakthrough. Some sign along the horizon of research. But there were no hints. There were no loopholes.

Prognosis: death.

There were no exceptions.

Deirdre could smile because she was only a child and could not comprehend what was happening to her body. She knew she would have to "go away" someday, but she didn't know what that really meant.

Smiling was the hardest part of the game.

> *Come along, Josephine, In my flying machine.*
> *We'll go up in the air …*

How can I explain the feelings of dread and depression that enveloped me every time I entered Sunny Dale? I was surrounded by ancients. Bent, gray, hobbling creatures forever muttering over events long forgotten or families never seen. And always repeating their statements, always repeating their statements, as if it were I who were hard of hearing and not they. The Home was a waiting room for Death. Waiting and waiting, until they had done with waiting. Here is where the yellowed skin and the liver spots belonged. Here! Not on the frame of a ten-year-old.

The fourth time I saw Mae Holloway, she crept up behind me as I opened the door to the clinic. "Morning, doc," I heard her say.

"Good morning, Mrs. H.," I replied without turning around. I opened the door and stepped through. Inevitably, she followed, humming. I wondered if this was going to become a daily ritual. She planted herself in the visitor's chair. Somehow, it had become her own. "The show just ended," she announced. "Oh, it was a peach." She waved a hand at my desk. "Go on, set down. Make yourself pleasant."

It was my own fault, really. I had shown an interest in her tiresome recollections, and now she felt she had to share everything with me, as if I were one of her batty, old cronies. No good deed goes unpunished. Perhaps I was the only one who put up with her.

But I did have a notion that could wring a little use out of my sentence. I could write a book about Mae Holloway and her musical memories. People were fascinated with how the mind worked; or rather with how it failed to work. Sacks had described similar cases of incontinent nostalgia in one of his books; and if he could make the best-seller lists with a collection of neurological case studies, why not I? With fame, came money; and the things money could buy.

But my book would have to be something new, something different; not just a retelling of the same neurological tales. The teleology, perhaps. Sacks had failed to discover any meaning to the music his patients had heard, any reason *why* this tune or that was rememb-heard. If I kept a record, I might discover enough of a pattern to form the basis of a book. I rummaged in my desk drawer and took out a set of file cards that I had bought to make notes on my patients. Might as well get started. I poised my pen over a card. "What show was that?" I asked.

"*Girl of the Golden West*. David Belasco's new stage play." She shook her head. "I first seen it, oh, years and years ago, in Pittsburgh; before they made it a highfalutin' opera. That final scene, where Dick Johnson is hiding in the attic, and his blood drips through the ceiling onto the sheriff … That was taken from real life, you know."

"Was it." I wrote *Girl of the Golden West* and *doubling episode* and made a note to look it up. Then I poised my pen over a fresh card. "I'd like to ask you a few questions about your music, Mrs. Holloway. That is, if you don't mind."

She gave me a surprised glance and looked secretly pleased. She fussed with her gown and settled herself into her seat. "You may fire when ready, Gridley."

"You *are* still hearing the music, aren't you, Mrs. Holloway?"

"Well, the songs aren't so loud as they were. They don't keep me awake anymore; but if I concentrate, I can hear 'em."

I made a note. "You've learned to filter them out, that's all."

"*If You Talk in Your Sleep, Don't Mention My Name.*"

"What?"

"*If You Talk in Your Sleep, Don't Mention My Name.* That was one of 'em. The tunes I been hearing. Go on, write that down. Songs were getting real speedy in those days. There was *Mary Took the Calves to the Dairy Show* and *This is No Place for a Minister's Son*. Heh-heh. The blues was all in a lather over 'em. That, and actor-folks actually kissing each other in the moving picture shows. They tried to get that banned. And the animal dances, too."

"Animal dances?"

"Oh, there were a passel of 'em," she said. "There was the kangaroo dip, the crab step, the fox trot, the fish walk, the bunny hug, the lame duck … I don't remember them all."

"The fox trot," I offered. "I think people still dance that."

Mae snorted. "All the fire's out of it. You should have read what the preachers and the newspapers had to say about it back then. They sure were peeved; but the kids thought it was flossy. It was a way to get their parents' goat. 'Bug them,' I guess you say now."

"Kids? Isn't the fox trot a ballroom dance for, well, you know—mature people?"

She made her sour lemon face. "Sure. Now. But today's old folks were yesterday's kids. And they still like the music they liked when they were young. Heh-heh. When you're ninety or a hundred, sonny, you'll be a-listening to that acid rock stuff and telling your grandkids what hell-raisers you used to be. And they won't believe you, either. We tote the same bags with us all our lives, doc. The same interests;

the same likes and dislikes. Those older'n us and those younger'n us, why, they have their own bags." A sudden scowl, halfway between fright and puzzlement, passed across her face like the shadow of a cloud. Then she hunched her shoulders. "Me, I've got too many bags."

She'd get no argument from me on that. "Have you heard any other songs?" I asked.

She folded her hands over the knob of her walking stick and rested her chin on them. "Let's see … Yesterday, I heared, heard *Waiting for the Robert E. Lee* and *A Perfect Day*. Those were real popular, once. And lots of Cohan songs. 'Oh, it was Mary, Mary, long before the fashion changed …' And *Rosie O'Grady*. Then there was *Memphis Blues*. Young folks thought it was 'hep.' Even better than ragtime."

She shook her head. "I never cottoned too well to those kids, though," she said. "They remind me of the kids nowadays. A little too … What do they say now? 'Close to the edge.' Ran wild when they were young 'uns, they did. Hung around barbershops. Hawked papers as newsies. Worked the growler for their old man."

I looked up from my notes. "Worked the growler?"

"Took the beer bucket to the saloon to get it filled. Imagine sending a child—even girls!—into a saloon! No wonder Carrie and the others wanted to close 'em up. Maybe folks my age were a little too stuck on ourselves, like the younger folks said; but at least we had principles. With us, it wasn't all just to have a good time. We fought for things worth fighting for. Suffrage. Prohibition. Birth control. Oh, those were times, I tell you. Maggie, making those speeches about birth control and standing up there on the stage that one time with the tape over her mouth, because they wouldn't let her talk. I helped her open that clinic of hers over in Brooklyn, though I never did care for her attitude about Jews and coloreds. Controlling 'undesirables' wasn't the real reason for birth control, anyway."

"Mrs. Holloway!"

She looked at me and laughed. "Now, don't tell me your generation is shocked at such talk!"

"It's not that. It's …"

"That old folks wrangled over it, too? Well, folks aren't born old. We were young, too; and as full of piss and vinegar as anyone else. I read *Moral Physi-*

ology when it first come out; though Mister did try mightily to discourage me. And, later, there was *The Unwelcomed Child*. Doc, if men had babies, birth control would never have been a crime."

Folks aren't born old … I squared off my deck of index cards. "I suppose not." My generation had been as strong as any for civil rights and feminism. Certainly stronger than the hard-edged cynics coming up behind us. It sounded as if Mae had had a similar generational experience. Though, that would put her in the generation *before* the hell-raising Lost Generation. What was it called? The Missionary Generation? Maybe she was older than she looked; though that hardly seemed possible. "Let's get back to the songs—" I suggested.

"Yes, the songs," she said. "The songs. Why, I recollect a man had a right good voice … Now what was his name …? A wonderful dancer, too."

"Ben Wickham?" I suggested.

"No. No, Ben was later. This was out Pittsburgh way. Joe Paxton. That was it." She tilted her head back. "He was a barnstormer, Joe was. He knew 'em all. Calbraith Rodgers, Glenn Curtiss, Pancho Barnes, even Wilbur Wright. Took me up oncet, through the Alleghenies. Oh, my, that was something, let me tell you. The wind in your face and the ground drifting by beneath you, and the golden sun peeking between the shoulders of the hills … And you felt you were dancing with the clouds." She sighed, and the light in her eyes slowly faded. "But he was like all the rest." Her face closed up; became hard. "I come on him one day packing his valise, and when I asked him why he was cutting out, all he would say was, 'How old is Ann?'"

"What?"

She blinked and focused moistened eyes on me. Slowly, before they could even fall, her tears vanished into the sand of her soul. "Oh, that's what everyone said back then. 'How old is Ann?' It meant 'Who knows?' Came from one of those brain teasers that ran in the *New York Press*. You know. 'If Mary is twice as old as Ann was when Mary …' And it goes through all sorts of contortions and ends up 'How old is Ann?' Most folks hadn't the foggiest notion and didn't care, so they started saying 'How old is Ann?' when they didn't know the answer to something." She pushed down on her walking stick and started to rise.

"Wait. I still have a few questions."

"Well, I don't have any more answers. Joe … Well, he turned out worthless in the end; but we had some high times together." Then she sighed and looked off into the distance. "And he did take me flying, once, when flying was more than just a ride."

> As I was walking down the street, down the street, down the street,
> A handsome gal I chanced to meet. Oh, she was fair to view.
> Lovely Fan', won't you come out tonight, come out tonight, come out tonight?
> Lovely Fan', won't you come out tonight, and dance by the light of the moon?

☼

It was late in the evening—midnight, perhaps— and, dressed in housecoat and slippers, I was frowning over a legal pad and a few dozen index cards, a cup of cold coffee beside me on the kitchen table. I was surrounded by small, sourceless sounds. If you have been in a sleeping building at night, you know what I mean. Creaks and rustlings and the sighs of … What? Spirits? Air circulation vents? The soft groan of settling timbers. The breath of the wind against the windows. The staccato scritching of tiny night creatures dancing across the roof shingles. The distant rumble of a red-eye flight making its descent into the metropolitan area. Among such confused, muttering sounds, who can distinguish the pad of bare feet on the floor?

A gasp, and I turned.

I had never seen Consuela when she was not wearing nurse's whites. Perhaps once or twice, bundled in a coat as she sought one of her rare nights out; but never in a red and yellow flowing flowered robe. Never with her black hair unfastened and sweeping around her like a raven-feather cape. She stood in the kitchen doorway, clenching the collar in her fist.

"Consuela," I said.

"I—saw the light on. I thought you had already gone to sleep. So I—" Consuela flustered was a new sight, too. She turned to go. "I did not mean to disturb you."

"No, no. Stay a while." I laid my pen down and stretched. "I couldn't get to sleep, so I came down here to work a while." When she hesitated, I stood and pulled a chair out for her. She gave me a side-long look, then bobbed her head once and took a seat. I wondered if she thought I might "try something." Late at night; wife away; both of us in pajamas, thoughts of bed in our minds. Hell, I wondered if I might try something. Brenda had grown more distant each year since Deirdre's birth.

But Consuela was not my type. She was too short, too wide, too dark. I studied her covertly while I handled her chair. Well, perhaps not "too." And she did have a liquid grace to her, like a panther striding through the jungle. Brenda's grace was of a different sort. Brenda was fireworks arcing and bursting across the night sky. You might get burnt, but never bitten.

"Would you like something to drink?" I asked when she had gotten settled. "Apple juice, orange juice." Too late for coffee; and a liqueur would have been inappropriate.

"Orange juice would be fine, thank you," she said.

I went to the refrigerator and removed the carafe. Like everyone else, we buy our OJ in wax-coated paperboard containers; but Brenda transferred the milk, the juices, and half a dozen other articles into carafes and canisters and other more appropriate receptacles. Most people shelved their groceries. We repackaged ours.

"Do you remember the old woman I told you about last week?"

"The one who hears music? Yes."

I brought the glasses to the table. "She's starting to remember other things, now." I told her about Mae's recollections, her consciousness doubling. "I've started to keep track of what she sees and hears," I said, indicating the papers on the table. "And I've sent to the military archives to see if they could locate Green Holloway's service records. Later this week, I plan to go into the City to check the census records at the National Archives."

Consuela picked up the legal pad and glanced at it. "Why are you doing this thing?"

"For verification. I'm thinking I might write a book."

She looked at me. "About Mrs. Holloway?"

"Yes. And I think I may have found an angle, too." I pointed to the pad she held. "That is a list of the songs and events Holloway has rememb-heard."

After a moment's hesitation, Consuela read through the list. She shook her head. "You are looking for meaning in this?" Her voice held a twist of skepticism in it. For a moment, I saw how my activities might look from her perspective. Searching for meaning in the remembered songs of a half-senile old woman. What should that be called, senemancy? Melodimancy? What sort of auguries did High Priest Wilkes find, eviscerating this morning's ditties?

"Not meaning," I said. "Pattern. Explanation. Some way to make sense of what she is going through."

Consuela gave me that blank look she liked to affect. "It may not make sense."

"But it almost does." I riffed the stack of index cards. Each card held information about a song Mae had heard. The composer, songwriter, performer; the date, the topic, the genre. Whether Mae had liked it or not. "The first time she came to me," I said, "she was 'rememb-hearing' swing tunes from the 1930s. A few days later, it was music of the 'Roaring Twenties.' Then the jazz gave way to George M. Cohan and the 'animal dance' music of the Mauve Decade. Do you see? The songs keep coming from earlier in her life."

Memphis Blues, 1912. *A Perfect Day*, 1910. *Mary Took the Calves to the Dairy Show*, 1909. *Rosie O Grady*, 1906. Songs my grandparents heard as children. "East side, west side, All around the town …" I remembered how Granny used to sit my brother and me on her lap, one on each knee, and rock us back and forth while she sang that. I paused and cocked my head, listening into the silence of the night.

But I could hear nothing. I could remember *that* she sang it; but I could not remember the singing.

"It is a voyage," I said, loudly, to cover the silence. "A voyage of discovery up the stream of time."

Consuela shook her head. "Rivers have rapids," she said, "and falls."

Hello, my baby, hello, my honey, hello, my ragtime gal …
Send me a kiss by wire,
Baby, my heart's on fire.

Mae's morning visits fell into a routine. She settled herself into her chair with an air of proprietorship and croaked out snatches of tunes while I wrote down what I could, recording the rest on a cheap pocket tape recorder I had purchased. She hummed *The Maple Leaf Rag* and *Grace and Beauty* and the *St. Louis Tickle*. I suffered through her renditions of *My Gal Sal* and *The Rosary*. ("A big hit," she assured me, "for over twenty-five years.") She rememb-heard the bawdy *Hot Time in the Old Town Tonight* (sounding grotesque on her ancient lips), the raggy *You've Been a Good Old Wagon, But You've Done Broke Down*, and the poignant *Good-bye, Dolly Gray*.

She frowned for a moment. "Or was that 'Nellie Gray'?" Then she shrugged. "Those were happy songs, mostly," she said. "Oh, they were such good songs back then. Not like today, all angry and shouting. Even the sad songs were sweet. Like *Tell Them That You Saw Me* or *She's Only a Bird in a Gilded Cage*. And Mister taught me *Lorena*, once. I wish I could recollect that 'un. And *Barbry Ellen*. I learned me that 'un when I was knee-high to a grasshopper. Pa told me it was the President's favorite song. The old President, from when his Pappy fought in the War. I haven't heard those yet. Or—" She cocked her head to the side. "Well, dad-blast it!"

"What's wrong, Mrs. Holloway?"

"I'm starting to hear coon songs."

"Coon songs!"

She shook her head. "Coon songs. They was—were—all the rage. *Coon, Coon, Coon* and *All Coons Look Alike to Me* and *If the Man in the Moon Were a Coon*. Some of them songs were writ by coloreds themselves, because they had to write what was popular if they wanted to make any money."

"Mrs. Holloway …!"

"Never said I liked 'em," she snapped back. "I met plenty of coloreds in my time, and there's some good and some bad, just like any other folks. Will Biddle, he farmed two hollers over from my Pa when I was a sprout, and he worked as hard as any man-jack in the hills, and carried water for no man. My Pa said—My Pa …" She paused, frowned and shook her head. "Pa?"

"What is it?"

"Oh."

"Mrs. Holloway?"

She spoke in a whisper, not looking at me, not looking at anything I could see. "I remember when my Pa died. Him a-laying on the bed, all wore out by life. Gray and wrinkled and toothless. And, dear Lord, how that ached me. I remember thinking how he'd been such a strong man. Such a strong man." She sighed. "It's an old apartment, and the wallpaper is peeling off'n the walls. There's a big, dark water stain on one wall and the steam radiator is hissing like a cat."

"You don't remember where you were … are?" I asked, jotting a few quick notes.

She shook her head. "No. I'm humming *In the Good Old Summertime*. Or maybe the tune is just running through my head. Pa, he …" A tear formed in the corner of her eye. "He wants me to sing him the song."

"The song? What song is that?"

"An old, old song he used to love. 'Sing it to me one last time,' he says. And I can't sing at all because my throat's clenched up so tight. But he asks me again, and … Those eyes of his! How I loved that old man." Mae's own eyes had glazed over as she lived the scene again in her mind. She reached out as if clasping another pair of hands in her own and croaked haltingly:

"I gaze on the moon as I tread the drear wild,
And feel that my mother now thinks of her child …
Be it ever so humble …"

She could not finish. For a time, she sobbed softly. Then she brushed her eye with her sleeve and looked past me. "I never knew, doc. I never knew at all what a blessing it was to forget."

Come and sit by my side if you love me.
Do not hasten to bid me adieu,
But remember the bright Mohawk Valley
And the girl that has loved you so true.

☼

Later that day, as I was leaving the Home, I noticed Mae sitting in the common room and paused a moment to eavesdrop. There were a handful of other residents mouldering in chairs and rockers; but Mae sat singing quietly to herself and I thought what the

hell, and pulled out my pocket tape recorder and stepped up quietly beside her.

It was a patriotic hymn. *America, the Beautiful.* I'm sure you've heard it. Even I know the words to that one. Enough to know that Mae had them all wrong. *Oh beautiful for halcyon skies? Above the enameled plain?* And the choruses … The way Mae sang it, "God shed his grace for thee" sounded more like a plea than a statement.

America! America! God shed his grace for thee
Till selfish gain no longer stain The banner of the free!

The faulty recollection disturbed me. If Mae's memories were unreliable, then what of my book? What if my whole rationale turned out wrong?

Her croakings died away and she opened her eyes and spotted me. "Heading home, doc?"

"It's been a long day," I said. There was no sign on her face of her earlier melancholy, except that maybe her cheeks sagged a little lower than before, her eyes gazed a little more sadly. She seemed older, somehow; if such a thing were possible.

She patted the chair next to her. "Hot foot it on over," she said. "You're just in time for the slapstick."

She was obviously having another doubling episode and, in some odd way, I was being asked to participate. I looked at my watch, but decided that since our morning session had been cut short, I might as well make the time up now. My next visit was not until Friday. If I waited until then, these memories could be lost.

"Slapstick?" I asked, taking the seat she had offered.

"You never been to the Shows?" She tsk-ed and shook her head. "Well, Jee-whiskers. They been the place to go ever since Tony Pastor got rid of the cootchee-cootchee and cleaned up his acts. A young man can take his steady there now and make goo-goo eyes." She nudged me with her elbow. "A fellow can be gay with his fairy up in the balcony."

I pulled away from her. "I beg your pardon?"

"Don't you want to be gay?" she asked.

"I should hope not! I have a wife, a dau …"

Mae laughed suddenly and capped a gnarled hand over her mouth. So help me, she blushed. "Oh, my goodness, me! I didn't mean were you a *cake-eater*. I got all mixed up. I was sitting down front at the burly-Q and I was sitting here in the TV room with you. When we said, 'be gay,' we meant let your hair down and relax. And a 'fairy' was your girl friend, what they used to call a chicken when I was younger. All the boys wanted to be gay blades, with their starched collars and straw hats and spats. And their moustaches! You never saw such moustaches! Waxed and curled and barbered." She chuckled to herself. "I was a regular daisy, myself." She closed her eyes and leaned back.

"A regular daisy?"

"A daisy," she repeated. "Like in the song. Gals was going out to work in them days. So they made a song about it. Now, let me see …" She pouted and stared closed-eyed at the sky. "How did that go?" She began to sing in a cracked, quavery voice.

My daughter's as fine a young girl as you'll meet
In your travels day in and day out;
But she's getting high-toned and she's putting on airs
Since she has been working about …

When she comes home at night from her office,
She walks in with a swag like a fighter;
And she says to her ma, 'Look at elegant me!'
Since my daughter plays on the typewriter.

She says she's a 'regular daisy,'
Uses slang 'til my poor heart is sore;
She now warbles snatches from operas
Where she used to sing 'Peggy O Moore.'

Now the red on her nails looks ignited;
She's bleached her hair 'til it's lighter.
Now perhaps I should always be mad at the man
That taught her to play the typewriter.

She cries in her sleep, 'Your letter's to hand.'
She calls her old father, 'esquire';
And the neighbors they shout
When my daughter turns out,
'There goes Bridget Typewriter Maguire.'"

When Mae was done, she laughed again and wiped tears from her eyes. "Law's sake," she said. "Girls a-working in the offices. I remember what a stir-up that was. Folks said secretarial was man's

work, and women couldn't be good typewriters, no how. There was another song, *Everybody Works But Father*, about how if women was to go to work, all the men would be out of jobs. Heh-heh. I swan! It weren't long afore one gal in four had herself a 'position,' like they used to say; and folks my age complained how the youngsters were 'going to pot.'" She shook her head and chuckled.

"I always did find those kids more to my taste," she went on. "There was something about 'em; some spark that I liked. They knew how to have fun without that ragged edge that the next batch had. And they had, I don't know, call it a dream. They were out to change the world. They sure weren't wishy-washy like the other folks my age. 'Middle aged,' that's what the kids back then called us. We were 'Professor Tweetzers' and 'Miss Nancys' and 'goo-goos.' And to tell you the truth, Doc, I thought they pegged it right. People my age grew up trying to imitate their parents; until they saw how much more fun the kids were having. Then they tried to be just like their kids. Heh-heh."

I grunted something noncommittal. Middle-aged crazy, just like my uncle Larry. "I suppose there were a lot of 'mid-life crises' back then, too," I ventured. Uncle Larry had gone heavy into love beads and incense, radical politics. He grew a moustache and wore bell-bottoms. The whole hippie scene. Walked out on his wife for a young "chick" and thought it was all "groovy." I remember how pathetic those thirtysomething wannabes seemed to us in college.

Dad, now, he never had an "identity crisis." He always knew exactly who he was. He had gone off to Europe and saved the world and then came back home and rebuilt it. Uncle Larry was too young to save the world in the Forties, and too old to save it in the Sixties. He was part of that bewildered, silent generation sandwiched between the heroes and the prophets.

"Neurasthenia," Mae said. "We called it neurasthenia back then. Seems everyone I knew was getting divorced or having an attack of 'the nerves.' Even the president was down in the mullygrubs when he was younger. Nervous breakdown. That's what you call it nowadays, isn't it? Now, T. R. There was a man with sand in him. Him and that 'strenuous life' he always preached about. Why, he'd fight a circle saw.

Saw him that time in Milwaukee. Shot in the chest, and he still gave a stem-winder of a speech before he let them take him off. Did you know he got me in trouble one time?"

"Who, Teddy Roosevelt? How?"

"T.R., he was a-hunting and come on a bear cub; but he wouldn't shoot the poor thing because it wasn't the manly thing to do. So, some sharper started making stuffed animal dolls and called 'em Teddy's Bear. I given one to my neighbor child as a present." Mae slapped her knee. "Well, her ma had herself a conniption fit, 'cause the experts all said how animal dolls would give young 'uns the nightmares. And the other president who had the neurasthenia." Mae scowled and waved a hand in front of her face. "Oh, I know who it was," she said in an irritated voice. "That college professor. What was his name?"

"Wilson," I suggested, "Woodrow Wilson."

"That's the one. I think he was always jealous of T.R. He wouldn't let him take the Rough Riders into the Great War."

I started to make some comment, but Mae's mouth dropped open. "The war …?" she whispered. "The war! Oh, Mister …" Her face crumpled. "Oh, Mister! You're too old!" She covered her face and began to weep.

She felt in her sleeves for a handkerchief; then wiped her eyes and looked at me. "I forgot," she said. "I forgot. It was the war. Mister went away to the war. That's why he never come back. He never run out on me, at all. He would have come back after it was over, if he'd still been alive. He would have."

"I'm sure he would have," I said awkwardly.

"I told him he was too old for that sort of thing; but he just laughed and said it was a good cause and they needed men like him to spunk up the young 'uns. So he marched away one day and someone he never met before shot him dead and I don't even know when and where it happened."

"I'm sorry," I said, at a loss for anything else to say. A good cause? The War to End All Wars, nearly forgotten now; its players, comic-opera Ruritanians on herky-jerky black and white newsreels. The last war begun in innocence.

Her hands had twisted the handkerchief into a knot. She fussed with it, straightened it out on her lap, smoothed it with her hand. In a quiet voice, she said, "Tell me, doc. Tell me. Why do they have wars?"

I shook my head. Was there ever a good reason? To make the world safe for democracy? To stop the death camps? To free the slaves? Maybe. Those were better reasons than cheap oil. But up close, no matter what the reason, it was husbands and sons and brothers who never came home.

Oh, them golden slippers, Oh, them golden slippers,
Golden slippers I'm gonna wear, Because they look
* so neat;*
Oh, them golden slippers, Oh, them golden slippers,
Golden slippers I'm gonna wear To walk them
* golden streets.*

(to be continued in Issue 13)

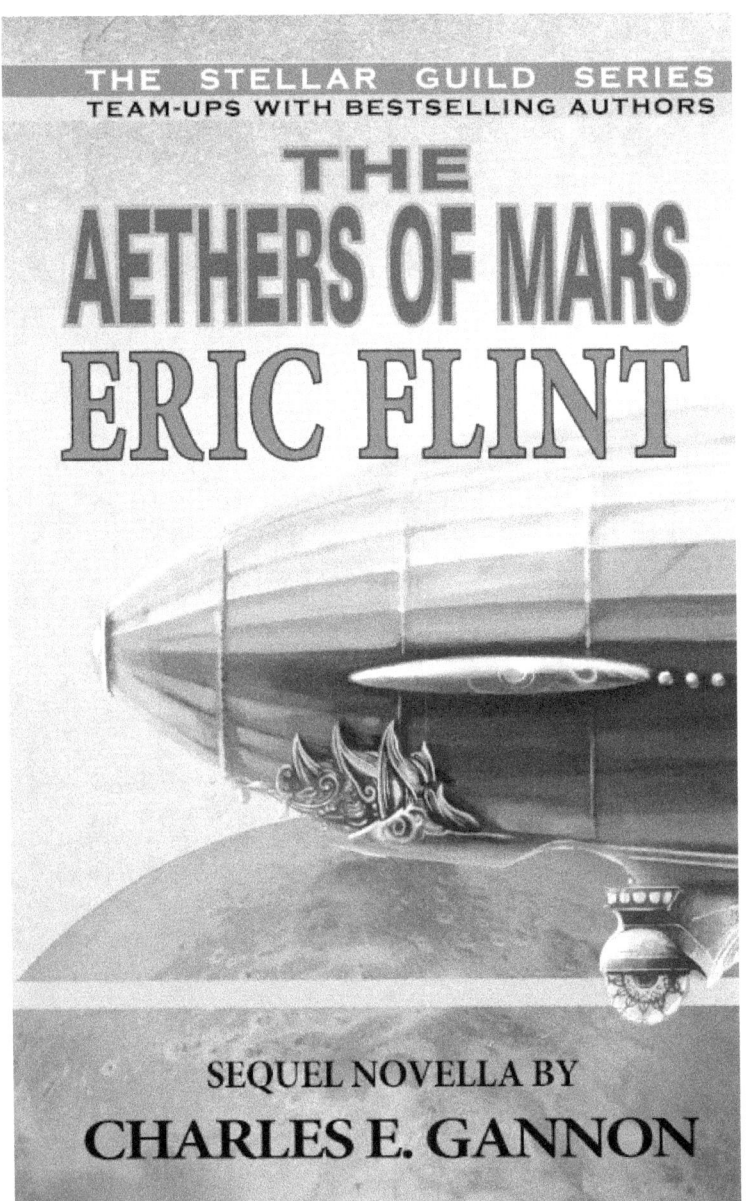

www.ingramcontent.com/pod-product-compliance
Lightning Source LLC
Chambersburg PA
CBHW082047220626
47052CB00007B/1247